Marisa Mackle was born in Armagh, Northern Ireland. She divides her time between Spain and Ireland.

Confessions of an Air Hostess

Marisa Mackle

little
black
dress

First published in paperback in 2007
by LITTLE BLACK DRESS
An imprint of HEADLINE PUBLISHING GROUP

A LITTLE BLACK DRESS paperback

5

ISBN 978 0 7553 3989 1

Typeset in Transit511BT by Avon DataSet Ltd,
Bidford-on-Avon, Warwickshire

Printed and bound in Great Britain by
Clays Ltd, St Ives plc

Headline's policy is to use papers that are natural, renewable and
recyclable products and made from wood grown in sustainable forests.
The logging and manufacturing processes are expected to conform to the
environmental regulations of the country of origin.

HEADLINE PUBLISHING GROUP
A division of Hachette Livre UK Ltd
338 Euston Road
London NW1 3BH

www.littleblackdressbooks.co.uk
www.headline.co.uk

This book is dedicated to my father, Eamonn Mackle

I'd like to thank God for everything. Also huge thanks to Catherine Cobain at Headline and all the Little Black Dress team.

Rule One: Smile and the world smiles with you, scowl and passengers will make your life hell.

Ten myths about cabin crew members:

1. We all love our jobs.
2. We also love smiling, even when presented with overflowing sick bags.
3. We're not remotely afraid of turbulence.
4. We eat the same food as the passengers.
5. We have a man in every port (we wish).
6. We don't get hangovers.
7. We don't mind getting up at 3 a.m.
8. We're not that bright so we need a calculator to work out the price of two coffees.
9. We all live very glamorous lives.
10. Our secret wish is to marry captains (even ugly captains).

Ladies and gentlemen, my name is Annie and today I'll be looking after you on your flight. Please do not give me any hassle as I was dumped on my way to the airport this morning, by text. Please do not be fooled by my heavy make-up, as without it I'd be a ghastly shade of green, the result of a vicious hangover. Please buy as much ladies' and gents' fragrance as you can, even though you don't particularly want it, as there's 20 per cent off today. Ladies, please don't be fooled by handsome Marco's charm; he's as gay as the Christmas fairy, and he wants to sell you a horrible Celtic brooch for the commission. Gentlemen, please don't think that sexy Sue thinks you're hot – she has been laughing about your toupee behind the curtain for the last twenty minutes but she's hoping you'll buy a hand-painted Irish tie, again for the commission. Please be careful when aiming for the toilet bowl as we have no cleaners on the flight. Cabin crew members are here primarily for your comfort and safety, and potty training is not included in the price of your cheap flight. Just to let you know, if you hand us complaint cards at the end of the flight, they will not be passed on to Head Office but will go straight into the bin along with your used napkins. Please do not ask us which country we are flying over at any stage of the flight – if we were that good at geography, we'd be, like, geography teachers or something.

Do not, absolutely do not, ask us which hotel we are staying at. If you are looking for that kind of entertainment, please ask the discreet concierge at your own hotel, which is hopefully at the other end of town to ours. Do not enquire whether we like our jobs as cabin crew and in return we will not ask you if you like your job in the bank or wherever the hell you work. Do not ask us where the best night spots in Dublin are as we will just tell you to go to Temple Bar – a place where we wouldn't dream of going ourselves. On your way home, don't complain that it rained all week in Ireland. We are not responsible for the weather, so tough luck if you got wet.

Please do not hand us your heavy black hand luggage, asking us to stow it away safely as you have a bad back. Our backs aren't the best either, and they will be even more damaged if we try to lift all your belongings and shove them into a tight overhead compartment. Please don't complain if you've ended up in the dreaded middle seat – no, we cannot ask another passenger to swap seats with you and it'll be a lesson for you to check in earlier the next time. Don't moan that we're not showing a film – it's a forty-five-minute flight, so what do you expect? And don't ask if little Johnny can visit the captain in his cockpit. The real reason the captain became a pilot was to spend as much time as possible away from his own little brats and, anyway, little Johnny could be a terrorist. We take no chances these days, as I'm sure you found out when that stupid-looking security guy at Dublin airport confiscated your shampoo.

The toilet is for one person only and no, you can't accompany your partner into the loo to help him with his medication. Yes, we understand that there are two yellow breathing masks in the toilet but these are strictly for parents and children.

Blankets are provided to keep you warm only and are not handed out so you can misbehave underneath them when the lights are dimmed. Any strange movements noticed will be reported to the captain. Well, he gets very bored in the cockpit after finishing the newspaper crosswords and suduko puzzles, so it's important to keep him entertained with amusing passenger stories.

Please don't tell us that your little girl would love to be an air hostess and ask us whether we have any advice for her. My advice would be to study very hard and become a doctor, or something useful. You see, our lives are not that glamorous, lots of us drink too much, we all socialise on week nights because weekends off are practically unheard of. At parties, people bore us to tears telling us about their own flying experiences and how they nearly died several times mid-Atlantic as their plane nosedived. As if!

Seriously, though, if you want a job that involves a lot of smiling and wearing red lipstick, why not become a clown? You'd probably get to travel the world with the circus and people don't shout at you because the plane is late or because you haven't got their pre-ordered, low-sodium, low-fat meal on board. And I bet the pay is much better, too.

One last thing: do not ask us if, when we land in water, anyone will hear you blowing your little red whistle. I doubt that they will. Anyway, I for one will be too busy swimming towards land as fast as I can.

Now, sit back, relax, and enjoy your short flight with us!

Rule Two: Behave professionally at all times. Even at the worst of times.

The plane roars down the runway at a thundering speed. All our passengers seem excited and are chatting eagerly amongst themselves as we then soar into the air en route to sunny Lanzarote. They are no doubt looking forward to spending a lazy fortnight in half-empty Irish bars in Puerto Del Carmen or Playa Blanca, watching Sky Sports on big screens and drinking San Miguel while comparing Lanzarote to the resorts they visited last year (like Santa Ponsa in Majorca or Playa De Las Americas in Tenerife) with other sunburnt Irish couples that they meet at the naff welcome meetings. Still, I'd rather be them than me. I am wondering how I'm going to cope now that my life has collapsed all around me. How could Niall cruelly dump me by text? How will I tell my mum? She loved Niall. Granted, she'd never met him as he was a Southsider who would never dream of venturing all the way to Swords on the Northside where my parents live in a semi-detached house on a quiet estate. But I'd told her all about him and she approved. She liked the fact that he worked as an accountant, didn't smoke, didn't drink and wanted children. Just not *my* children it would seem.

Cathy, my fellow air hostess, who is sitting beside me applying electric-blue eyeshadow, notices the tears spilling on to my hands streaking my fake tan.

'Are you OK?' she enquires.

'No, I'm crying because I'm happy,' I say with more than a hint of bitterness. 'I just love spending my weekends making sure happy couples arrive in comfort and safety at their sunny holiday destination.'

She looks at me blankly. 'Are you being sarcastic?'

'Of course I am. Yesterday I was out celebrating my longest relationship in years. I was telling my friends that I couldn't believe Niall and I had lasted three long months. We were even thinking of getting a little dog together. We were going to call her Molly. And then this morning at 7.07 a.m. I received a text telling me it was all off,' I said shakily before bursting into tears.

Cathy put a skinny arm around my shoulder. 'My poor baby,' she cooed. 'What an absolute bastard! What an unbelievable coward. If he's such a loser, maybe you're better off without him.'

'I am,' I sniffed, 'aren't I? He didn't deserve me. Didn't deserve all the love I had to give him. I just wish I hadn't given him a thousand quid to help him find his feet.'

'You did that?' Cathy looked at me wide-eyed.

'I know. I'm such a stupid fool. He was sick of his job and his boss.'

'So you gave him the money and he found his feet no doubt.'

'Yes; it seems they took him all the way to the airport

where he booked a one-way flight to Australia. Now apparently he loves it so much over there he's not coming back.'

'I hope he gets buggered by a kangaroo,' Cathy spat.

'Thanks, Cath.' I smiled weakly, wiping my wet cheeks with the back of my hand. 'Is my mascara all streaked?'

'Nothing that a Kleenex can't quickly sort out.'

'Thanks. And thanks for listening to me. I will survive this, you know.'

'I know. You go, girl. And don't worry; there are more men just around the corner.'

'I just wish I knew which corner. But I'll get back out there with a smile on my face. Life goes on. Fuck the bastard!'

With that the deafening sound of applause came from down the cabin. A startled look appeared on Cathy's face.

'What? What's going on?' I shrieked, my hand flying to my mouth.

'Oh. My. God,' said Cathy slowly. 'We forgot to switch off the microphone!'

Rule Three: Let safety be your number-one priority.

I wake up the following week to the sun streaming though my window and an irate message on my answerphone from Sylvie my supervisor. My heart immediately fills with dread. Sylvie is a witch who seems hell-bent on making my life hell. Apparently, when she first joined the airline, like a hundred years ago when air hostessing was the most glamorous job in the world and guaranteed you a rich husband, she was a raving beauty and all the pilots were wild about her. But now her looks have gone to pot and she has acquired the face that she deserves – pinched, spiteful features, thin, mean-looking mouth and hawk-like eyes accentuated by naff bottle-green eyeshadow.

While all her contemporaries used their glamorous status as globe-trotting air hostesses to nab wealthy businessmen and get dazzling sparklers for their engagement fingers, Sylvie married late in life, and is now divorced and sour as hell. Her main preoccupation these days seems to be torturing younger fun-loving girls. Girls like myself who simply joined the airline for an easy life of luxury hotels, swimming pools and sunny locations, not realising that working through the night with a teapot in one hand and a tray with jiggers and sugars in the other, is bloody hard work.

According to her sharp, short message, she wants to meet me at 12 p.m. Looking anxiously at my watch, I realise I have exactly two hours to make myself look normal and get out to her poky little office at cabin crew headquarters at Dublin Airport. So I make myself look presentable but not too glamorous and head to Busaras to catch the Airport Express.

For once I am early. I pause outside the tall, grey, un-welcoming building where a bunch of cabin crew members are taking the opportunity to sneak a quick cigarette before their overnight in Paris. They all stand huddled against the wind, identical in their uniforms, their black overnight wheelie cases nearby. Their hair is all swept back into ridiculously old-fashioned buns. They could all be members of a 1960s girl band.

'Hey, Annie.' One of them smiles as I approach, looking for a lighter. 'We've just been talking about you. You're a legend, do you know that?'

I raise an eyebrow.

'Cursing into the microphone like that,' she laughs. 'You've some balls on you, woman. Fair play to you.'

'But that was an accident,' I say, reddening. I am getting embarrassed now. I don't want to make my mortify-ing faux pas my claim to airline fame. How much do they know? I don't particularly care about the microphone incident but the thought that everyone in the airline knew

I'd been dumped by text, was absolutely mortifying. How would I live ever that one down?

'So any plans for Paris?' I ask quickly, trying to change the unpleasant subject.

'I'm just going to take it easy,' says Sophie, the older air hostess, a striking sallow-skinned girl in her thirties. 'When you've two toddlers at home the last thing you feel like doing is partying in somebody's hotel room. I'm going to have a long hot bath with a glass of wine and enjoy the latest Cathy Kelly without the sound of little fists thumping on the door.'

'It depends on the cockpit crew, I suppose,' says Elena, who is a former beauty queen and only goes for drinks if there's a single pilot among the crew. This girl suffers from serious pilotitis (an addiction to pilots) and wouldn't waste a night in Paris chatting in some hotel bar to a bunch of girls when she could be getting her beauty sleep. 'Are you not working today?'

'I'm on a day off.' I grimace. 'I'm just in to meet Sylvie Savage for a chat.'

'About what?' asks the third girl incredulously.

'Oh, just about life and stuff, I guess.' I have to laugh at their surprised faces. 'I'm joking, of course. You hardly think I'm in here to collect a bonus for my good behaviour? No doubt I'm in for a good old bollocking about something or other. Well, have a good trip, girls; I'm off to meet the devil herself.'

I take the lift up to the third floor examining my spots in the harsh mirrors. Man, the lighting in here is terrible. Either that, or I look like shit.

I'm still a good five minutes early but Sylvie makes me

wait outside to suffer in silence until she's ready to see me. Her face is like thunder when I'm finally granted entry. God, what have I done now?

Her beady eyes bore through me. I uneasily shift from one foot to another. There's another seat in the room but she doesn't invite me to sit down. 'What's the meaning of this?' She's holding up a neatly written complaint card but my eyesight isn't that good so I don't know what it's all about.

'Can you explain?' I try to keep my voice steady. Today is my day off so I don't want to spend the entire day in this stuffy little room going around in circles with a woman who seems to hate my guts.

I sit down. She inhales swiftly and her eyes narrow until they look like slits in her over-made-up lined face.

'I've had a complaint from a respectable family man who is a regular traveller. He says you used foul language on a flight to Lanzarote a couple of weeks ago. He also says for the rest of his holiday his innocent young son kept asking him about the word "bastard".'

She almost winces as she says the word. What a prude! That's bloody ridiculous. What era is she still living in? Would she not think of retiring gracefully? Bastard isn't even a curse word. It's in the dictionary.

'That was a mistake,' I admit, realising that this was an argument I wouldn't win. 'I was talking about something private at the time. I had no idea that the microphone was on. Anyway, most of the passengers laughed. They thought it was funny.'

Sylvie bristles. 'Well, this man didn't find it remotely funny. In fact, he was so offended that he is now looking for a refund on his plane tickets and a written apology from the airline.'

'Jesus, he needs to get a life!'

'Would you mind not taking the Lord's name in vain? Can't you be professional for once in your life? You are in the wrong here, Annie, and you know it. You have let the company down, not to mention yourself and whatever's left of your reputation. The consequences for your actions will result in your suspension for a week without pay.'

What? Is she kidding me? She cannot be serious. It soon dawns on me that she is. Oh great, I think. Maybe I could go away somewhere for a spa break or something. Or tidy my room. Or do something useful like get driving lessons.

'If you are disciplined three times, we will be forced to terminate your contract,' Sylvie spat almost gleefully.

Now, that isn't so good. Where else could I get a job where I spend most of my time looking into a mirror reapplying my lipstick? Who would pay me to swim up and down a glorious pool in Santa Monica as part of my job? Or to hang out in London hotels during rugby internationals? And who would make the repayments on my crippling mortgage? I bought an inner-city two-bedroomed box for the price of a mansion in any other country! Shakily I get to my feet. 'It won't happen again, Sylvie, I promise,' I mutter, hating myself for grovelling. 'Thank you.'

God, why am I thanking her? Isn't it bad enough that she'd made me feel like a piece of crap stuck to the sole of her stiletto heel? I slink out of the office feeling more depressed than I have in a long time. My heart is heavy. Oh well, at least I will be able to dine out on the microphone story for years to come. That is, if anybody ever invites me anywhere ever again. I'm still reeling over the fact that Niall dumped me without so much as a simple explanation. Why? I mean, we're all adults here. I can take rejection the same as the next girl, but I would prefer it to my face. The thing that really gets me about Niall dumping me, is that it was done in such a cowardly fashion. What did he expect? That I would make a scene? That I would fall to my knees and beg him to take me back, that I would change? As if I was *that* desperate. Anyway, it was Niall, not me, who had done all the chasing to begin with. I'd met him in a club on a night out with the girls. He had approached me on the dance floor and had impressed me with his wit and cheeky smile. I'd been reluctant to hand over my number to a stranger at first, but Niall hadn't taken no for an answer. Then he'd texted me and phoned me about twenty times a day before proclaiming his undying love for me. Our problems only began when I told him I loved him back. Immediately he started to cool off and the texts dwindled to a couple a week, usually informing me that he couldn't meet me because of rugby training. The more he ran away the more I ran after him. Until I got that final text to tell me it was over. He'd invited me to a dreary place called Dumpsville, population: me.

Since Niall and I have split up (I tell people that we split up, of course, not that I was ditched), the invitations haven't exactly been pouring in. People don't seem to feel comfortable with a new singleton sitting amongst them. It makes them feel uncomfortable, for some reason. As if they've found out I've some kind of unpleasant disease. Even all Niall's friends' girlfriends, whom I'd quite reasonably thought were my friends, too, have deserted me. No doubt they are just waiting to befriend his new flame, the fickle bitches.

'We'll definitely have to meet up for a girlie night soon,' a couple of them, Rose and Sarah, promised me when they bumped into me in the street, without ever specifying a date. I think they're avoiding me in case I ask awkward questions and they have to tell me the truth. What was the truth anyway? Was Niall with somebody else now? Were they both lounging around Bondi beach drinking cool beers without a care in the world while I struggled to get my dignity back in depressing old Dublin, alone? Was she accompanying him to barbecues, holding his hand and laughing at all his silly jokes? Is her mother as excited as my own had been about dating such a good catch? Maybe his new girlfriend is Australian, an Elle MacPherson lookalike with impossibly long, tanned limbs. Is he using my money to buy her flowers? The thought just sickens me.

My head spinning, I cross the road quickly in my new pastel-pink strappy Jimmy Choo sandals. I'm wearing a baby-pink cardigan, too, with faded denims, as I read in some psychology book once that pink makes people warm to you. Obviously it didn't work on Savage. Maybe she is colour-blind. I totter across the road, lost in the depths of my own sad little world and fail to notice the big, shiny, black Mercedes coming at full speed around the corner. Too late. It screeches to a halt. The noise of it throws me and I stumble, crashing to the ground and hitting my face on the kerb with a thud. Darkness follows.

*

I come round with a thumping headache, feeling that somebody has slashed the side of my face with a knife. I'm aware of being rushed to the medical centre, but thankfully I'm OK. What isn't OK is that, when I look down, I see the heel has come off one of my brand-new sandals. God, I'll be working overtime for a year to pay for another pair.

I'm placed on a bed which is very comfortable. So comfortable it makes me want to go to sleep.

'How are you feeling?' asks the middle-aged nurse holding a wet cloth to my aching cheek.

'Fine, fine,' I say, feeling dizzy. There's a man awkwardly standing next to me in a beautifully cut navy suit. He has dark hair going slightly grey around the temples. He has the bluest eyes I've ever seen and they seem full of concern.

'Who's Jimmy?' he asks slowly. He has an English accent. A very grand one, as though he could be related to the royal family. Or read the BBC news.

'Jimmy?' I blink a few times. Really, he was very attractive. Where had he come from and why was he asking me weird questions? Was he the new airport doctor?

'You asked for Jimmy . . . I didn't quite catch the surname. I was wondering whether I could phone him for you, perhaps. My name is Oliver Kane. I knocked you down.'

'Did you? Were you the guy in the Mercedes?'

The kindly nurse interrupts. 'Do you want to give us Jimmy's number? Is he your boyfriend?'

'No, my boyfriend was Niall and I certainly don't want you to phone him. He's in Australia for a start.' I sit up in the hospital-type bed. Ouch. My head really hurts. 'I'll be fine. I'd better get home. Where are my shoes?'

I look down sadly at my destroyed sandals. 'Oh my poor Jimmy Choos!'

The nurse and the well-dressed man look at each other and exchange secret smiles.

'Your sandals,' they say in unison.

'Yes they're my Jimmy Choos. Oh, I see what you mean. Shoes, not a man.'

'Can I give you a lift somewhere? You're not going to be able to walk home in those,' says the man with the cute eyes, or Oliver, as I suppose I should call him.

'No, I'll get a taxi,' I assure him. 'I'm OK, honestly. Is there a bathroom in here? I'll just go and get myself cleaned up.'

The sight of my face in the bathroom mirror gives me a shock. One side of my face is very badly scratched. I look as if I got into a fight with a big wild vicious cat – and lost.

I come out into the medical room again. 'My face . . .' I start to whimper. This day is just not turning out to be good for me.

'I'll write you a note,' says the nurse hurriedly. 'You'll clearly be cosmetically unfit for a week, so you won't have to work.'

'Oh, but that's no use,' I insist. 'I've been suspended for a week, anyway, so could you give me the same medical cert for a fortnight?'

I know I'm probably chancing my arm, but what the hell? I may as well get something out of this. I've had the day from hell and I could always go away on a nice holiday or something for all my trouble.

'Sure,' the nurse says immediately. 'That'll be no problem.'

'In the meantime, do you mind if I lie down for half an hour or so? I feel a bit drained. Thank you so much for being so kind.' I take the gentleman's hand and squeeze it. I feel the cold touch of a wedding ring. Oh, pity. But sure, it's inevitable, isn't it? Single men in Ireland are a rarity. Especially good-looking ones.

When I wake up again the nice man is gone. I feel much better now, although my cheek still stings a bit.

After I've freshened up, the nurse hands me my sick note (yippee!) and an envelope.

'What's this?' I enquire. Hopefully, I won't have to fill out a load of forms or anything to be released. My day off has nearly come to an end and I've absolutely nothing to show for it. I didn't even get to go to the dry cleaners, the post office or Dunnes Stores to buy underwear. See what an exciting life I lead? Those are the things I normally do on a day off. And sometimes for extra excitement I get the 41 bus to Swords to visit my folks and help my dad out in the garden.

'Mr Kane left you some money for your taxi home. He had to rush off to a meeting.'

'Oh,' I say, ripping open the envelope. He must be a busy man! As the envelope tears open, a load of €20 notes start floating towards the floor. I stare at them in stunned silence. There must be some mistake.

'Where does he think I live? London? A taxi into the city centre would only cost €20 at the most. This is ridiculous. I'll have to give it back. Did he leave a card or something?'

'Apparently not.' The nurse shrugs. 'I'd take the money, though. He could have killed you.'

'But he didn't,' I protest. 'And he was very kind.'

'And good looking.' The nurse winks.

'And married!' I counter.

She conveniently ignores that last comment. 'Give the money to charity if you feel so guilty about it.'

I stuff the notes into my back pocket and fish my mobile out of my bag to ring a taxi. I can hardly walk up to the taxi rank with no shoes, can I? What a funny man, I think to myself. But very generous. Pity he never even said good-bye!

'Well, I'd better be going,' I say, giving the nurse a hug. I know she didn't really have to give me such an extended sick note, so I'm terribly grateful. 'Thanks for everything.'

'Do you want to know where he is staying?'

I hover at the door ready to leave. 'As I said, he's married.'

'OK,' the nurse says. 'Fair enough.'

'Bye.'

I wander outside but it has started to rain. And no sign of my taxi. Maybe I should go back and ask the nurse for an umbrella.

'I thought you'd come back,' says the nurse, giving me a knowing smile.

'I was wondering if you have an umbrella. It's freezing and it's lashing and my feet are bare.'

'Do you want to know the name of that hotel?'

I shrug nonchalantly. 'Oh go on then, it doesn't make any difference, but obviously you're dying to tell me.'

'The Conrad Hotel, Earlsfort Terrace.'

'OK, thanks for that. Not that I would dream of popping in to say hello.'

'Of course not,' says the nurse demurely. 'Well, anyway, have a nice weekend.'

Rule Four: Keep your opinions to yourself.

I'm on the plane to Malaga. Only this time I've kicked off my impossibly high heels and my face is completely devoid of all that heavy make-up I'm usually forced to slap on my face. Yes, I'm a passenger this time. A standby passenger – I only got on the plane at the last minute because there were a few empty seats. Thank God for the no-shows! I'm sitting in row one guzzling champagne mixed with orange juice. I feel as though I'm drinking in the office and it's a naughty feeling indeed! I'm so looking forward to a week of sunshine and sangria. There's something fantastic about heading for the sun when the rest of the country sits on buses with fogged-up windows and rain-sodden umbrellas sitting on their laps.

Well, who could blame me for escaping? I've two weeks off work so what's a girl to do? I didn't want to hang around Dublin anyway, not the way I look at the moment. People might think I was self-harming myself with a razor blade over the break-up with Niall. As if! I have so moved on from him. He's history. I don't even think about him. Call me a liar, and you'd be telling the truth. Would you believe

I got a cheque from him yesterday for two hundred euros, saying he was sorry about everything that had happened but still giving no explanation as to why he screwed me over the way he did. I cashed the cheque and immediately sent him a text reminding him he still owed me another eight hundred euros. I mean, the cheek of him. I'm not that bloody forgetful! Still, the two hundred euros will help pay for my hotel in Spain. I'm so glad to be going away. It's October and the autumn chill has really begun to set in. The brown and golden leaves covering the footpaths are slippy and soggy and everything looks a bit bleak, especially in the city centre where I live, my bedroom overlooking a road congested with traffic most of the time.

It will be good for me to go away and find myself. My case is full of my favourite chick-lit books, trashy magazines and pots of cellulite creams, face creams, exfoliating creams and luxury bath oils to pamper myself with. I'm all set now as I booked a hotel in an Internet café on O'Connell Street last night. It looked fabulous on screen so I hope the reality lives up to its cyberspace image. My flatmate Edel thought I was mad when I told her.

'But what'll you do over there all day by yourself?' she asked wide-eyed. 'I mean, is it safe?'

Edel is probably the best flatmate a girl could have. She's not the tidiest girl in the world, but at least her messiness is confined to her bedroom, and she takes her turn washing up and watering the plants. To be honest, I'd rather share with somebody like her than a neat freak who writes her name on milk cartons and stuff. I once had a room-mate like that. She used to hoover the flat at 3 o'clock in the morning and keep her rolls of toilet paper under the bed, carrying them to and from the bathroom whenever she needed them. Then, one day, when I was out of bread and 'borrowed' a slice of hers she hit the roof and shouted at me for having no respect for her and robbing her blind. The relief when she finally packed up and left was only enormous. Edel, on the other hand, from a small Wexford town, is a sweet girl if a little naive at times. I mean, she has only ever gone abroad twice in her life, once to an uncle's funeral in Manchester, and another time she went for a job interview in Bristol which she didn't get. She dropped out of Montessori college this year and now works in a shoe shop in Henry Street, which makes her feet swell because she's wearing fancy high heels all day. Those same shoes also give her a bad back from all the bending down trying to squeeze the feet of all the wannabe Cinderellas into tiny delicate dainty slippers. She is also terrified of flying, although she is doing 'fear of flying' hypnosis sessions at the moment, which are supposed to be brilliant. Every time I leave the apartment to go to work, she says she'll say a prayer for me in case the plane goes down. I know she says it to make me feel better but it's so annoying. I mean, how would she like it if I kept praying that she didn't get knocked down by a bus crossing O'Connell Street?

Anyway, why wouldn't I go away? It's not like Spain is a really dodgy, dangerous place. And besides, since Edel hooked up with grungy wannabe artist Greg from Leitrim, the pair of them are beginning to be a little irritating because they watch TV every night in my tiny flat. I'd thought I was letting out a single room to a single girl and now Greg, whom Edel met on the Internet of all places, stays over so much I feel he should be contributing towards the rent. Edel assures me that he's looking for work. But looking at the TV all day with his dirty sneakers parked constantly on my cream Habitat couch that I took out a substantial loan to pay for, won't find him a job, will it? However, at least he doesn't wash so he doesn't use any hot water, which is good, and he does have his uses. For example, he runs out to the shops to get us heavy stuff like briquettes for the barbecue which we can't carry for fear of ruining our clothes, or when we're simply just too cold or lazy to move our arses and run to the shops for a pint of milk and the *Evening Herald*. His brother Mickey, cute but only nineteen, works in a video shop so we rent DVDs for free and we get half-price on the tanning booths upstairs. Mind you, Greg does well out of me too – all those duty free cigarettes and bottles of booze I bring home go down a treat with himself and his hairy, smelly mates. Oh, hopefully by the time I get back from my holidays he'll have sorted himself out. As I said, he's not a bad creature, just somebody who's beginning to over-wear his welcome a little.

I relax back in my seat and order another drink. Thankfully I don't recognise any of the crew today so I don't need to explain where I'm going or the reason why I've been suspended. It's shameful enough being in the bad books without also being gossip fodder for the whole airline in the process. Also, I'm sitting right in front of the loo, so I can see if it's vacant without walking all the way up the aisle and standing at the front cross-legged in front of all the passengers.

Thankfully the seat next to mine is also free so I don't have to chat to anybody about why I'm going on holidays on my own. People always presume that a pal let you down at the last minute, that you're a total Billy-No-Mates, or that your cad of a boyfriend must have stood you up at the airport at the last minute. But there are huge advantages to heading off on your tod. There is absolutely nobody I can think of whom I'd like to share a small hotel room with for twenty-four hours a day, seven days a week. First of all, if it rains you are literally stuck with them and, after a day or two, all your news and gossip has been exhausted. Second, if they snore loudly, turn on the light in the middle of the night, or flush the loo, then your sleep is broken. And third, if they're the type of people who want to visit museums or go on ghastly bus tours, then you might just have to kill them. Don't know about you lot, but any time I've gone on a so-called romantic holiday it has ended in tears. A weekend I can do, no problem. Any more than that is torture.

By the time I fairly stumble off the plane after the two-and-a-half hour journey mostly spent staring out at the clouds, the champagne has gone to my head. But the warmth of the sunshine beating down on my face as I cross the airport ramp makes me feel very glad I'm here. Immediately I feel as though I'm getting a second shot at summer. Only two and a half hours away from Dublin. Why don't I do it more often?

At the carousel in the airport I take off my thick navy bomber jacket and stuff it in my wheelie bag. I then head out of the airport and make my way over to the train station which is a good ten-minute walk away, including a trip over the busy road. I drag my case over the pedestrian bridge to the train stop. The sun, high in the sky, is still beaming down. The temperature must be in the mid-twenties and the clouds are practically non-existent. With any luck a train will be here soon, I can quickly check into my hotel and I'll be sunning myself on a beach in hours.

After purchasing my cheap ticket from the automated machine, I carry my bag down the steps, sit on a bench and wait. There's nobody else on the platform apart from a tall dark-haired man nearby who has a fit body and a rucksack on his back. Maybe it's my imagination but I feel I'm being stared at. Slowly I raise my head and catch his eye. He smiles. I nod. I don't want to smile too much and encourage him in case he's a weirdo. Mind you, he doesn't look like a fruitcake. He's got the longest, darkest eyelashes I've ever seen and piercing green eyes. He's also already sporting a decent tan, especially compared to my pale freckled skin. He must be Spanish.

I notice he's got a map in one hand. Odd. If he's Spanish, surely he'd know his way around the place. Then again, he could be from Madrid or somewhere.

'Excuse me?' he asks in a clear South Dublin accent as I nearly fall off the bench in surprise. 'Do you know how far Fuengirola is from Marbella?'

His face is picture-perfect, with high cheekbones and a squarish jaw sporting day-old stubble. When he speaks he reveals teeth that could be in an ad for cosmetic dentistry. I feel self-conscious all of a sudden. Dammit, I wish I'd put on a bit of make-up earlier. What will he think of my scratched face? And are my eyes bloodshot after the three – or was it four – champagne snipes?

'The train's final stop is Fuengirola,' I explain, squinting at him through the sunlight. 'Then you'd have to get a bus or a taxi to Marbella, which is about twenty minutes away.'

'Thanks,' he says, pushing a lock of jet-black hair from his face and frowning slightly as though weighing up the pros and cons of both options. He's ridiculously good looking. 'By the way, did I see you on the plane from Dublin?'

Ooh, stalker alert. Good stalker alert, mind you. He can follow me around as much as he likes. How flattering that he noticed somebody like me, considering I'm wearing not a screed of make-up and look like a Scissors Sister on a bad day. I can feel myself redden. Gosh, it is warm.

'Yeah that's right. Very early start, wasn't it? Like getting up in the middle of the night. It's a killer.'

'But you should be used to early starts.' He grins as my heart does a double flip. He knows what I do for a living? Scary!

'I work in the same airline as you. I recognise your face. I joined the company as a pilot last year. My name's Danny.'

No way. Where has he been hiding? Few of our pilots are remotely attractive. True, a lot of them look fairly dashing in their smart uniforms and caps but as soon as they take their caps off to reveal their rapidly receding hairlines, and change into their civvies you sadly notice the beer bellies and lack of muscles.

I open my mouth to say something but nothing comes out. I wonder what age he is. He looks youthful. I don't do younger men. Well, usually I don't. But I'd probably make an exception this time.

Eventually my voice comes creeping back. 'Really? My name's Annie. Isn't that a coincidence?' *Danny and Annie*. Oh, I like it!

'Yeah, I noticed you from around. I don't think we've flown with each other yet.'

'No, I don't recall . . .' I trail off as if I'm trying to remember. Of course I didn't bloody work with him. I'd never miss this cracker. If he was driving the plane, I'd be in and out of the cockpit begging for a go of his joystick!

'Are you on holidays or . . . meeting friends?'

'Friends, that's right,' I say hurriedly, and then mentally bite off my tongue. Now what the hell did I go and say that for? Am I trying to look like I'm Miss Popular? Still, the thing is that, deep down, I am a little embarrassed at the fact that I'm holidaying all by myself.

With my temperature suddenly having shot up, I'm beginning to feel two damp patches accumulate under my arms, which is a pity because I'd love to take off my cardigan.

'What about you?' I ask hastily. 'Are you meeting friends?'

'Yes, they're actually training to be pilots in Jerez but they're driving down to Marbella to meet me for a few days. We should all meet up for a few scoops later. Would your pals be on for that?'

I feel a smile freeze on my face. What can I say? Pretend that my non-friends are nuns and that they don't drink or that they don't like boys? But instead of just coming clean I end up digging a bigger hole for myself.

'That'd be great.' I beam. 'Let's all go down to the port and have a mad night out!'

'Are the other girls hosties too?'

'Oh no,' I answer quickly. 'One's a model and the other's a singer. They're crazy party girls. They could drink you under the table!'

I'm beginning to warm to my invisible friends. In fact, it's a pity they aren't here actually. We could have had such a laugh, especially since now I feel like a complete loser heading off for a week of fun and frolics for one. Am I a loser? No, I can't be. I've loads of friends but none of them would have been able to come away at such short notice.

Danny the pilot whips out his mobile phone as the train roars into the station at terrific speed. We hop on together and I give him my number. He's probably being polite and won't phone at all.

'I'll ring you later on, then. What are your plans for this afternoon?'

Yikes, that a bit keen, isn't it?

'Well I'm a bit tired after my flight and everything . . . maybe tomorrow night then?'

That should give me a bit of time to figure out how to quietly dispose of my made-up pals. Maybe I can say that they got sunstroke and were holed up in the hospital in Marbella. Or else I could say that we changed our minds and went out the first night and were then too hungover to party again the second night. Of course I could come clean and tell him that, hahaha, I didn't have any friends, but I doubt that would wash. Anyway, why is he so interested in meeting my friends? Am I not good enough? Suddenly I feel lacking.

The train rumbles out of the station. I sit at the window

for the view and Danny sits next to me, his thigh dangerously close to mine. God, he is handsome though.

The weather is simply gorgeous. I cannot believe how glorious it is, especially since it's October. There isn't a single cloud in the sky. Why doesn't everybody live here? There's plenty of room. If the airline had a cabin crew base here in Malaga, I'd definitely sign up. What isn't there to love? The weather is heavenly, the people are nice, and the food is scrumptious, so you could eat salads all day and still be thin and you could walk everywhere and it would be pleasant instead of a chore. Oh, and it's cheap, too, much cheaper than Dublin, where it seems as though you can't sneeze on the streets these days without there being a charge.

'Wouldn't it be great to live here?' says Danny, echoing my thoughts. He's taking off his jacket to reveal a sturdy pair of bronzed, toned arms under a flimsy light pink-striped cotton shirt. 'I always think the pace of life really slows down in sunny climates. Nobody seems to be in a hurry like in capital cities. I suppose the weather has something to do with it.'

'Mmm,' I agree, desperately wanting to take off my cardigan. I'm boiling inside and I'm sure my face is red and sweaty, but I'm afraid the whiffs of my underarms might knock out the delicious Danny. If only those idiots at the airport hadn't confiscated my can of deodorant. Listen, it was quite obvious I wasn't going to blow up the plane with it. I reckon those guys are so badly paid that they sell all those banned aftershaves and perfumes on eBay.

'So where are you guys staying in Marbella?' I ask.

'We're staying in the Coral Beach. Do you know it?'

'Yeah, I do, I've stayed there before. It's a nice hotel, decent-sized heated pool, and right on the beach. It's only about five minutes from Puerto Banus in a taxi. Wow, you're really living it up for the week.'

For a moment I feel sorry that I didn't check in there. Mind you, I didn't particularly want to be staying in a place where the probability of bumping into fellow Paddies would be high. The best thing about holidays is being able to slob around an apartment with oil in your hair and sunning yourself on your balcony while rubbing anti-cellulite cream into your tummy. It's not the time where you want to be making sure your bikini coordinates with your flip flops and matching beach bag, with a face full of melting make-up.

'So why Fuengirola?' Danny asks.

'I love the prom there. I love the way I can stick on my iPod and walk for hours listening to music and looking out at the ocean.'

And it's a lot cheaper than Marbella, I think without feeling the need to state the fact aloud. Now, I know some people mistakenly look at Fuengirola as a place crawling with time-share merchants who lurch among the fish and chip shops and tacky pubs with plastic bulldogs on the outside, but you can't deny that it's pretty good value – some pubs sell you a glass of wine for a quid, and it seems to be happy hour all day long. Anyway, it's different in the winter time. The huge crowds have disappeared until the following summer and the place seems to be full of retired people who walk at a snail's pace, wear socks and sandals and carry small white plastic bags around with them. I love old people because they remind me of my grandparents when they were alive, bless them.

It's just so chilled here that I fit right in with my romance novels, my sunglasses and penchant for ice-cold white wine. Now, I wouldn't like to go to Fuengirola on my honeymoon or anything, as only Mauritius would do for such a momentous occasion, but for a week or so lounging around doing nothing, you can't beat it. Already I'm getting excited at the thought of strolling along the prom with the warm breeze in my hair.

'Can't you walk around Marbella too, though?'

'Yeah, but the prom isn't as long.' And I might bump into somebody I know! And the bars are a bit pricey too, I add silently.

Unfortunately I have to be frugal at the moment, although it completely goes against my nature. I mean, inside I feel like I should be a rich person, and I really identify with all of those footballers' wives I read about who go shopping all day, in theory if not in practice. But while I'm still an air hostess (the lifestyle might be glamorous, but that doesn't impress my bank manager) with a crazy mortgage (whoever thought giving one hundred per cent loans to impoverished shopaholics was a good thing?), I can't be paying top dollar for a round in a fancy bar. So that's why I stock up on duty free any time I fly out of the EU and buy lots of bulk items with unpronounceable names in Lidl.

Every year, I say to myself that next year will be different, that I will save at least some money, but I can never seem to. And any time I bring down my credit card debt, they just seem to raise my credit. Like now my credit is ten grand, which means I can walk into any garage and 'buy' a brand spanking new car with this piece of plastic, even though I'm skint.

I don't know where I went so wrong. I mean, people on flights who aren't from Ireland always ask me about this Celtic Tiger we're supposed to be enjoying as a nation but I haven't even been whipped by the animal's tail. And now some economists on the news are saying he's already gone, and I just think, how could he? The bastard didn't even leave me a tip when he was here.

My mortgage is crippling me, but I bought a place because my sister Emily left me the deposit and I'd feel guilty buying clothes with the money she had saved. Also, everyone I spoke to was banging on about getting a foot on the property ladder before it was too late. So that's what I did. I got a foot on it, but the heel of my second foot is still well and truly stuck on the muddy ground. Property ladder? Everything I like in the property section of the paper costs at least a million quid, so even if I do sell my little apartment at a profit, it's not going to make a damn bit of difference, is it? So where do I go from here? Will I just wait until my parents eventually leave their Swords home to me? Is that my only chance of ever getting something with a garden? Then again, they probably won't even leave it to me. No doubt they'll leave it to me and my siblings, and they'll want to sell it, and I won't even be able to buy them out. God, it's so depressing.

'Do you think the sea is still warm enough to swim in?' asks Danny as the train speeds towards built-up Torremolinos. We both crane our necks for glimpses of the blue ocean between the sky-scraping apartment blocks.

'We could try, after a few stiff whiskies, I suppose,' I

giggle. 'But I doubt it's as inviting as it looks. After all, look around us, it's winter time here. Everybody's wearing their winter woollies.'

It was true. The passengers on the train, mostly Spanish, were wrapped up in duffle coats, scarves and beanie hats. There was precious little chance of them diving into the Mediterranean sea to cool down. They must really think the Brits and the Irish are stark raving mad stripping off and shivering on windy beaches as they themselves scurry along head down complaining of the dropping temperatures.

'Have you ever gone skinny dipping?' Danny beams and I blush at the thought of him picturing me naked and running along the strand. Does he imagine me as toned and buffed, or flabby and blotchy skinned? Anyway, it's a bit of a personal question, considering we've only just met. I mean, we haven't even snogged yet. Crikey, what am I thinking? First, this guy is so devastatingly handsome he probably has an equally stunning girlfriend; second, he's shown as much interest in my non-friends as he has in me; and third, he could be only talking to me because I'm Irish and I happen to work in the same airline as him. On the other hand, I, the saddo that I am, am imagining watching the sun set with his strong arms wrapped around me.

'Yeah, all the time,' I lie, looking out of the window, terrified of making eye contact. Why not exaggerate a bit? It's not as if I really intend hooking up with him in my 'get-to-know-myself' peaceful holiday. 'There's something very liberating about swimming around in the nip, isn't there?'

I smile innocently at him. His hand brushes against my thigh, sending a frisson of excitement down it. 'Saucy girl,' he laughs. Talk about being over-familiar! If he wasn't so good looking he'd get a smack in the face. Isn't it awful the way people with symmetrical features get away with everything. If Danny was a short pudgy redhead with a beer belly, a hairy back and out-of-control nasal hair, I'd probably have got him arrested. In fact, if he'd any of those traits I'd have escaped to the furthest carriage by now.

There are many stops before we reach Fuengirola. I stare out the window and notice only a couple of clouds languishing in an otherwise unbroken blue sky. The nearer we reach our destination, the more loathe I am to get there. Now that it's nearly lunchtime, my stomach is beginning to rumble quietly and I quite fancy a plate of chips with lashings of vinegar and a bit of lingering over a nice glass of cool dry white wine. Wouldn't it be fabulous to share it with Danny? He's definitely a bit of a scamp but naughty boys are much more fun – in the short-term, anyway. And I'm on holidays.

'Well, here we are,' I announce, with not much enthusiasm, when the train finally pulls in at Fuengirola and everybody gets off purposefully. Only Danny and I seem reluctant to get out. Being a gentleman, he gallantly lifts my wheelie case on to the track and then carries it up the narrow steps with his own rucksack on his back and me following gratefully behind. I'm not as tired as I felt this morning when my annoying cuckoo alarm clock blasted me out of it and I thought I was going to simply die at the thought of dragging myself out of my warm bed complete with electric blanket. Only the thought of a week wearing T-shirts and shorts made the ordeal more bearable. But now, with the sun beaming down on me, I've got a new lease of life. I've arrived safely and I hope I can find my hotel all right. I printed off a map from the Internet earlier, but as I'm not great at reading maps, and I would rather die than ask somebody directions, I'd best make my way towards the beach as the hotel is on the sea front. I wonder whether Danny has decided to take a taxi or a bus to Marbella.

Neither, apparently. Danny says his friends aren't arriving until later on tonight so he may as well keep me company. Oh goody. Hopefully, he will want to accompany me to my hotel. But do I let him into my room? I can't let him see me unpack as I've brought all the clothes I was originally going to donate to charity shops with me. But then I figured I'd get one last wear out of the rags, leave them behind, and stock up my empty case with booze for the way home. Well, it's a much better idea than bringing home smelly, damp suntan-oil-drenched towels, isn't it? Now I've nothing glamorous to wear. I've left behind my two favourite dresses because I wore them on the last two nights I shared with Niall, and in the back of my head I suppose that if they'd made me look at all hot, he wouldn't have dumped me.

'Let's just dump these bags in your hotel and find a bar and get drunk, huh?' Danny ruffles my hair with a mischievous glint in his eye. How could I resist? Anyway, at least getting drunk doesn't involve me having to shave my legs. Imagine if he'd suggested a swim or a spot of sunbathing? Now, that would be taking things too far. Maybe we can find an outdoor terrace somewhere to sit and watch the world go by?

'Sounds like a plan,' I agree, too flattered to turn down his offer. I mean, it's not as if I'm looking too hot at the moment. The scratches on my face are still visible even though they don't sting any more. Danny, on the other hand, looks like a mini God. Still, he seems to fancy me a bit which is great. I can only imagine what a ride he looks in his uniform. 'The thing is, though, I'm not exactly sure where this hotel is. I know it's by the sea as I requested a sea view, but that's about it.'

'Come on, let's find it,' says Danny, leading the way, still holding my case. I must say I find it very appealing when a man takes the lead. Especially when he looks like Danny.

Fuengirola is actually full of pretty little laneways with interesting-looking gift shops, boutiques and quirky restaurants. It's only when you get to the long stretch of promenade that you notice the tacky karaoke bars and hideous 'cafés' serving real Yorkshire pudding and tea and crumpets. We pass them all and I notice Danny's forehead is gathering tiny beads of sweat. I offer to wheel my case myself but he won't even hear of it. Aw, what a dote!

Finally, I see my hotel looming into the air. I recognise it from the picture on the Internet. Majestically, the building towers over every other one on this stretch of beach, and it looks magnificent. Thank goodness, because I paid well for it, and I was getting a bit nervous there for a minute as we passed one grotty-looking run-down hotel after another. If I'd had to stay in one of those kips, I'd have been better off staying at home.

The lobby is very impressive with cut-glass chandeliers

hanging from the ceilings and flower arrangements in tall vases dotted around the place. I'm thrilled that I splashed out now, even if my bank manager won't be. When I go to check in the girl behind the desk looks from me to Danny.

'A single or a double?'

'Oh, a single,' I say hurriedly, not wanting to give her the wrong idea, or her to charge me more than I had originally intended. Still, I'm quite honoured that she thought Danny and myself were a couple. Do we look like a couple? Does he not look like my younger, more handsome brother or something?

We get into the lift and press the button to the fourteenth floor. I almost feel dizzy in the lift as we seem to shoot up towards the roof in the glass elevator. The fancy lobby certainly seems such a long way down.

'I like this place,' says Danny, grinning from ear to ear. 'I could see myself living in a place like this.'

'Now, don't push your luck, hon.'

A loud ping indicates that we've reached the right floor. My room is directly opposite the lift. I slip my hotel-room key card into the slot and the door opens easily. Rushing to the sliding doors, I pull them back eagerly and step out into the warmth of the balcony. The view is breathtaking. You can see for miles and miles. Fishing boats bob along the bay, tiny white dots in the ocean. Couples stroll along the beach, some with excited dogs running around in circles. Some kids struggle with a huge red and white kite. The sun loungers are for the most part deserted, though. Only the serious sun worshippers seem to be availing themselves of the last of the summer rays. I take a deep breath of sea air, taking off my shoes and resting my feet on the heated tiles of the balcony. Oh, it's good to be here. Really it is. Thanks, Mrs Savage, you stupid old cow, I think. If it wasn't for you I'd be back in dreary Dublin picking my toenails or something equally as dull.

'Well chosen, Annie, this place is class,' murmurs Danny in my ear, wrapping his strong arms around my waist.

I can't answer. I'm speechless, although whether that's because of the scenic view or the closeness of a six-foot hunk beside me, is anybody's guess. My heart is hammering in my chest. How am I supposed to react?

'Quick, take your clothes off . . .' he whispers.

I turn around to face him. He looks quite taken aback by the obviously cross face on me. 'Now listen here—' I begin, but he puts a middle finger on my lips to shut me up.

'I mean,' he says, 'I mean I want you to get into the shower and get changed as fast as you can. I'll meet you down in the hotel bar in fifteen. Drinks on me, I promise.'

'OK, I'll see you in fifteen.' I nod. 'But, please, let's go outside. We're on the Costa Del Sol, for God's sake!'

'Deal.' He smiles, putting his hands back in his pockets like a cheeky schoolboy. 'Don't be long.'

I strip off hurriedly and run a hot shower. I'm in holiday mode already and can't wipe the smile off my face. A week ago who would've thought I'd be here in a luxury hotel with a sexy toy-boy in tow? Some girls have all the luck, huh?

*

I step out of the shower, my long hair dripping down my back and I catch it in a towel. Wrapping myself in a fluffy white bathrobe and slipping my feet into matching white hotel slippers, I step back out on to the balcony again. I can't stop smiling. I wish Niall could see me now, the prick! Danny's much better looking than Niall. I'll have to arrange to bring him to Niall's local pub once he comes home from Australia. He'll have to come back sometime, whether he likes it or not, when his visa expires. His mum told me that he'd only gone for a year when I phoned her to see if she knew anything about my missing money. She sounded horrified. Niall's trip apparently wasn't just a spur-of-the-moment decision – he'd been planning it for ages and had told her he'd got a loan from the Credit Union. His mother had even gone guarantor for him! So obviously my thousand euros were just a bit of extra pocket money, then. Huh! But she assured me that Niall would be back next year in time to be groomsman at his brother Peter's wedding. So I'll be waiting for him, looking slim and gorgeous with all my confidence back. Wouldn't it be great if I turned up at Niall's local after one of his rugby matches with Danny on my arm? Now *that* would make his jaw hit the floor.

I'd love to stay out here all day, dreaming of plotting my revenge on Niall while watching people leisurely stroll the never-ending prom underneath my balcony, but the pub beckons, as does my handsome man. I wrap my hair in a second towel to thoroughly dry it, sit down on the edge of the double bed and smother my thighs in delicious-smelling white chocolate cellulite cream. I've been bold recently, and not drinking the required eight glasses of water a day which help to rid the body of unsightly orange peel, apparently. So say the beauty magazines, anyway, and

I devour them on a regular basis, looking for a quicker and easier fix than giving up beer and chocolate. The problem with all those slimming magazines, though, is that they're crammed with photos of food which always make my mouth water.

Now smelling a lot fresher and feeling wide awake, I slap on some flawless finish, smear some scarlet lipstick over my lips, and brush my eyelids with copper eyeshadow. There, that's my face sorted. Then I empty the contents of my suitcase on the bed and they tumble out looking a lot more crushed than when I first packed them. Honestly, I don't think I brought anything really decent to wear. Because I have to dress up in a formal-looking suit, and wear unflattering flesh-coloured tights and high heels every day as part of my job, on days off, all I feel like doing is slobbing around in tracksuits, even on holidays in an upmarket hotel.

I try on my 'skinny jeans', but doing exactly as they say on the tin, they're not very accommodating when I try to fit my own thunder thighs into them. So much for the bloody cellulite cream. I spent almost a week's wages on it!

A phone call to my room makes me jump. Who on earth knows I'm here? I didn't even give my own mother the number of the hotel.

'Hello?' I answer tentatively.

'Baby,' coos the deep well-spoken voice. 'I was afraid you'd fallen asleep. I've ordered you a cosmopolitan but the ice has almost melted.'

I pick out a cream chiffon skirt (about five seasons out of date, but Danny, being a bloke, will hardly notice now, will he?), a simple black tank top, and a light black wrap-over cardigan with a hole under the arm which, with any luck, Danny won't notice. Then I slip my bare feet into black strappy sandals adorned with diamante butterflies. They're nice, but not a patch on my ruined Jimmy Choos which are now in a bin somewhere. Tears fill my eyes as I remember how much they cost me in Brown Thomas. Stop it, Annie, I tell myself; there is no point even thinking about them now.

It's so nice not to have to wear horrible restricting nylon tights for a change. I whip out a fairly blunt razor blade from my wash bag (I think it must have belonged to Niall at some stage), and give my fuzzy legs a quick going over.

Finally ready, my hair still damp, but respectable, I grab my shoulder bag, leave the bedroom and call for the lift. I glance at my watch. At this stage Danny will probably be on his second pint and the ice in my cocktail will have well and truly disappeared.

I sashay into the bar which is empty apart from Danny. I'm right – he has ordered himself a brand new pint. My cosmopolitan looks perfect. I sit myself up on a stool as Danny hands me my glass.

'Cheers.' Danny raises his pint. 'To a fun holiday.'

'And to coincidences,' I add. 'Fancy meeting you here! Can you believe I've never bumped into you on a flight?'

'No, I can't. To think of all the fun we've been missing on overnights.' He winks, and I feel myself blushing again. Jesus, girl, I think, would you get a grip!

It doesn't take me long to down my cocktail. It shoots straight to my head, squashing a few brain cells in the process, no doubt.

'Wow, you can really knock them back,' says Danny, clearly impressed. 'But if we stay here all night paying hotel prices, we won't be able to afford any more nights out and will have to stay in bed for the rest of the holiday with just a couple of bottles of supermarket wine to keep us company,' he says suggestively, placing the warm palm of his hand on my bare leg.

As I said before, if this guy wasn't hot, he'd be considered a serious lech. But he has lovely green eyes, is tall, tanned, and because he's so goddamn handsome he can get away with murder. Besides, I'm kind of in lust. And I'm on holidays, unexpectedly yes, but on holidays all the same. And if you can't throw caution to the wind when you're away there's no hope for you. I push his hand away playfully. 'Get away you.' I drain the last drop from my glass. 'Have you not got a girlfriend or anything?'

Danny does a bad impression of trying to look mournful, but it doesn't wash. He knows he's as handsome as anything.

'Nope, do you?'

'No, my last bird dumped me.'

'You know what I mean.'

'The part about being dumped is true, though,' I admit. 'And it's only recent so I'm pretty fragile at the moment.'

'What you need is a real man,' says Danny, standing tall and puffing out his chest exaggeratedly.

'I agree.' I smile back, fluttering my eyelids. 'Wow, what did they put in that cosmopolitan? It's gone straight to my head!'

'You didn't have to drink it so quickly,' Danny teases.

But I ignore his suggestion. I'm enjoying being alone here with him, and anyway, just one or two more drinks can't hurt, can they?

The next thing I know, it's the following morning. I wake with the strong morning sun streaming in through a crack in the curtains, and Danny's legs tangled up in mine. I reach down with one hand, my finger tips trailing his six-pack abs. Oh God.

Panicking, I sit bolt upright in the bed, pulling the sheet up to cover the naked top half of my body. Danny's eyes remain closed. I look at my watch. 7 a.m., 8 a.m. Spanish time. I realise I'm still wearing my pink thong. Thank goodness for small blessings.

'We didn't, did we?' I croak, my voice gravelly, my tongue feeling like a furry, dirty old piece of carpet.

Danny's still sleeping and doesn't seem to hear me. I rack my brains to try to piece the previous night's events together. After the cocktails in the bar everything seemed a bit fuzzy. I remember heading out into the blinding sunshine complete with designer sunglasses and alcohol warming up our stomachs. Linking arms, we crossed the road over to the vast impressive-looking beach.

'I just want to dip my toe in the water,' I remember laughing, 'just to check if it's warm enough for swimming in.'

'But it's too early for skinny dipping,' Danny had answered flippantly with a mock earnest look in his eye. 'We'll have to wait until dark. We don't want to be arrested. Not on the first day of our holidays anyway.'

'God, you've such a dirty mind,' I said, giving his tall

frame a shove. 'Did your mother never wash your mouth out with soap and water when you were young?'

'My mother's got a far filthier mouth than me. Come on, last into the sea is a hairy ape.'

Then I raced him to the sea. It didn't look very promising. Despite its inviting deep blue colour there wasn't a single other human being in the water. If that wasn't a sign, then what was?

I kicked off my sandals as Danny hunched down, struggling to remove his socks and shoes. I won. So I wasn't a hairy ape after all.

'Come on in,' I beckoned with mock encouragement. 'The sea is not only glorious, it's boiling!'

I shudder now as I remember how cold the water was. I had waded in as far as my knees, despite my skirt getting wet as the waves crashed against my legs. Of course, I'd completely forgotten about my instant fake tan which instantly washed away as my lower legs turned blue with the cold. It was absolutely bloody freezing.

'So what did I win?' I stood in the water with my hands on my hips.

'OK, the rest of the drinks are on me this evening,' he offered. 'But I'm not letting you off that easily. You can get them tomorrow night.'

'Tomorrow? Who said anything about tomorrow, Mister? What do you think this is? A long-term relationship?'

'You wish.' He grinned retreating from the icy sea.

'Chicken!' I accused.

'Ah, Jesus. I came here for a tan, not to try and get pneumonia, you cheeky brat.'

I followed him out of the water shivering. The sun was going down and a strong wind had begun to circulate. I could feel the goose pimples covering my legs at an alarming rate. What was I thinking?

We made our way back up to the prom, and dried off on a bench underneath a palm tree. I was beginning to feel hungry. Starving, actually, and cold. I wanted to sit somewhere warm, snug and cosy, in a corner with a jug of decent sangria in front of me. I didn't even care if it was an Irish pub with 'The Fields of Athenry' playing in the background, or a British pub full of geezers wearing Union Jack T-shirts. I just wanted some food and some more drink.

I rub my eyes and look over once again at the sleeping Danny. My head feels as if somebody is thumping it and my stomach feels queasy. Maybe I should have gone back to the hotel after our paddle in the sea. Then I would have got a nice sober night's sleep, alone. Suddenly my phone rings and I jump out of bed to answer it before it wakes Danny up.

I take it into the bathroom and shut the door.

'Hello?'

'Where on earth are you?'

'I'm in Spain, Mum,' I whisper.

'Speak up. What are you doing there? I called round to your flat yesterday and Edel said you'd disappeared off to Spain.'

'I didn't disappear, Mum, I came here for a bit of a break.'

'You shouldn't have done that without telling myself or your father. Anything can happen when you go off like that on your own without telling anybody where you're going. Irish people get murdered over there. I often read about it in the paper.'

'But they're drug-related murders, Mum,' I say wearily. 'As if they're going to break into my room with a shotgun.'

'Well you be careful, do you hear me? We've already lost one daughter and don't want to lose another. Don't go swimming by yourself in case you get a cramp, and don't talk to foreign men, Annie, they're not like Irish men, you know. When they hear your accent, they think you're easy, and will try to get you into bed.'

'I'll keep that in mind, Mum.'

'And Annie? When you're over there, will you pick me up some lined washing-up gloves? I can never seem to get them here and Mrs Joyce across the road says every time she goes to Benidorm she picks up half a dozen to keep her going.'

'OK, Mum, and don't be worrying about me. I'm fine. I love you, OK?'

'OK,' she says grudgingly, without telling me she loves me back.

At this stage I'm wide awake and reckon I might as well have a shower to freshen up. I sincerely hope my hangover won't get worse as the day progresses. I turn on the water and step into the bath, trying to remember how on earth I ended up in bed with Danny. After coming out of the sea I recall sitting on bench complaining about my cold feet. Danny then grabbed one of them, took off my sandal and started rubbing it between the palms of his warm hands. Ah bliss!

'Better?' he enquired.

'Much better.' I nodded, thanking God I'd just had a pedicure done in a top beauty salon before I came out here. 'Now do the other one,' I added cheekily.

'I am your majesty's servant,' he said, lifting my foot up really high and kissing my big toe.

A couple of passers-by threw us some odd looks but I didn't care. I was having such a good time. Eh . . . Niall who?

Eventually we started walking briskly back to the prom again. 'I'm starved,' I announced. 'I haven't eaten anything all day.'

'Did you not eat the meal on the flight?'

'You are joking, aren't you? I haven't eaten airline food in five years. I couldn't even look at it without feeling sick.'

Danny stopped in his tracks and put his hands on my shoulders. 'We have a problem then,' he said without smiling. 'I was going to bring you to a pizza place but I didn't realise you were such a fussy eater. How about we find somewhere Spanish and order paella instead?'

'Nah, pizza is fine, as long as we don't go to one of those places that display dodgy photographs of the meals at the door of the entrance. God, I'd rather starve than do that. Anyway, I feel like chips or something. Fat greasy chips. Plenty of soakage. I reckon tonight is going to be a long one.'

'That's what I like to hear. But, wait a minute, what flight are your friends arriving on? We don't want to miss them. Have they not phoned you yet?'

Indeed, I had completely forgotten about 'the girls' who were supposedly in the sky, somewhere in Europe at the moment on their way to meet me. I had to think quickly.

'Oh, eh, did I forget to tell you? They rang when you were down in the bar waiting for me. One of them got an early modelling job in the morning for like a few hundred euros so they've changed their flights to tomorrow.'

I searched his face for traces of disappointment but found none. Phew! In fact, believe it or not, he looked almost happy to have me all to himself.

'What about your own pals, though?' I quizzed him. 'Won't the lads be worried about you?'

'Not at all, I texted them earlier when you were in the shower to say I'd probably be late and to go on ahead and eat without me. I'll catch them later no doubt. The best thing about Marbella is that the nightclubs stay open till after six, so there's no rush.'

'Well, just as long as you don't go getting ideas about dragging me to some manky club until the early hours. I came here for a rest, remember?'

'Oh sure sure, you granny you.'

With that, he linked my arm in his and we crossed the road again. Five minutes later we were sitting in a cute little pizza place on one of the side streets as the friendly Spanish waiter lit a candle and placed it in between our place settings. Aw, how romantic!

Danny looked even better in the dimmed lights with the flicker of the candle dancing on his picture-perfect face. He was so scrumptious. Yes, he was quite cheeky with a bit of a mouth on him but that was part of his appeal. I gave him a full ten marks out of ten for sexiness. Just the man to mend my badly broken heart, if only for one night.

There were only two other people in the restaurant. A middle-aged couple sitting over by the window. I noticed they were halfway through their desserts so I craned my neck to see what they had ordered. No matter how hungry I am, I can always manage to fit in my sweets! The restaurant was so quiet because, I suppose, it was off-peak season, so the few bars and restaurants that had remained open, were struggling for business until the season started again.

I scrub my hair thoroughly with shampoo and begin to feel marginally better as I rinse out every last soapsud. Now, the real trick will be to apply a full face of make-up before I emerge from the bathroom again.

I remember last night Danny ordering a bottle of Rioja with no complaints from me. The waiter expertly poured a bit for me to taste. I duly obeyed before giving him the nod to fill up my glass.

'Cheers.' We clinked glasses before gulping back the contents. Now I kind of wish I'd paced myself a bit more, as my tummy gives a slight grumble.

We smiled at each other awkwardly. This is bizarre, I remember thinking. I felt as though I was on a first date, only I hadn't had time to prepare. It felt like a dream or something, and we were centre stage.

'Isn't this fantastic?' I said to Danny. 'The best thing about being a shift worker is that you can party on week nights when everybody else is getting ready for bed.'

'Yeah, but the bummer is during the summers whenever everybody else is heading off on their holidays and we have to bring them there,' he replied.

'But it's cheaper off-season, and there are no queues for restaurants and the temperature isn't so unbearable that you can hardly breathe. Oh, and there are no kids running around, which can only be a good thing.'

'Don't you want kids?'

'Not just at the moment, thanks,' I answered quickly, taking another mouthful of wine. 'They're fine in small doses but take up an awful lot of time.'

'Do you have nieces and nephews?'

'Yeah, actually,' I said, my face brightening. 'I've a nephew called Ben, He's four. I'm his godmother, too. Actually, he's an exceptional kid. I look after him a lot. His mother ... his mother ...' I found myself breaking off, suddenly unable to continue. Oh God, I think as I massage in some conditioner in order to soften my hair, that was awful the way I choked up while talking about Emily. But unfortunately I had just found it impossible to hold back my emotions. In fact, I can never seem to be able to talk about my elder sister without bursting into tears. Even now, I swallow hard, I can't hold back the tears. But I don't want to cry now. Definitely not now. I've cried for far too long.

'How about you?' I remember asking, wiping away a stray tear, desperate to get the focus of conversation off me. I simply couldn't bear to talk about Emily's death. Not with Danny, not with anybody, in fact. I don't even discuss her with my parents or with my other sister. Maybe the rest of the family discuss her when I'm not around. But I don't know because I never ask them. The deep-rooted emotions are still too raw, even after all these years.

'I'm an only child.' Danny looked straight at me and

handed me a fresh napkin. 'So any grandchildren depend on me.'

'Why? Are your parents really that anxious for you to get a move on?' I surprised myself by giggling.

'Not really, I'm only twenty-six.'

Ohmigod. Only twenty-six! Two years younger than me. The word 'cradle snatcher' immediately sprang to mind. Then again, lots of women dated younger men, so it was no big deal. I thought of the beautiful Demi Moore. Her husband Ashton is way younger than her and they both seem madly in love. Where there was a will, there was always a way. And Cameron Diaz was a lot older than Justin. Mind you, I'd heard they'd put their relationship on hold for the time being, so maybe that wasn't the best example.

'Anyway, my parents are divorced so it's not like they're discussing the possibility on a regular basis. Somehow I doubt my mum would like to be a granny any time soon. I think she hasn't even come to terms with the fact that she's even a mother,' he said quietly, his demeanour dramatically changing suddenly. He took his glass of wine to his lips and sipped it thoughtfully without looking at me. I sensed that he was having trouble discussing the subject. I needed to change the topic of conversation. Fast.

'So do you often go away with the lads?'

Danny looked startled for a second as if my question had taken him completely unawares. 'No, actually,' he answered after a short pause. 'I never go away with them. I suppose I've always had a girlfriend to go away with. I guess I'm a romantic fool, in that I'd much prefer candlelit dinners and sharing my room with a beautiful woman than a pair of snoring lads sleeping off their hangovers.'

I felt myself reddening again, or maybe that was just the heat in the restaurant. At least I hoped it was the heat. Else this guy was going to think I was a complete idiot.

'So what's new this time? Why did you decide to go away with the boys?'

He looked sad again. 'It wasn't exactly my first choice. I told you, I just got dumped. This holiday was supposed to be a romantic trip with my girlfriend, but she met somebody else and I found out about it. I persuaded a couple of the lads to join me on the holiday 'cos I'd already paid for a hotel room and didn't want that to go to waste. Like, obviously, I wasn't going to go away by myself.'

'Oh yes, obviously.' I nodded vigorously. 'Could you imagine? You'd feel like such a weirdo.'

Danny's eyes bore into me and I was becoming so hot I was afraid I might faint.

'Excuse me?' I called over the waiter. 'I wonder if I could possibly have a glass of iced water?'

'And one for me too?' asked Danny. 'It's hot in here, isn't it?'

Oh thank God it wasn't just me. I was beginning to feel totally paranoid. But the funny thing was that Danny didn't look a bit hot or bothered. The colour on his face, unlike mine, hadn't changed even slightly. Oh to be blessed with sallow skin.

We ordered pizza and chips, with lots of ketchup on the side (very Spanish, not), and guzzled more wine. It was going down a treat. Danny was great company, easy to talk to, and very funny. How could some woman have unceremoniously ditched him for another bloke? It didn't make sense. I mean, they didn't make lots of men like Danny these days. She must have been mad. I wondered if she was an air hostess? Lots of pilots went out with air hostesses, although not in my case. I always did my best not to mix business with pleasure. Then again, it wasn't too difficult. Lots of pilots were pretty boring and went on about planes too much. It was enough to put anyone into a near coma. Danny was different, though. His conversation was deep and meaningful, and becoming more meaningful with every drop he drank, I hasten to add. He wasn't afraid to share his emotions, and that was very endearing. Maybe it was because he was an only child. No wonder he'd always had a girlfriend. This was probably the first time he'd been single since he was a teenager. He was the type of guy girls would shamelessly chase. At least I'm not like that, I told myself smugly, draining my glass of wine and letting Danny top it up again. At least I had my pride, even though love had eluded me for most of my life. Until I met Niall, I'd worried that I'd remain championing the sad singleton cause for ever. Then I mentally kicked myself for letting the image of Niall creep back into my head. Immediately I banished any thoughts of him. I was on holidays. And he was history. Adios.

Antonio, the friendly waiter, reappeared at our table to make sure everything was OK.

'Everything's perfect,' I assured him, and Danny backed me up.

'How long are you here for?'

Danny and I answered in unison.

'A week.'

'Where are you staying?'

'Not far from here,' answered Danny, mentioning the hotel.

'Oh, that's a very nice place. Well, I hope you both enjoy your stay.'

'We will,' we answered again at the same time and I forced myself to look down at my plate again, to stop myself from going red. The waiter had obviously thought we were a real couple, just like the hotel receptionist had earlier. How embarrassing!

The waiter left us to enjoy the rest of our food. Not being able to think of anything else to say, I concentrated on slicing up my vegetarian pizza meticulously. For the first time since we met that afternoon, the silence hung in the air between us. It felt awkward so I drank more for the sake of having something to do.

We continued to eat and drink in silence and I noticed the Spanish waiter had turned on some light music, maybe in an attempt to get us to leave. No doubt he has a home to go to, I remember thinking, feeling sorry for him.

'Well that was scrumptious,' I said eventually, popping the last morsel of food into my mouth and wiping my greasy lips with a paper serviette. 'I'm stuffed. How about you?'

'I could still fit in some dessert,' Danny said enthusiastically, looking around for the menu.

Well, that's a good sign, I thought. It meant he wasn't rushing off to hail a taxi. You can always tell a date is going well if the other person opts for dessert. If they ask for the bill, well, it usually means curtains.

'Do you not think your man wants us to hurry up and leave?' I whispered, anxious that we might be delaying him. At least he hadn't started putting chairs upside down on tables, though. I just hate when people do that.

Danny looked at his watch. 'Not at all. Sure, it's not even nine yet. The Spanish people eat very late.'

Then, as if on cue, a group of six people entered the restaurant and asked for a table near the window. The waiter rushed to accommodate them, all smiles.

'See what I mean? At this time of year they're happy for any business at all. No doubt senor has a family to feed.'

I sat well back in my chair, feeling more relaxed. With the extra customers now speaking in loud English accents it kind of took the pressure off us.

'Can you fit dessert into that tiny stomach of yours?'

'Oh Mr Charmer, don't you ever stop giving compliments?' I grinned.

'I'm only so generous when the lady in question truly deserves them. I think I'm going to go for the vanilla ice cream with hot chocolate sauce. Will I ask for two spoons?'

I hesitated slightly. Was that such a good idea? Already I could feel my waistband tighten significantly.

'Go on, you only live once.'

Despite my initial good intentions, I relented. How could I have refused anything with that much delicious chocolate in it? Anyway, I was quite pleased at the thought of sharing Danny's dessert. There was something quite intimate, quite 'coupley' about a man and a woman eating off the same plate, I thought. Just as long as he didn't expect us to spoon-feed each other. Now, that would have been taking it all a step too far.

As we waited for the waiter to come back with our order, I asked Danny whether he was worried about his friends. It seemed that they hadn't been in touch yet. I wondered if they were having so much fun that they'd forgotten all about him. Maybe they weren't as attractive as he was, and therefore didn't really mind that he wasn't around to provide stiff competition for the ladies down at the port.

'They're big boys,' Danny said, shrugging off my concern. 'Well able to look after themselves. Anyway, I'm enjoying myself here, so why spoil the moment?'

'So what do you want to do after we've finished here? Do you want to go and find a bar somewhere?'

I looked at him anxiously, willing him not to refuse. Suddenly I didn't want him to go anywhere and leave me all alone. When I'm alone it's almost impossible not to think about Niall and the cruel way that he dumped me, so I was eager not to let that happen. Life was more bearable when busy or in good company.

'Your wish is my command,' he said, opening his arms invitingly. I don't know if the wine had anything to do with it but suddenly I was overcome with an urge to lean over and kiss Danny on the lips. Something held me back, however. I was a little worried about making a fool of myself so early on in the night. Anyway, despite his fairly consistent suggestive comments, I had no proof that Danny actually fancied me even the slightest bit. Maybe he was just a natural flirt. I reckoned it was quite likely that he was on the rebound, just like myself. I didn't want to push it. What's meant for me won't pass me by, I told myself.

The waiter arrived back with the ice cream, two spoons and two shots of sambuca.

'On the house.' He grinned. 'Please.'

'Oh God! If I drink this I'll keel over,' I groaned once Antonio was safely out of earshot. 'He must think we have stomachs made of iron.'

'Come on, you big wuss,' insisted Danny, picking up his shot glass, throwing back his head and emptying the contents down his throat in one go.

'You're a bad influence,' I said before relenting and doing the exact same. I felt the strong alcohol go straight to my head which started to spin. I got up unsteadily and excused myself to go to the ladies'. In the mirror I remember staring at my reflection which seemed to look nothing like me. At least I hoped not. When I got back, the bill had been paid for.

'You shouldn't have,' I muttered gratefully, adding a hefty tip. I felt warm inside and out. I felt like dancing. I felt like skinny dipping. I felt like doing anything other than going back to my hotel room. To that big empty double bed. Alone.

I step out of the shower and roll all my hair into a big bath towel. I can't see my reflection in the mirror because it's all fogged up but hopefully I don't look as bad as I feel. The shower has done wonders for me. At least I feel alive now. I wonder whether Danny has woken up yet and whether he remembers where he is, or remembers me, even. I sit down on the side of the bathtub and take the razor to my legs, as I seemed to have missed a bit yesterday. By the time I am finished, Danny will hopefully have risen from his deep sleep.

*

As we left the restaurant last night amid profuse thanks and gentle pleas from the waiter to return once again during our holidays, Danny reached out a hand to me and it seemed like the most natural thing in the world to slip my hand into his. We strolled leisurely along the prom with the full moon lighting up the dark, and now distinctively less inviting sea. A cool sobering breeze played around our ears and to the odd passers-by walking their dogs, we probably looked like a young couple very much in love. Maybe even a honeymoon couple. Nobody could have guessed that only hours beforehand we'd met as strangers on a train platform.

Danny suggested hitting a bar en route back, but the wine had made me feel slightly drowsy so I quickly suggested a night cap in the lobby of my luxurious seafront hotel. I reckoned that was a much more appealing alternative to a few bevvies in a dingy tourist-type karaoke bar. I really wasn't in the mood for listening to some out-of-tune drunk screeching 'Dancing Queen' or 'Sweet Caroline' into a microphone. The hotel bar was half full when we arrived back. Well-dressed pensioners were lazily clapping along to the hotel entertainment – a man doing fairly bad Frank Sinatra impressions – so we took stools up at the bar. I ordered a Jameson on the rocks and Danny opted for a double.

'Thanks for a lovely night,' I murmured, this time not shoving his hand away when he placed it on my thigh. 'I really enjoyed the whole evening.'

'It's not over yet,' said Danny. 'Don't be wishing your life away, baby.'

It took just three badly sung Sinatra tunes for us to

finish our whiskies. I noticed that Danny couldn't keep his eyes off me and vice versa. I reckoned that both he and I knew how the night would eventually end at that stage. There was no point even pretending otherwise.

'Do you want to go upstairs and collect your bag?' I asked airily, trying to focus on Danny's face but due to the record-speed consumption of generous measures of Jameson, I was beginning to see double at this stage. I didn't know how my wobbly legs were going to succeed in eventually getting me up to my room.

'Sure,' said the two Dannys. 'I'll collect my gear and then get the receptionist to call me a cab. The boys probably think I'm lying on the edge of a Spanish motorway somewhere between the airport and Marbella,' he added with a glint in his eye.

And they couldn't have cared less, obviously, I thought to myself, as I stood up and followed him shakily to the lift, my arm linking his. Both he and I knew fine well that Danny wouldn't be going to meet any of 'the boys' tonight.

Once we got out of the lift, it took me a good five minutes fiddling around in my bag to find my room card. I took out my credit card, my House of Fraser customer reward card, my Boots card and my Tesco card, until, finally, I found the right one. I fumbled awkwardly with the lock and finally we were in the room. Danny conveniently chose to ignore his bag sitting at the foot of my bed, and I didn't remind him that it was there.

'I feel manky,' he said, plonking himself down on the foot of the bed. 'At least you got to have a shower earlier.'

'You can have a shower here before you go,' I offered. 'Smarten up for the boys.'

I caught Danny's eye which seemed to be smiling.

'You sure you don't mind?'

The thought of Danny stripping off was making me feel hot in all the right places. I gestured to the second fluffy bathrobe which was hanging in my wardrobe. 'Be my guest.'

He took a step towards me and cupped my face in his hands. He took a moment to look deep into my eyes. 'On one condition,' he said softly.

If he asks me to join him he can feck off, I thought hazily. I didn't feel I knew him well enough to let him see the cellulite on my ass just yet.

'Don't push it . . .' I warned.

His eyes widened. 'I wasn't going to ask you anything too difficult, lady . . . what kind of a cad do you think I am?'

'I don't know. I don't know you . . . yet.'

'Can you get us some ice from outside and pour us two more Jamesons from the minibar? One Coke should do us both.'

'Is that all?' I asked, almost disappointed.

'No, that's not all,' he toyed with a strand of my blonde hair. 'A packet of peanuts would go nicely with the drinks.'

'I think I could manage that,' I replied hoarsely.

He made his way to the bathroom, and soon after that I heard the tap running and saw the steam swirling out into the bedroom. His head appeared at the door and he looked at me quizzically. 'Don't go anywhere, OK?'

I smiled and opened the door of the mini-bar to retrieve Danny's order as commanded. Go anywhere? Huh? Wild horses couldn't have dragged me away the way I was feeling.

After fetching the Jameson and pouring it into two glasses, I quickly took the opportunity to change into a pink negligée with cute little lace trimming on the bust-line. I then lay down on the huge double bed, having retouched my lipstick and brushed my hair ready for Danny's return from his shower. How lucky was I that I packed this saucy little number? In fact, the only reason that I packed it was because it was so light I could have rolled it up in a ball to fit into a purse, never mind a handbag. However, I hoped I wasn't giving him the wrong idea by getting into bed. That wouldn't have done at all. Whatever he might have been hoping for, I was adamant this was not about to turn into Danny's lucky night.

I love getting into hotel beds with crisp clean white sheets for the first time. As an air hostess we get to stay in fabulous four- and five-star hotels all the time, but I never get tired of it. Granted, it's a pain packing all the time for the different weather conditions. Obviously packing heavy jumpers for a couple of nights in bitterly cold Chicago in wintertime is a lot different to packing bikinis and trendy T-shirts for sunny LA, but there is something lovely about checking into a huge hotel room with a big comfy double bed. For those couple of nights that super trendy room is yours, your very own home.

I like to think I'm blessed with a lively imagination. Sometimes it works to my advantage; if I'm waiting for a bus or something I don't get bored because I can imagine myself on a luxurious Caribbean island somewhere, but at other times it can be a hindrance. For example, when a date doesn't show, I always picture the worst – usually the guy in question in bed with a supermodel type. However, nothing, and I really mean nothing, could have prepared me for the vision of Danny when he stepped back into the bedroom, his jet-black hair damp, his torso taut, tanned and smooth, and a fluffy white towel loosely covering his modesty.

I let out a long, slow, appreciative whistle.

'Stop that,' Danny lifted up his arms and smoothed his hair off his face, looking like a young Sean Connery, 'you'll end up giving me a big head.'

I propped myself up on the bed with my right elbow and raised an inquisitive eyebrow. 'You're trying to tell me you don't already have one?'

Danny flopped down on the bed and playfully pinned my arms backwards. Little droplets from his hair fell lightly on to my face. 'Hey, you're not by any chance trying to get me wet, are you?'

He lowered his beautiful face, planting his full luscious lips on mine. 'You got it in one.'

Fully made up now, I walk tentatively back into the bedroom. The strong morning sun is streaming in through a crack in the curtains. I slip back into bed, my body still damp.

Danny opens one eye and grins at me. 'So, how was it for you, gorgeous?'

Oh God, what does he remember that I don't?

'We didn't, did we?'

'Believe me, if we did, you wouldn't have to ask,' whispers Danny, opening his other eye playfully. 'Don't be rushing me, we only arrived yesterday.'

I sink back down on the mound of soft pillows once

more and Danny rolls on top of me, smothering me in light butterfly kisses. 'You're gorgeous,' he says as I do my best to suck in my stomach.

'No, I'm not,' I protest, throwing my arms around his neck.

'OK, you're not. You're a boot. Hey, I hate girls who put themselves down. Especially when they know they're divine.'

'Right,' I relent. 'I am fabulous, then. By the way, have the boys not phoned yet to see where you are? Anybody would think they didn't like you or something.'

'Anybody would think *you* didn't like me. Are you trying to get rid of me or something?'

Maybe it's because I'm still reeling inside due to Niall's recent sudden departure, or because my confidence in true love and men is at an all-time low, but it seems a bit surreal that this beautiful specimen is sprawled out on my bed, his tanned body a stark contrast to the dazzling white sheets. After all, I'm not even really supposed to be here. I'm supposed to be at work. But I'm not. I'm suspended, and rather than sitting in my noisy city-centre flat feeling sorry for myself and vowing that I'll soon be airline employee of the month to make amends, I'm living it up in a fabulous hotel with a love god. How life works in mysterious ways!

I wriggle myself away from under Danny's muscular body and slip off the bed.

'Going somewhere?'

'Yep, I'm going to go for a swim.'

'In the sea?'

'No, silly, I don't have a death wish. Not yet, anyway.

There'll be time enough at the end of my holiday when the prospect of going back to work rears its ugly head. In the meantime, there's a heated pool and massive open air jacuzzi on the roof top of this hotel, which is a far more appealing option.'

'You're kidding?'

'Do you honestly think I'd joke about something like that?' I ask folding my arms self-consciously across my breasts. He doesn't know me well enough to see me naked. In fact, nobody does until I shed another five pounds. Oh, I wish I hadn't polished off that pizza last night.

'Well, at least a swim would lessen the hangover,' says Danny sitting up in the bed. 'Not that I have much of a hangover, mind you.'

'Do you not?' I ask in amazement. How can he not have a hangover? He drank twice as much as I did last night, and I admit to fairly knocking them back. I envy people like him who can drink for Ireland and not suffer any side effects.

'I'm used to it.' He grins. 'It'd take a lot more boozing for me not to be able to get out of bed. Seriously, I feel fine. Ready to do it all over again. Hey, did we totally clear out the mini-bar last night or is there anything left? We could have a couple to kick start the day. Hair of the dog and all that.'

I'm not sure whether he's joking or not.

'Are you serious?' Nah, he must be pulling my leg. I mean, I couldn't possibly drink anything else until I at least got some grub into me. 'I don't know about you but my hangovers seem to get worse with age. They're not so bad somewhere like here where the weather's good but in

Dublin they kill me. There was a time I could party all night, not go to sleep and then go ahead and do the same thing all over again the following night. That's just not an option any more. And besides, on an airplane you can hardly sit at the front of the plane puking your guts out into a sick bag while the passengers are eating their meal.'

Danny laughs. 'At least you can scoot into the bathroom and close the door,' he points out. 'Spare a thought for the poor cockpit crew. Vomiting really isn't an option in such a confined space.'

I'm imagining Danny leaning across and emptying the contents of his previous night's dinner into a horrified captain's lap and my stomach starts to heave.

I block my ears dramatically. 'Stop it!' I screech. 'I might not have a raging "I'm-never-drinking-in-my-life-ever-again thumping headache", but I'm still feeling a bit delicate all the same. You hungry?'

'Not any more. I'd prefer a swim.'

I reach out and shake his hand. It's a deal.

We are the youngest people by far on the pool terrace, the average age being about ninety. The sun is beating down and unlike yesterday, which was bright and clear, there are a few clouds gathering menacingly in the sky. The sun, however, seems determined to shine through them so it's all good. Danny looks so sexy in his wine-coloured swimming trunks that I'm convinced even some of the old dears are giving him the once over from beneath their straw sun hats. At least he isn't wearing Speedos.

Danny peels off his robe like he's in an aftershave ad

and I noisily pull out two sun loungers, placing them near the wall to provide shelter from the breeze. I wish I had a digital camera right now so I could take a picture of him, or even better, get somebody to take a sweet photo of the two of us and I could subtly use it as my profile picture on my bebo page. Wouldn't that just make everyone ill?

We've just laid out our towels when a uniformed bartender comes running up with a silver tray. Wow, this is very classy indeed. 'Would you like something to drink?'

'Well, come to think of it, I am very thirsty. I'd love an orange juice, plenty of ice, put it on room 1412's tab. What about you, Danny?'

'I'll have the same. Plus a bottle of champagne. I'll pay cash, please.'

I look at my watch and then incredulously at Danny. It isn't even 11 yet!'

'Is there a set of rules I don't know about? Let's start as we mean to go on, babes. Now, get out of that robe and show off your pretty swimsuit.'

I obey his orders and then Danny stands up and takes my hand.

'Where are we going?'

'Over to the Jacuzzi while there's nobody in it.'

I follow him over and tentatively dip my toes into the rush of warm bubbles. Then we both get in fully and sink deep down into the hot water until just our heads are bobbing over the water surface.

'Put your hands where everyone can see them, Danny,' I warn.

He rolls his eyes upwards and lifts his arms towards the sky. 'Really, Annie, have you no faith in me?'

The bartender arrives with our glasses of Bucks Fizz on a silver tray. Danny reaches over and takes the glasses, offering one to me. We raise them in unison.

'To us.' Danny smiles.

'Well, why not indeed?'

'And to happiness.'

'*Our* future happiness? Oh God, you're so corny.'

'But you love me really,' he says, tipping his glass against mine. 'Don't you?'

'Danny,' my feet playfully intertwine with his under the water. 'I don't even know you. I don't even know your second name.'

'It's Savage, Danny Savage.'

'Oh,' I say, knocking back the champers and frowning. 'I've only ever met one other Savage in my life. Savage by name and by nature.'

He looks at me oddly. 'Really?'

'Yeah. Do you not remember me telling you about her last night? She's the reason I'm here on holidays, hahaha. The old bat is my supervisor at work.'

'Is she?'

'Yeah, she suspended me for no good reason, the stupid cow. Actually, the word "cow" is far too good for her. She's a bitch. A savage bitch!'

I wait for Danny to laugh. Or even give a smile. But he doesn't. Not even the slightest smile. And as the horrible realisation of what I've just said hits me, my heart seems to hit the bottom of the whirlpool with a thud as my sad little world momentarily stops turning on its axis.

'Is . . . is . . . she's not related to you by any chance?' I ask with a horrified smile. But there isn't even a trace of joy in his frozen face. Instead I'm met in return with an icy-cold stare.

'I believe the person you are referring to is—'

'Oh my God. She's your mother, isn't she?'

Rule Five: A second on your lips, a lifetime on your hips.

I'm pounding the prom. Really charging ahead, sidestepping children on tricycles and avoiding roller skaters. My arms are swinging determinedly by my side. I will get fit. I will, I will, I will. Anyway, walking at this pace makes me think and I need to figure out a few things. Like why Danny bolted on me yesterday as soon as I mentioned his mother. OK, I could have been a bit more complimentary about the old wagon but I wasn't *that* bad. Considering she suspended me for no good reason, I think I was rather kind when talking about her.

But Danny didn't see it that way at all. We finished the champagne in near silence in the Jacuzzi, and then he got out, dried himself, gathered up his things, called a taxi and left for Marbella. He muttered something about calling me, but how can he possibly call me? He doesn't even have my mobile, for God's sake. I have his, of course, but as if I'm going to ring him! I feel confused more than anything else.

Maybe I am better off being single. After all, there's

nothing wrong with being single – it's just the pressure from attached people that really gets to me. Why do they insist that singletons get married? Would they like it if we pressurised them to divorce?

Anyway, I'm better off without the divine Danny. Yes, he was a great kisser but there's more to life. And yes, he was drop-dead gorgeous, but of course there's more to life. And he was great fun, but there was more to . . . I stop dead in my tracks. Hang on a minute, is there more to life? More what? More holidays reading books in my bed at night because it isn't exactly the done thing to go for a candlelit dinner and then head off clubbing all on your own, is it?

The only thing going against Danny is that he's slightly younger than me and his mother is the battleaxe from hell. He isn't even as sleazy as I'd first thought. I mean he didn't even *try* to shag me! I sit down on a nearby bench to try and get my breath back and analyse it all. Why didn't the bastard try to jump my bones? Wasn't he attracted to me? If he'd been a gentleman he would have tried at least to give me the chance to turn him down and tell him that I was a girl with morals. But no, he hadn't even made a move. So much for that? Maybe he just hadn't fancied me. Maybe he was into supermodels who never drank more than a half-glass of champagne. Maybe he saw me as more of a ladette. Somebody with whom you could have drinking games but not, God forbid, actually go on a date with. I feel used for all the wrong reasons. Maybe I'm just not attractive to members of the opposite sex. Maybe I'm only good for borrowing money off, or going on mad, boozy sessions with when there is nobody else available. I stand up as a lone hot tear slides down the side of my face. I'd better keep on moving.

I end up walking the whole promenade, all five miles of it, my arms swinging furiously as I pound the pavement, frustrated thoughts swimming in my head. At least the results of my heartache will have helped me burn off a few calories, for which I should be grateful. Say what you like about broken hearts, but they help shift weight a damn good faster than any diet known to man. At this rate, by the time I get back to Dublin, I'll be a skinny little rake.

Talking of weight loss, incidentally, you wouldn't even believe the pressure on air hostesses to remain slim. On the initial application form which I filled out on joining the airline, it was clearly stated that one of the requirements was that 'weight should be in proportion with height'. But what they really mean by this is that you should be slimmer than the average person, and be able to squeeze past a cart in the middle of the aisle without any difficulty. And to make sure that we are truly humiliated in front of bored passengers during the safety demonstrations, we are forced to remove our jackets and hold up a safety belt above our heads, with our shirts neatly tucked into our waistbands. If, of course, for some bizarre reason, we do fill out a bit, we cannot simply go down to clothing stores to pick out a bigger size. No, it's a lot trickier than that. You have to fill out a detailed form, detailing the reasons for your weight gain, and then arrange a meeting with your supervisor to see how you can both rectify 'the situation'. Can you imagine me phoning Savage on my return to explain that I need a new uniform as my belt will now no longer fit due to excess consumption of whiskey, wine, chips and pizza on holidays with her son? On the plus side, I could tell her that now I'm back in Dublin I'm in need of some urgent calorie-burning exercise so could she please give me her son's mobile number? After all, I believe that you can burn up to five hundred calories during a rigorous one-hour sex session. Some chance, huh?

I arrive back at my hotel, sweating like a pig. My hair is scraped back off my face, giving me an instant council flat facelift and I'm wearing tracksuit bottoms from Champion Sports, teamed with a fading five-year-old navy Polo shirt. Still, I'm looking forward to soaking in a nice long hot bath with lots of bubbles, a good book, and a vodka and Diet Coke which I bought in the local supermarket around the corner. Well, I need something to cheer me up, don't I? I think the porter gives me an odd look as I shoot past him holding my plastic bag, but maybe I'm imagining it.

Up on the fourteenth floor, I wearily push open the door of my room. It's as neat as a pin with fresh towels on the bed, and all traces of Danny gone . . . it's as if he was never here at all. Maybe he wasn't? Maybe it was all a hallucination after all. I kick off my runners and lie on the bed staring at the newly painted white ceiling. Suddenly I'm overcome with self pity. What on earth am I going to do with my life? I've recently been dumped by the man I once thought I was going to marry, and then thrown aside by a man I'd at least hoped to have a no-strings-attached fling with. What's more, I've been suspended by his vitriolic mother who will probably have it in for me for the rest of my life in the sky, and my face still hurts where I was knocked down by that Oliver Kane's damn car. Hmm.

He was another man who walked out of my life, or drove out of it, even. He was hot, come to think of it, really hot, with looks like a film star. I wonder where he ever disappeared to.

So here I am on holidays on my own and I'm so sad that I even have to pretend to strangers that I have a bunch of friends who don't exist. Hot tears fill my tired eyes and a lone one escapes down my scratched cheek stinging it in the process. Suddenly I wish I wasn't alone. A pathetic singleton. When I'm alone I always find myself thinking about my older sister Emily, the person I worshipped for twenty-five years until cancer ravaged her young body three years ago. She was my heroine, the woman who could do no wrong. I never thought that there would be a time in my life when she wouldn't be in it. Even when I'm at home in Swords with my parents, I keep expecting the front door to burst open and Emily to walk in full of news. She was a great talker and a great listener. She was also brilliant at giving me sound advice on men. Now that I am on my own again, I seem to be making a right mess of my love life. I can't realistically talk to Mum as she just thinks any old man would be good enough for me, as long as he isn't a drug addict and talks to her about golf and the garden plants. She always said that looks don't matter because most men lose their looks at some stage. She says that personality is what counts and that they should be good providers. When poverty comes through the door, love flies out the window, is her no-nonsense approach. So, as you can see, Mum isn't the best person when it comes to discussing matters of the heart, and Dad is even worse.

Any possibilities I ever introduced to him, he would describe as 'harmless'. But 'harmless' is such a non-compliment, it's almost an insult.

They were both delighted, of course, when Emily met Robert, a respectable economics student from 'a good home' at the age of twenty at a UCD party in Hollywood Nights at the Stillorgan Park Hotel and married him four years later. Baby Ben arrived a year later making the family complete and we all doted on him, especially me, the cherished godmother.

When the news of Emily's breast cancer came weeks after baby Ben's birth, I went into denial. I just couldn't get my head around the shocking news and spent hours on the Internet researching the subject. Emily couldn't die, she just couldn't. She was so young, so strong, so pretty with all the answers to other people's problems. Most of all, mine.

The truth became more of a reality when Emily's hair drastically started falling out during chemo and she asked me to go to the hairdressers with her to help choose a special wig. Emily's shiny golden hair had been her crowning glory. When we were children I used to envy her flowing locks and the fact that her hair, unlike mine, was never unruly. Emily was always in control, even when it came to her hair. To see her without it left me distraught. When, three weeks before she passed away, she lay on her hospital bed, and, weighing just under six-and-a-half stone, she took my hand and asked me to always look out for Ben and not take it badly if her beloved Robert ever remarried, I promised her that I would make sure her wishes were fulfilled. And the day she passed from this cruel world into the next, and I held her hand as she departed peacefully with a serene look on her young, wise, but frighteningly gaunt face, I still could barely accept that 'my rock' had disintegrated. She'd been so proud of me and had taken tons of photos of me in my air hostess uniform the day I'd passed my airline training course. She had also been the one to persuade me to take my studies further in case I ever decided to hang up my wings. That's why, two years after her untimely death, I'd enrolled in a PR course which I hated. Because I knew that she knew it'd be good for me.

The tears are flowing now, as I lose myself in the painful memories, but I don't even try to stop them. I rarely let myself cry or even remember. It's too painful and it makes me feel weak and worthless. Emily never cried, at least not in front of any of us. Perhaps she cried behind closed doors, but I'll never know whether she did or not. Maybe that's a good thing. All my memories are of my big sister always smiling despite the odds. Three weeks after her death, I received a letter from her solicitor. She had left me enough money for a deposit for my first apartment. Until then I'd never really considered growing up and moving out. Providing for something as boring as my future had never even occurred to me. Emily's passing made me realise that there wasn't always going to be a future. Even in her darkest hour Emily had always been thinking of others. Her death made me face reality. Now, I was my parents' eldest child. I had to act responsibly.

I look at the large bottle of unopened vodka sitting on the hotel desk beside the silent phone. It's just begging to be opened. I've already checked the answer phone in the hope of a message from Danny, but to no avail. Now I feel I could drink the vodka straight without the Coke. Or with

Coke I could still down a couple of glasses. Perhaps it could knock me out so that the pain, still raw even after three years, would ease. Instead I pick myself up off the bed, and make my way to the bathroom to run a hot bath. It's a much safer option with fewer consequences. Emily wouldn't thank me for getting drunk in her honour.

I open the bathroom door and, to my complete surprise, I notice a huge bouquet of flowers, tied in a lavish red ribbon languishing in the bath. I lift it up in amazement. Where on earth has that come from? The attached card reads, 'Sorry, love D.' It makes me cry even harder.

Rule Six: Forgive, forget but tell him to flip off.

In the dining room I hover at the breakfast counter filling my plate with fresh fruit. I also grab a glass of fresh orange juice. Sitting back down and ordering a pot of black coffee from a smiling waitress, I wonder whether I should phone Danny to thank him or simply just send a text. To do neither would be plain rude, but I don't want to get myself into a situation where he's trying to meet all my imaginary friends again. Suppose he wants us all to come up to Puerto Banus for the night to party in the popular Sinatra's and then on to the ultra-chic nightclub, Olivia Valera's?

Maybe I could say that the girls came out for a night, but then had to go home urgently to wash their hair? Nah, too complicated. God, I don't know what to do! I devour all my breakfast with the gusto of somebody who has just finished a hunger strike. Every mouthful of juicy orange, kiwi, melon and pineapple goes down a treat. I manage to resist at all costs the buttery croissants located near the fresh rolls, and sip my strong, piping hot coffee instead.

I think I'll send him a short text and hopefully that'll be the end of it. I mean, for all I know, he might not even want to see me again. Maybe he just sent the flowers out of kindness, or worse, guilt?

After finishing my plate clean and draining the coffee dregs, I head back to my room, quickly change and head up to the rooftop pool. Then I fish my mobile out of my beach bag and compose a quick text.

Thx 4 flowers. 2 kind. Enjoy rest of ur hols, A. x

I wait for him to reply but after a few minutes of agonising anticipation I realise that it's not going to happen so I have a quick swim, and then decide to leave the infuriatingly silent phone in my room while I go out for another walk.

Just under an hour later, when it's becoming too hot to walk any further, I turn back towards my hotel. It's going to be another boring long drawn-out day, but at least the sun is going to be shining. If it was overcast, I don't think I could handle it.

No sooner am I back in my room than the phone rings. Frantically I reach out for it. It's him. Oh God. Panic sets in.

'Hello?'

He sounds genuinely thrilled to hear from me.

'My God, I was worried that I'd seen the last of you. I've phoned you three times over the last hour. How's your head?'

'Much better today, thanks,' I answer coolly even though my heart is racing. 'I wasn't drinking last night. How's yours?'

'Not great. The lads and I fairly overdid the drinking at the port last night.'

Now why isn't that such a surprise?

'Tut, tut.'

'Hey, the last thing I need from you is a lecture; that's my mother's job!'

I feel myself flinch at the mention of his mother as the unwanted image of her spiteful little face enters my head.

'What are your plans for today, then?' I enquire swiftly moving the subject on to safer ground.

'Well, guess what? One of the lads here knows a guy with a yacht moored at the port. We're taking it over to Gibraltar for the day. Wanna join us?'

I nearly drop the phone in surprise. Now this is a totally unexpected suggestion. I'd been planning a lazy geriatric-style afternoon by the pool sipping beer and reading the day-old British tabloids. Funny how, when you go away in order to escape all the madness, you still crave all the celebrity news from the likes of Posh and Becks and – don't tell anyone – Jordan!

'When does the boat set sail, captain?' I find myself giggling. I've never actually been on a yacht but I've always admired the spectacular vessels all competing with each other down in the marina any time I've been drinking in the port. I've often wondered about the type of people who owned them. The other halves, so to speak. It must be wonderful to be that rich. Anyway, this is obviously my once-in-a-lifetime chance to sample a slice of it. And it's a trip I would be mad to refuse. Oh, what a difference a day makes. Last night I fell asleep sobbing my heart out. Today, however, is a brand-new day, the sun is shining and I'm up for another crazy adventure.

'In about two hours. Are the other girls there yet?'

'Eh, no, sorry, yeah . . . yeah, they arrived last night. They're shopping – they're actually in Malaga at the moment. They got the train into the city earlier.'

'Did they?' Danny sounds surprised, as if he couldn't possibly imagine why anybody would come all the way over here just to go around stuffy shops trying on clothes and shoes.

'It's much better value over here, though,' I point out in my imaginary friends' defence as my heart starts beating faster. 'The El Corte Inglés department store in Malaga is massive, even bigger than the one in Puerto Banus.'

'OK, whatever,' he says, still sounding baffled. 'So when can you get a taxi to the Coral?'

'How about I meet you outside Sinatra's at two p.m.?' I suggest, thinking quickly on my feet. There's no bloody way I'm turning up in my manky old clothes. If I'm going on a trip on a swanky yacht with a group of hot guys, I've got to at least look the part. I've got less than two hours to get to Puerto Banus, find a decent clothes shop and get myself kitted out.

Rather than ring a taxi when I'm so pressed for time, I decide to hail a passing one on the street outside. Within minutes I'm in a white cab racing along the motorway towards Marbella.

Twenty minutes and we're there. I ask the driver to drop me outside El Corte Inglés where I then proceed to run around grabbing seriously bling jewellery, and a pair of monstrously high strappy silver sandals. I doubt I'll be able to walk very far in them, but hey, I'll be on a yacht, so I won't be walking very much! With my bags in hand I rush down to the port and race past the various bars and restaurants until I reach the small Armani shop. I quickly glance at my watch. I have approximately twenty minutes in which to buy a knock 'em dead outfit.

I try on about six different Armani suits until I finally find the perfect one. It's a charcoal-grey which fits me like a glove. I also choose a delicate pink camisole for underneath. I feel like a superstar. The whole ensemble comes to over €800. That, added to the €350 I've already spent in El Corte Inglés, means that I've spent more impulsively in an hour than I normally spend on myself in three months. I hand over my credit card quickly before I can change my mind. The guilt I can live with as the adrenaline I'm feeling now is priceless.

I reach the front of Sinatra's bar at the exact same time as Danny. He's wearing a white T-shirt, a pair of faded blue Levis and red sneakers. He looks scrumptious.

We wrap each other in bear hugs like long-lost friends. Is this really somebody I'd never even met a few days ago? I think, clinging to him a bit more possessively than intended. It's hard to believe.

'You look amazing,' he says sounding genuine. I had quickly run into the Ladies' in a nearby cafe to put on all my finery. The look is completed by huge Jackie O-style Chanel sunglasses that I'd picked up in New York on one of my trips. I totter along unsteadily behind Danny as we make our way to the berth where the yacht is being moored. *Princess Caroline* is dazzling white, so clean you could eat off it, and the most beautiful vessel I've ever laid eyes on.

Danny introduces me to his two friends (at least they're real, unlike mine), who are almost as handsome as himself. Immediately one of them, a tall, blond muscular chap with cheeky blue eyes and picture-perfect teeth hands me a flute of champagne from the bar. His name is Greg.

'Let's start as we mean to go on.' He grins. 'Dan's told us all about you.'

'He has?' I ask, catching Danny's eye. 'All good things, I trust?'

'Absolutely. By the way, Danny, when are the others coming on board?'

Others? What others? I shift uncomfortably on the pristine white leather seat. I hadn't realised such a big crowd had been invited along. Is there going to be a party on board? I sip some more of my champagne as if I haven't heard the question.

'This is nice, isn't it?' says Danny sitting so close to me that his thigh touches mine, sending pleasurable shivers down my leg all the way to my red-painted toenails.

'It's perfect.' I smile. 'We should do this more often.'

'Do you want a tour of the boat?'

'What? You mean there's more?'

'Put your glass down and come with me.' He offers his hand.

Downstairs are two cabins, a single and a twin. Outside the tiny windows the blue sea is bobbing up and down. There's also a tiny kitchen, and a cute backroom with a shower. It's adorable.

'I'm in love with this boat,' I say with open admiration.

'Ditto. Do you want to check out the cabins again?'

I give the back of Danny's hand a playful slap. 'Not just

yet, thanks, you cheeky brat! Come on, let's go back upstairs and be sociable.'

Upstairs a surprise, or rather a shock greets me. There are two girls with unnaturally skinny waists looking very much at home on the white leather seats where Danny and I had been sitting only a few moments ago. They are bronzed, wearing simple tank tops and tiny shorts, revealing long golden legs up to their armpits.

One of the girls stares blatantly at me. 'Oh, do you work in real estate?' she says in a bitchy, whiny voice. She has platinum-blonde hair scraped back from her face in a severely high ponytail. Her brunette pal sniggers.

'No, why?'

'Oh . . . no, nothing; I just presumed with the suit and all that you were probably working.'

I can feel myself flush. I look completely out of place here. Everyone else looks as though they could be going out on a paddle boat or something, whereas I look as if I'm going along for an interview as a secretary in an office. How could I have got it so wrong?

Danny puts a protective arm around me. 'I think she looks fabulous.' He squeezes me and plants a kiss on my forehead.

'Is this your new girlfriend, Danny?' asks the brunette with a barely disguised disdainful look.

'Yeah,' he says without hesitation. 'Annie, meet Attracta and Jane. We met them out last night.'

'How do you know Danny?' asks the blonde, Jane, looking decidedly peeved that her catty comments have backfired.

'We work in the same airline.'

'Oh, so you're a trolley dolly, I mean, air hostess. God, I don't know how anybody does that for a living.'

'I love it. Thousands of girls send in their CVs every year but it's very hard to get in. Why?' I shoot back defensively. 'What do you do?'

'I'm in sales,' she says with an arrogant toss of her ponytail.

'Really? That must be tough on your feet walking from door to door . . .'

'I work in corporate sales,' she scowls, 'so I'm hardly walking the streets.'

Whatever . . .

'I'm a model,' says the other girl with an abundance of confidence, holding out a slender hand for me to shake. It nearly breaks when I grab hold of it. 'Very pleased to meet you.'

Well, I doubt very much that she is, but for the sake of peace, I nod in agreement.

'Annie's here on holidays with another model,' Danny says, suddenly remembering. 'You two might know each other, Ireland being so small and all that.'

Oh bloody hell, time for more excuses. Quick, Annie, quick.

'What's her name?'

'Naoise, but you probably wouldn't know her. She does mostly promotions, you know, handing out flyers for nightclubs, doing press calls for seasonal scratch cards, bikini shots in Stephen's Green – that kind of work.'

'Oh, I probably wouldn't know her then,' sniffs Attracta, wrinkling her nose as if I'd just announced that my friend worked in the accounts office of a clamping office. 'I just do the catwalk shows. But you might know her, Jane,' she said turning to her blonde friend. 'You used to do a bit of that kind of work, didn't you? Handing out flyers at traffic lights and stuff?'

Jane's face is like thunder. She gives a strangled self-conscious laugh. 'That was a very long time ago when I was a poor student trying to make ends meet,' she says, quickly gulping her champagne as Danny pops open another bottle of bubbly to no doubt try to ease the atmosphere, which you could almost slice in half.

The third guy on the boat is called Emmet and he's slightly shorter than the other two strapping lads but he's got a really tanned, happy face and cute dimples on his cheeks. He's a rugby player, apparently, and plays for Clontarf rugby club.

'Have you enough champagne there?' He sidles up to me, grinning.

'God, yeah, I'd better be careful with this stuff, I don't want to be throwing up over the side of this beautiful boat.'

Jane shoots me a pained look. I really don't think she likes me being here. Why? Have I done something wrong? Apart from showing up in a suit, which needless to say probably cost more than the contents of her entire suitcase. How was I supposed to know it was such an informal occasion? The people I see on yachts in *OK!* magazine always look like Joan Collins or Mariah Carey. I was afraid I'd be underdressed, for crying out loud!

'OK, all aboard,' says Greg, untying the rope to push the boat out. 'We're not expecting any more women, are we, Danny?'

Everyone laughs except Jane who scowls for Scotland.

I don't really get the joke but I laugh anyway to try to fit in. I wonder what happened last night when the boys met the girls. Am I being left out of some big secret here or something?

Emmet goes on deck and the next minute we are manoeuvring our way slowly out of the harbour. It's really exciting. People stop to look. Some take photos with their digital cameras, children point and a few wave at the departing boat. I wave back. I feel like a celebrity.

Once safely away from the other boats, with a loud roar of the engine, we take off towards the middle of the ocean at terrific speed. I hold on to Danny's arm as the wind blows through my hair and the sun beats down generously. Now, this is what I call a real holiday. Thanks, Mrs Savage. I grin to myself. I definitely owe ya one!

Despite Jane's peevish face constantly glowering at me, I'm having a great time. The champagne is flowing, a bit too freely, maybe, but who cares? It's not like anybody has to go to work in the morning. Attracta, as it surprisingly turns out, isn't as stuck-up as she first appeared, and the champagne seems to be loosening her up. At one stage she even demands the boat to stop, then steps on deck, peels off her tank top to reveal the most impressive set of boobs I've ever seen in my life (they must be fake, five grand's worth of silicone at least), drops her shorts to the floor and dives head first into the water. Everyone stares in amazement. I mean, the water's not exactly hot. I reach down and sample it with my own fingers. Yes, definitely too nippy for me. Moments later she mounts the small steel steps back up to the boat like a bona fide Bond girl, and you can't help but notice her nipples straining against her flimsy see-through bikini. I hope the boys have the decency to look away to protect her modesty, but no chance of that. They stare open-mouthed but for once, Jane takes her hostile attention off me and glares disapprovingly at her best friend. Throwing her a towel with such vigour that I'm afraid she'll knock Attracta off the boat, she snaps, 'Go down stairs and get dressed before you freeze to death. You'll die of flipping pneumonia!'

Greg fetches the attention-seeking Attracta a soft black bathrobe and wraps it around her shivering, voluptuous body. 'Let's get you downstairs and into some warm clothes,' he says, giving her a rapturous hug. Attracta gives Jane a sly wink before heading downstairs and calling for somebody to make her a hot whiskey.

'Is your model friend as much as a diva as that?' Danny asks me.

'Oh ten times worse. She modelled on the Brown Thomas supermodel show in the RDS a few years ago and managed to get Naomi Campbell thrown out of her changing room because there wasn't enough room for both their egos.'

'You're joking,' Danny says, open-mouthed.

'Of course I am,' I reply, at which both Danny and Emmet dissolve into laughter. Stony-faced, Jane refuses to see the funny side.

The boat starts up again, thanks to Emmet at the controls, and speeds off at a terrific pace. I look back at Puerto Banus becoming smaller by the second. It feels so liberating to be in the middle of the ocean. So romantic – apart, of course, from Jane's steely-grey eyes boring into us. I wish she'd just cop off with Emmet or something and leave us alone. Greg and saucy Attracta show no sign of re-emerging from the downstairs area and it's probably just as well that the engine is loud enough to drown out any possible moans from below deck.

Danny stands up and offers to play some music. 'What's your taste?' he asks me, ignoring the others.

'Girls Aloud.'

'Any particular song?'

'I really like "I think we're alone now".'

Jane and Emmet exchange awkward glances.

Danny sticks on Girls Aloud and the music blares loudly. I'm sure they can hear it back in the port. I feel like dancing only there's not that much room on the yacht. It has everything else. Only a dance floor with a disco ball in the middle is missing.

'Who owns this place, anyway?' I ask. Certainly these guys are too young to own a super yacht like this.

'A guy called Kane. Fucking loaded. He doesn't have time to use it himself so Emmet gets to bring it around the place for him.'

'Like where?'

'Monaco, Nice, wherever. He only spends, at the most, a week a year on this beauty.'

'I suppose he's too busy making money,' muses Jane. 'What does he do for a living?'

'No idea. He travels a lot, that's all I know. You might know him to see from flying around. That's him over there.'

He nods to a picture on the wall behind my head. I turn around. There's a picture of a very handsome man – in his early forties I'd guess – with one arm wrapped around a stunning blonde woman, presumably his wife. He looks awfully familiar. I must recognise him from the papers or something. Lucky sod, whoever he is. Imagine owning this boat. Then again, if he can't take off time from work, then what's the point really? Why can't people have money and time? Why does one always have to choose?

And then the penny drops as I realise with shock that it's Oliver Kane. My Oliver. About five years younger but just as handsome. God, to think I'd kind of fancied him. As if I'd have been in with a chance! His wife is divine and he's obviously some kind of billionaire. Who did I think I was kidding? I pick up the photo frame and scrutinise the photo. Oliver has a dreamy look in his eye. What a kind face he has. His wife is obviously one lucky woman. I wonder briefly should I tell the others about my chance encounter with the owner of this yacht and how he knocked me down. Or would they think it was too much of a coincidence? I decide to keep the story to myself. Oliver will be my little secret. For some strange reason I just don't feel like discussing him with any of this lot. It would almost feel like I was betraying him or something.

Suddenly Attracta appears at the top of the stairs, dressed in Greg's clothes and with a coy look on her face. He's right behind her looking fairly pleased with himself.

'Twenty minutes,' observes Danny checking his watch. 'Good going, guys. I suppose you're both looking for a cigarette?'

'Shut up, loser,' Greg reaches over and slaps his head playfully. 'For your information we were just talking.'

'For your information, any information is more than we need to know.'

Danny opens a packet of cigarettes and offers them round. Nobody takes one so he leans over the water and lights one himself. I join him on deck and raise my face to the sun. Vanity has prevented me from smearing sun block on my nose so I have to be careful not to get burnt and end up resembling Rudolf, the red-nosed reindeer.

'You having a good time?' He looks at me endearingly but I notice his eyes are fairly bloodshot. Is that just from today, I wonder? Or are the effects of last night kicking in? Or both?

'Yeah, it's amazing.' I smile, reaching up and ruffling the top of his head. 'I couldn't be happier. So,' I probe a bit because I can't help myself, 'what's the story with Greg and your woman Attracta? Are they an item?'

'Yeah, since last night, anyway. He seems really into her but y'know he hasn't said anything to us. Blokes don't gossip the way you girls do. We're not into *feelings*.'

'That's rubbish, you guys have feelings too; you're just incapable of expressing them sometimes.' I nick his cigarette and take a long drag from it before exhaling slowly. 'So what about Jane?'

'What about her?'

'Does, or rather did, she fancy her chances with you?'

Danny looks genuinely surprised, as if the idea hasn't even occurred to him. 'What makes you think that?'

'She keeps staring at you.'

'Well, it's not that big a boat. She has to look at something.'

'You know what I mean. I reckon she came on board thinking she was going on a date with you or something.

She's making me feel about as welcome as a fart in a packed elevator.'

'Just ignore her.'

'OK, I will.' He's right, actually. Why am I always being so paranoid? I mean, Danny has invited me because he wants to be with me and presumably enjoys my company. If he'd wanted to be with Jane he wouldn't have invited me along. Somehow I doubt she'd play hard to get with him.

'And besides, I think Emmet is kind of into her so maybe the two of them will get together.'

Hmm. I don't think there's a remote possibility of that happening. The chemistry between them is about zero and all of Jane's conversation seems to be directed at Danny. At my Danny.

'Here, let me have a last drag of that before I'm finished. I wish cigarettes weren't so bloody cheap out here. I'd love to quit this disgusting habit once and for all.'

'Ditto,' he says, rubbing his eyes. 'Jeez, I'm kinda tired now. I reckon I only ended up getting about three hours sleep last night, if even that.'

'Where did you go?'

'Some disco bar on the port, I can't even remember the name of it now.'

'Is that where you met the girls?'

'No, we met them in Sinatra's and then they came dancing with us later.'

'I see.'

Now it's all making a bit more sense. Danny was probably flirting with Jane all night. Why am I even saying probably? Of course he was. The guy wouldn't have been able to help himself! I know I haven't known him very long but I've known him long enough to know he wasn't playing with his beer mat and talking about planes for the evening.

'And Attracta snogged Greg?'

'Yeah.'

'And where was Emmet?'

'He went home early. He'd had seafood at dinner and I don't think it agreed with him.'

'So it was just the four of you in the club?'

'And a few hundred others.'

'You know what I mean.' I give him a playful dig in the ribs. 'She probably thought there was a bit of double-dating going on.'

'That's her problem, then. I'm not a mind-reader, you know?'

He puts his hands on my shoulders, bends down and his lips touch mine, sending tremors of excitement down my whole body. We stand there hugging each other for what seems like an eternity, until Emmet joins us on deck.

'Sorry to interrupt you love birds, but I needed a bit of fresh air.' He lights up a cigarette, inhales deeply and then blows out a cloud of grey smoke slowly.

'How's your tummy?' I enquire.

'So, so . . . I should have stuck to the golden rule about not trying out shellfish in a foreign country. Especially when there's a planned boat ride the following day. But I'm managing. The beer's going down a treat, anyway. Hey, I can see the Rock of Gibraltar already.'

We all turn to look. And true enough, in the distance the magnificent rock looms up from the sea, jutting into the skyline and towering over the nearby countryside. It's awesome.

Soon Attracta, Greg and Jane all join us as we stare in the direction of the Iberian Peninsula.

Jane fishes out a digital camera from her oversized D&G handbag. She hands it to me. 'Can you take a picture of all of us?'

Reluctantly, I take the camera from her and click while they pose. I notice she puts a possessive arm around Danny's waist while I snap. The nerve of her! After the group stops grinning for the photos, Jane finally lets go her grip on Danny and steps forward.

'Thanks, Annie,' she says, giving me a smug smile while taking back the camera and putting it in her bag. The message is loud and clear; she doesn't want my mug in any of her pics reminding her of my unwanted presence. I decide I'm going to ignore the slight, and just concentrate on enjoying the rest of my day trip.

The guys decide to anchor the boat about a mile out to sea. Most of the group lie out on deck while myself and Danny cosy up inside.

'I wish it was just the two of us here,' I whisper.

'Me too, babes, Do you know how horny you make me feel?'

'No.'

But as I lean forward and kiss him I can feel how horny he is by his straining jeans zip.

'Let me show you the downstairs cabins . . .'

'But I've already seen them.'

'Let me show you again,' he says, scooping me up in his arms. 'I don't think you got to see everything.'

If you've never made love on a gently rocking boat, you should try it sometime. It's the most pleasant sensation in the world. Especially if your willing partner in crime is the delicious Danny. I hadn't meant to jump into bed with him immediately of course, but we just lay down in each other's arms chatting, and the next minute we were kissing again and I removed my suit in case it got crushed, and Danny removed his jeans in case they got crushed – well, that was his excuse anyway – and one thing just led to another.

Mind you, I'm sure all the champagne had something to do with it, but making love to Danny seemed like the most natural thing in the world. He was a giving and generous lover, and without exaggeration the best I've ever had. And just to clear things up really quickly, I haven't had many. And although I usually stick to the golden three-month rule, this time I succumbed two months and twenty-seven days early. You probably would have too, if you knew how gorgeous he was.

We must have fallen asleep for a few hours because it's dark when I open my eyes again, and peering through the porthole I can see the stretch of the Costa Del Sol sparkling in night lights and the sea seems almost black. We're no longer floating but just cruising along at a nice, comfortable speed.

'A cent for your thoughts?' Danny says with one eye open when he spies me staring outside.

'I'm wondering how we're going to explain our lengthy absence to the others,' I reply, squinting at my watch. 'Talk about being unsociable, we've been down here for hours.'

'They're adults.' Danny gets up and reaches for his

boxers which are under my bra on the floor. 'I'm sure they're well able to entertain themselves. As long as we had fun . . . did we have fun?'

'I know I did,' I say, wrapping my arms around his waist and nuzzling my face in his abdomen. He smells of saltwater.

'C'mon, let's go back upstairs and let them know we're still alive.'

We dress, I slap on a bit of make-up and try unsuccessfully to comb the tangles from my bed head, and then rejoin the others who are sitting on deck, wearing warm clothes. As far as I can make out, we are just passing Estepona en route to Puerto Banus. There is a distinct chill in the air now and the dark waves bash against the side of the boat.

Thankfully, nobody mentions our long absence, and Jane astutely ignores us. Greg is making hot whiskies and has produced bumper bags of crisps and nuts. We tuck in gratefully.

'So, Annie,' says Attracta, addressing me for the first time since I met her, 'what are your plans for the rest of the holiday? Anything exciting?'

'I suppose I'll just be taking it easy.' I shrug, feeling slightly uncomfortable with all eyes on me now, anxious to hear of my plans. How can I top a ride on a yacht? 'I know when I get back to work there'll be precious little chance of any time off. The Christmas period is always manic as you can imagine.'

'I suppose so. Everyone goes away then, don't they? Myself and my family always take off to Barbados on St Stephen's Day and stay there until after the New Year.

There's not much work for models at Christmas time, unless you dress up as Santa and hand out flyers on Grafton Street. Do you remember you did that one Christmas, Jane?'

Two bright pink spots appear on each of Jane's pinched cheeks. She looks livid, as though she's just been forced to swallow a bag full of razor blades. I bite my lip to stop a grin spreading across my face. I wish I had my hands on her fancy digital camera now. 'Attracta . . .' she begins but then simply just sighs, as if to comment would demean her. Then, however, instead of taking out her fury on her best friend who has deliberately insulted her, she seems to want to tear shreds off me instead.

'Will you be heading out with your friends tomorrow night?'

'Eh, I don't know, I suppose I will.'

'Where will you go, though? Fuengirola's such a kip. Full of nasty little fish and chip shops, and stalls selling buckets and spades. I can't think of any upmarket bars around there.'

'Well, I really like it,' I say defensively. 'The beach is fantastic and the place is very clean and safe, and there are no poseurs to impress. Anyway, there's more to life than just drinking your head off at every opportunity.'

'The hotel the girls are staying in is stunning,' Danny adds. 'You couldn't beat it. It's as nice as our hotel. Where are you two staying by the way?'

'Oh, Jane has a place here. On the Golden Mile. All the rich and famous have pads there, like Antonio Banderas and Melanie Griffiths and Sean Connery. Even King Fahd had a summer house there. Look, there it is now in the distance.' We all look across to the shoreline where a gold and white replica of the White House stands in all its majestic glory, shimmering in fairy lights. It is absolutely spectacular.

'Wow, now that's amazing,' I murmur. Imagine being rich enough to build that palace!

'Jane's place isn't that big but it's not small either,' Attracta pipes up again. 'How many bedrooms again, babes? Five? Six?'

'Seven. Of course it's not mine. It's my old man's.'

'We could all have stayed there,' says Danny pouring more whiskey into his glass.

Jane gives him a flirtatious smile. 'Indeed. Maybe next time.'

I stand rooted to the spot in annoyance. What a brazen little hussy she is, flirting with my man like that, right in front of my eyes. I'd love to give her ridiculous-looking ponytail a good tug!

'It's a pity you're heading out with your friends tomorrow,' says Jane, looking directly at me with a tight, spiteful smile, 'because I was going to invite everyone around to our place tomorrow evening. You'd love it, guys,' she adds, turning her attention to the others. 'We have our own heated outdoor swimming pool lit with floodlights and a fully stocked bar. You, especially, Danny, would be in your element.'

I flinch but nobody seems to notice.

'I'm sorely tempted,' Danny muses. 'But I've got to be at Malaga airport early tomorrow morning. Crew control rang earlier. They're desperately short-staffed and they need me to fly to Edinburgh the following evening.'

I feel my heart sink. Danny hasn't mentioned his change of plans to me. When did he get the call? Why didn't he tell me earlier? Why does he have to announce it in front of the others? Is he lying? Is he just looking for a chance to escape now that he's had his wicked way with me? Is it because I'm not thin enough? Suddenly my head is swimming with my own insecurities.

'Don't worry about getting to the airport in time,' Jane coos. 'Daddy leaves a car for us in Marbella to use, a Beamer,' she adds unnecessarily. 'I'll wake you up and drive you to the airport the following morning. No problemo.'

'Well, if you're sure,' says Danny, not even looking at me, 'if you're sure it's not too long a drive.'

'I love driving in Spain,' she answers like a flash.

She must be lying. She's just showing off. Everyone, at least every foreigner used to driving on the other side of the road, knows that Spain is a nightmare to drive in. Especially on the motorway to the airport where people seem to drive like lunatics with a death wish. And what does she mean she'll wake him up? Will she put him in a spare room and set his alarm clock? Or will he be lying next to her anyway, so close that she can simply reach out and nudge him? Suddenly I feel sick. Danny finally seems to notice me. 'Are you OK?' He looks concerned.

'I've felt better,' I mutter, as my stomach begins to heave involuntarily. I rush downstairs to the bathroom and lock myself in as we pull into the port.

'I feel much better now,' I tell Danny as we sit at the water's edge. The others have gone home to change in preparation for another few drinks later back at the port. Danny is trying to persuade me to stay out for a few beers but the thought of any more alcohol makes me feel queasy. I've had a long day and now I'm dreaming of my bed.

'You can come back with me if you want,' I say, leaning my head on Danny's chest as he strokes my hair softly.

'If I come back you might not ever get rid of me,' he murmurs into my ear.

'That's OK.'

'No, it wouldn't be a good idea.'

We remain sitting on the wall in silence for another ten minutes or so. The stars hang low in the sky above. I shiver slightly. Danny takes off his jacket and wraps it around me. I'm feeling kind of sad now. This might be our last evening ever together. But why am I even thinking of such depressing thoughts? Of course it's not the end. We live in the same country, the same city even. Danny and I work for the same company. Snap out of it, Annie, I tell myself, anybody would think you had a jail sentence hanging over you.

Eventually I speak up again. 'So are you going to go to Jane's party?' I ask, willing him to say no but guessing he'll say yes.

'Maybe.'

'She's got the hots for you.'

But Danny doesn't seem to hear me. He seems distracted. I look up at his face, at his perfectly chiselled cheekbones. His strong, full lips are set in a straight line. He looks different, but not in a good way. He looks strained.

'Is there something on your mind, Danny? Do you regret what happened earlier?' I ask nervously.

'No, not at all, nothing could be further from the truth.'

'So tell me what's on your mind. You've suddenly turned very quiet.'

'I don't know if I should tell you . . .' he says, trailing off. 'It still hasn't sunk in yet really.'

I'm alarmed all of a sudden. What could possibly be so terrible? What's this big secret he's hiding from me? Have I done something wrong? Does he think I'm some kind of shameless hussy? Has he in fact got a wife back in Dublin whom he forgot to mention? Or four children by different women? The worst scenarios are racing through my mind. He's got to stop torturing me like this.

'Danny,' I say, taking his hand in mine. It feels icy. 'Danny, whatever is on your mind, you can tell me. I'm a big girl, you know. Hey, you never know, I might even be able to help.'

'You won't, believe me, you won't,' he says, sounding adamant. But his voice is breaking. All his confidence seems to be shattered. How could somebody undergo such a personality change in such a short a time?

'I'm waiting . . .' I probe gently. 'A problem shared is a problem halved. Remember?'

He looks at me, his eyes full of wild panic. I'm startled. What on earth could have happened?'

'When you were in the bathroom getting changed,' he said quickly, his words almost stumbling into each other, 'I got the call that every young guy dreads. I got the call that my mother warned me about over and over again when I was a teenager . . .' he broke off.

My mind is reeling. Nothing is sinking in. 'From work . . . ?' I ask.

'No, not from work,' he says sounding exasperated. 'From my goddamn ex, Fiona.'

'B . . . but . . .'

'She's pregnant, Annie,' he says, pushing me away from him and putting his hands over his face. 'She's pregnant and I don't know what I'm going to do about it.'

Rule Seven: Don't worry if you don't know all the right answers. Neither does anybody else.

The sauna is sweltering and I'm sweating like crazy. Good. It'll take a hell of a lot of sweating to remove the last traces of alcohol from my system. To think I was coming here to be healthy, and to drink lots of water and eat lots of fruit and vegetables! So much for that! I've been on a rollercoaster booze fest ever since I got here and now I want to get back to Planet Earth as quickly as possible.

Danny has gone home. He texted me at the airport before he got on the plane. I didn't text him back. I couldn't. I can't even think about him without becoming totally overwhelmed. I sort of feel that the whole thing . . . meeting Danny . . . the trip on the yacht . . . was all a bit of a dream, which rapidly turned into a nightmare.

My head is pounding with questions without answers. Like, when did he get that call from his ex? Was it before or after he made love to me? Did he end up going to the party last night with my new enemy Jane? Or was he frantically trying to call his ex in order to talk about things?

Anyway, why am I even trying to figure things out? It's none of my business. Danny's nothing to me. Just a fling. A meaningless fling with a guy who'll soon be a dad and will probably get back with his ex for the sake of his child, and barely remember me, the silly air hostess whom he shagged on somebody else's yacht.

I shudder despite the intense heat of the wooden sauna. I feel kind of disgusted with myself. OK, I was on holidays, I was in lust, there was a lot of drink taken, but it was still a kind of slutty thing to do.

The heat is too much. My nose feels like it's burning. I feel dizzy. I get up and push open the door, welcoming the cool air that hits my face like a wake-up call.

I make my way towards the nearby indoor Jacuzzi. It's empty, which is a big bonus. Somehow I don't feel like making small talk with strangers from Wales in a pool full of forced bubbles just at the moment. And the outside Jacuzzi would only remind me of the happier times I'd shared with Danny. Was it really only a couple of days ago when we'd sat there drinking champagne like a real couple without a care in the world? It kind of feels like a faraway dream now.

As I sit with the spray of the furious bubbles dampening my warm face, I silently talk to Emily, my dead sister, who always had all the answers to everything. I ask her what I should I do and close my eyes to hear her soothing words from above.

As far as I can gather, Emily is telling me not to beat myself up over recent events, which she points out are beyond my control. She tells me to relax, enjoy the rest of the holiday, and above all to work on a tan. She says life's too short for regrets, and she's right. Emily, of all people, knows about the brevity of life.

Feeling a lot more upbeat now, I haul my body from the Jacuzzi, wrap myself up in the hotel robe, and head outside to the rooftop where I pull out a deckchair, and lie out underneath the glorious sunshine. As I dry off, I realise that I shouldn't be mourning the loss of Danny as he'd never been mine to start with anyway. We were just two people whose paths happened to meet unexpectedly and now we've gone our separate ways. Period.

I close my eyes and begin to relax. It's my last day here so I'm not going to let anything or anybody ruin it. Instead of feeling angry about Danny I should feel sorry for him. After all, his mother is the devil reincarnate and his ex is unexpectedly up the duff. He won't have a happy Christmas this year, that's for sure.

A high-pitched male voice suddenly interrupts my thought. 'Move into the bar area for the fun quiz,' he squeals, ringing a bell for ultimate effect. 'It'll be starting in five minutes.'

I open my eyes and squint up at him. He's a tall skinny lad with spiky dark hair and a gold hoop in his left ear and a camp-as-a-row-of-tents smile.

'I'm going to give the quiz a miss today, I think.' I say politely. 'If you don't mind . . . maybe tomorrow.'

'Nonsense.' He takes my hand and almost hauls me off my lounger. 'We'll have no people ducking out of the quiz today. There's a fantastic prize at the end of it.'

'What is it?'

'A bottle of locally produced Spanish wine.'

Oh God. Please don't mention wine. Or any type of alcohol for that matter.

'I don't have a choice, do I?'

'No, not really. Where are you from, anyway? England?'

'Ireland.'

'Same thing though . . .'

'Eh . . . no,' I say indignantly.

We have to get into groups of four. Everybody wants me to be in their group for some strange reason. I'm flattered. I feel so popular all of a sudden. It's a difficult decision but eventually I choose the table nearest to me consisting of two women and a man, all in their eighties.

'OK, everybody,' screeches Mr Entertainment himself. 'Has everybody got a pen and a sheet of paper? Good, good, quiet now, please. We need everyone's full attention. The questions start NOW!'

'Question number one: Who is the lead singer of Take That?'

The elderly people at my table look totally confused.

'Is it that Irish fellow? Ronan Keating?' asks one of the women frowning.

'No, it is Gary Barlow, remember the pudgy one?' I say.

She couldn't. 'Are you sure it isn't Ronan Keating, the one with the strawberry-blond hair and the sideburns?'

'No, definitely not. He was in a different band altogether.'

'Were you a fan?'

'Absolutely not,' I insist, appalled at such a suggestion. God forbid!

'Question number two: What year did the Second World War end?'

'Nineteen thirty-nine?' I venture hopefully.

The trio look disgusted. 'Nineteen forty-five, you silly girl,' the man hisses in my ear. 'Shame on you.'

I'm about to take him on. Eighty-something or not, he shouldn't be having a go at me. After all, he didn't even know about Gary Barlow. But then I see a twinkle in his eye and realise he's winding me up. 'I fought in the war,' he explains. 'So I should know my dates.'

'Really? I'm sorry I don't know my dates too well. If I'd been any good at history in school, I'd probably be a historian or a tour guide or something.'

'Ssshhhh!,' says Mr Entertainment with the ridiculously spiky hair.

I glower back at him.

'Right, then. Question number three . . .'

Justin Timberlake's 'Sexy's Back' rings from my bag underneath the table. As I frantically open it to switch off my mobile phone, Mr Entertainment roars, 'Could everybody PLEASE ensure that ALL electronic devices have been switched off at this present time?'

Jesus, would he ever keep his hair on? He must have been an air steward in a previous life. No other job allows such unnecessary hysteria. Honest to God.

Eventually I locate my phone under a bottle of factor 2 (like, who am I kidding?) suntan oil and hit the 'off' button.

'Sorry about that,' I mutter smiling around apologetically.

'Right, then. If everybody is QUITE ready,' Mr E

pauses to glare at me, 'we'll move on swiftly and without further ado . . .'

'Question number three: Who is the father of Kate Moss's daughter?'

'Who's Kate Moss again?' The two women at my table frown, looking confused.

'Is that Kate Moss the model or Kate Mosse the author?' I say, putting up my hand.

At this stage I think Mr E is going to explode. Oh well, that'll teach him for preventing me from developing my tan in peace. Hopefully tomorrow, when he's organising the weekly charades, he'll leave me to my own devices.

'I think Johnny Depp is the father,' somebody pipes up.

'Or is it that waster who's always on drugs? Pete something or other.'

'No, definitely not,' I shout back. 'I should know, I regularly read *Hello*! and *OK*! And *Grazia*, *Heat* and *Now* and . . . all of those magazines, really. The father is Jefferson Hack. I know because I remember thinking they were quite an odd couple at the time.'

Everybody scribbles down his name. Suddenly I realise what I've done and press my hand to my mouth in mock horror. I glance surreptitiously over at Mr E and can see imaginary smoke bellowing from each ear.

'Anybody who shouts out the answers to the questions will be AUTOMATICALLY disqualified,' he yells looking directly at me.

I've been put firmly back in my box. I promise to be a good girl for the rest of the quiz.

'Question number four: Who was the first man to ever land on the moon?'

I zone out at this point. Who bloody cares? More to the point, who was just ringing me on my mobile? Could it have been Danny ringing to inform me that Fiona's unexpected pregnancy was in fact a hoax and he now has the all clear to date me? Oh God, Annie, stop torturing yourself . . .

'Question number five: How many members in the girl band Girls Aloud?'

'Five,' I mutter without hesitation, 'the three good-looking ones, the blonde who promotes push-up bras and the redhead.'

My team dutifully writes down the correct answer.

'Question number six: How many legs does a cockroach have?'

'Let me go back down to my bathroom and check the fellow on my wall,' I mutter, laughing at my own joke.

'Question number seven: What is Tara Palmer-Tompkinson famous for?'

'Beats me.' I shrug.

'Question number eight: What was . . . ?'

And on and on and on he drones until I've practically slipped off my chair and fallen into a coma. I'm exhausted, all quizzed out, and want to get back into the sauna as quickly as possible. I reckon there's still copious amounts of alcohol left in my body which needs to be sweated out.

'And the winners are at' – it nearly kills the scowling Mr E to say it – 'table number four.'

My newfound companions whoop for joy and a bartender comes flying over with the chilled bottle of wine and four large wine glasses but I can't look at the wine without my tummy feeling queasy so I ask for an iced water instead. Then I check my mobile phone. There's a missed call from my flatmate, Edel. I frown at the phone. That's weird. I wonder what she wants. I hope she hasn't gone and locked herself out of the flat or anything. As far as I know her unemployed boyfriend secretly has a key. He shouldn't have, of course, as he's not a tenant, and I own the damn place, but I kind of turn a blind eye to it to keep the peace.

I don't particularly want to ring her back if I don't have to, as I've got hardly any credit on my phone and she's on a different network to me. When I do ring people back on holidays, usually at exorbitant costs, they end up asking me silly questions like how the weather is. But what if it's urgent? Like what if something's happened to a member of my family or the flat has been burnt to a cinder? Oh dammit anyway, I decide to go downstairs and use the payphone in the hotel lobby. Edel answers the phone in our flat immediately.

'Oh it's nothing serious,' she's at pains to point out as I silently curse her from dragging me away from the precious sunshine. 'It's just that there's an interesting parcel here for you. Do you want me to open it up and tell you what it is?'

Who on earth could it be from? 'Oh yes . . . I mean, no, you'd better keep it for me as a surprise so I'll have something to look forward to when I get home.'

'Are you sure?' Edel asks, sounding a bit disappointed.

'Oh go on, then, you nosy cow!' I can't help but laugh.

'Oh goodie,' she squeals and I can hear the sound of paper being torn frantically. 'By the way, are there any men out there?'

'I've seen one or two walking around,' I mutter evasively.

'You know what I mean though,' she insists.

'No, no, there's nothing to report.'

I think that talking about Danny over the phone would only be futile. I'm doing my best to try to forget him at the moment. Discussing him in detail would only prolong my pain and eat into my credit card too.

'It's a pair of shoes,' she says.

'Are you sure? How odd!'

'Yeah but wait, just let me open the box.'

The next minute a screech sounds down the line which almost bursts open my eardrum.

'What?' What is it, I wonder, has Edel fallen or been electrocuted?

'It's a pair of Jimmy Choos.'

'Really, like my old ones?'

'No, much better . . . wait for it. They're the very latest ones. Brand new to the market. I know. They cost a fortune. I saw these ones in *Vogue*. You lucky bitch!'

'Describe them,' I insist, practically drooling at the mouth. As a self-confessed shoe addict, I'm practically hyperventilating.

'They're cream in colour, and satin, encrusted with Swarovski jewels.'

I close my eyes and with a sharp intake of breath, try to imagine them. 'What's the heel like?'

'It's steel, super sexy, slim and higher than anything I've

ever seen. You could wear these babies to the Oscars and walk away with the best-dressed prize.'

'But who gave them to me?'

'I don't know. There's no card or anything. But they were posted from the UK to you, care of the airline, if that's any use. The airline driver who usually delivers passengers' lost luggage got me to sign for them. Could you have won them?'

'No, no . . .' I don't enter many competitions. I always mean to, of course, but never get around to it. 'And I definitely didn't order them online. How bizarre! Are they definitely my size?'

'Yes, five and a half – oh, hang on a minute, there *is* a card here after all. I couldn't see it among all the packaging. Does the name Oliver Kane mean anything to you?'

'Oliver Kane?' I muse. Yes, indeed, that name *does* means something to me. For some strange reason every time I hear it I feel an odd tingle in my spine. But why? Who exactly is this chap? I know nothing about him except that he seems to be very important, rich, gorgeous, happily married, and almost killed me with his big fancy car. So how did he suddenly become part of my life? Is he some kind of fairy godfather? There are too many coincidences. After all, if he hadn't knocked me down, I wouldn't have gone on holidays, I wouldn't have ended up on his yacht making love to another man in his bedroom, and now he's gone and sent me a brand-new pair of Jimmy Choos? What kind of man would even remember the name of the label of the pair of sandals I was wearing? And why do I feel an almost warm, fuzzy feeling at the sound of his name? This is just ridiculous. He's got a stunning wife for goodness' sake and I am the type of person who despises women who chase unavailable men. It absolutely goes against everything I stand for. So why am I feeling this way? Good God, what on earth is happening to me?

Rule Eight: Learn how to apply your make-up in the dark, in five minutes.

The annoying cuckoo ring tone on my phone chirrups at exactly 3.30 a.m. on Wednesday morning. In a daze I reach over and press the snooze option, turn on the light and stare at the low magnolia-painted ceiling feeling sorry for myself until the cuckoo blasts me out of it again.

OK, I know I'm only going over and back to London today, but that's not the point, is it? The point is that I have to get up, make myself look glamorous, haul my unwilling self out to the freezing cold airport, feed and water a couple of hundred grumpy, exhausted passengers across the water and then do it all over again on the way back.

I look at my watch again – 3.46 a.m. God, I'm such a night owl. I am such a devil in the mornings. Mind you, it is still the middle of the night. Some people are only rolling into bed at this time. Why, oh why, do crew planning not grant my wishes to do late shifts, when I can sleep on in the mornings, have a leisurely breakfast and then go to work feeling normal? I know some people say it's great to be home by lunchtime so you can go shopping or do a bit of gardening or whatever. But how do they do it? How? By the time I drag myself in from the red-eye flights the only thing I want to do is crash out in front of the TV while stuffing my face with chocolate ice cream.

I'm just out of my steaming hot shower, wrapped in a flimsy towel with my hair dripping down my back, when the door bell rings loudly making me jump. I look out the window, craning my neck to see who it could be. That's weird, there's a taxi waiting on the kerb. Good Lord, how early is he? How wet am I? For goodness' sake I'm still undressed and unmade up. How can they torture me like this?

I holler out the window, the freezing air cruelly biting my shivering skin, my towel wrapped tightly around my bust in order to prevent the middle-aged cab driver from getting an early morning eyeful. 'Will you give me ten minutes?' I implore in my best little-girl voice.

The taxi driver grunts. 'We're picking up another three people, so hurry up.'

'I'll go as fast as I can,' I groan, scrambling around the room trying to locate my shoes and tights. My uniform is pressed and waiting in the wardrobe for me. At least I had the foresight to iron it last night.

In exactly eight and a half minutes I'm in the car, my hair still wet and no make-up on my face but that's fine. Hopefully there'll be a few traffic-light stops at which I can draw in my lips and colour in my eyelids. Normally it should only take twenty minutes to get to the airport but as we have to pick up other people at Drumcondra, Glasnevin and Santry respectively, it'll probably take us at least twice the time. Oh to have a little car so I'd be spared this bloody tour of the city on a regular basis. The only problem with driving, however, is that the staff car park is about ten miles away from the terminal and if you're away for a few days in the winter, there's a good chance your car won't start when you get back due to frost. So, no matter which way you look at it, transporting yourself to and from the airport is a bummer.

We stop off at a house in Drumcondra to pick up a check-in girl. Thankfully the taxi stops under a lamp-post so I can get out my flawless finish and wipe my face with it, hoping I don't leave any unsightly white patches of skin near my ears and that I have my neck covered. There really can't be anything worse than a brown face clashing with a deathly white neck! Then at Glasnevin when we stop outside a bungalow I take the opportunity to draw in my eyebrows with brown pencil. At Santry I paint a raspberry-coloured smile on my lips and insert a pair of simple studs in to my earlobes. Dangly earrings are not permitted while on duty. Now then, I'm finally beginning to look like a real live human being.

At the airport, I go quickly to the cabin crew rest area, check my cubby hole for any post (none), and then go downstairs to meet my waiting crew. We're on an airbus A320 this morning so there'll be quite a few of us working the flight. Let's hope the rest of the crew are a decent bunch. I wonder who the cockpit crew will be. Hopefully Danny won't be the co-pilot. I don't think I could face him this morning. I haven't even heard from him since I got back from Spain, so I think it's pretty obvious where I stand in his affections.

The door is already closed so I open it tentatively and poke my head around it to see if I've got the right briefing room. My face drops in shock at the sight of Sylvie's tight platinum bun. Mother of Divine God, why oh why does she have to be on my flight? God, there must be over a thousand cabin crew working in the airline, so why is life being so unkind forcing me to fly with such a weapon? I wonder does she know about me and Danny? Nah, no way. It's highly unlikely he would have sat down and had a heart-to-heart with her about me. I wonder does she have any idea that she's about to become a granny.

Sylvie wrinkles her nose in distaste at the sight of me which is very comforting, not. I quickly take my seat and nod politely at my fellow colleagues.

'Who is wearing that hideous perfume? It smells like room spray that has gone off! Could somebody quickly open a window?'

Er, that would be me. I gave myself a good old spritz before coming in, but do I own up? The hell I don't. I keep a studied gaze on the floor.

'If I've said it once, I've said it a million times,' she snaps. 'Strong perfume in the morning just puts our passengers off their sausages.'

I remain with my head lowered, my eyes glued to a spot beside my feet. Give me a break! It's only my first day back. Anyway my perfume isn't *that* bad. Sure, it may have gone off a bit considering I've had it for over five years and originally salvaged it from a bargain bin in a Miami store, but it's not going to kill anyone.

We've a full house on board today so we're going to be busy. The London flights are always a nightmare but the good thing is that when we're that busy the morning will fly.

We make our way out to the ramp. The icy wind cruelly nips my ankles as I board the steps to the plane. We've just about time to count the breakfasts, turn on the ovens, put the ice in the silver buckets, and place the newspapers in the racks, before the first of the passengers (mostly bleary-eyed business people) make their way on to the plane amid greetings of 'Good morning, do you have your boarding card there, please?'

Boarding takes an age with people carefully folding their overcoats and placing heavy laptops in the overhead bins. Thankfully I'm at the back of the plane so I can make myself a piping hot coffee while informing passengers via the back intercom to take note of the security and fire exits.

Soon everybody is seated and I take out my demo gear in order to show the passengers how to survive a ditching should we happen to plunge into the sea en route. Now, normally nobody ever takes any notice of the demo (although one day, maybe they'll wish they hadn't lifted their newspapers in defiance), but today we have a crowd of very enthusiastic Japanese passengers who stare as though they're being gripped by a riveting Hollywood movie. I feel like taking a bow when I'm finished.

Five minutes into the air the race is on to feed and water our passengers. We scramble into our nasty-looking unflattering aprons and put on our black oven gloves to unload the hot breakfasts into carts and put cartons of orange juice and water on top. There, we're ready to go.

'Tea, coffee, juice?' we sing as we push the carts, smiling as ever, down the cabin. 'Would you like ice with that?'

Most passengers are either asleep or in the process of nodding off so we are virtually ignored. That's fine by me, though. At least nobody is asking us how many feet we are above sea level or whether we've flown over Dover yet. Normally those annoying questions are left up to the charter flight passengers.

After that we come out with our plastic white bags shouting for 'Any empties there please?' A few people lazily lean over to discard their used tissues and empty bottles of cola which they bought before they got on board. I thank them profusely for their rubbish.

The next minute, I hear Sylvie making a standard announcement in her deeply affected accent about the in-flight shopping. Ah God, I can't believe she expects us to bring out the carts full of perfumes, aftershaves and teddy bears on such an early flight. People never buy anything on these commuter flights and I hate shouting out to them as if I'm pushing a pram flogging fruit and rotting vegetables on Moore Street.

As predicted, nobody reacts as we haul the carts along, shouting like fairground employees, and we make zero commission. Then the captain makes his announcement about imminent landing and prepares us for delays due to fog at Heathrow. Oh, what's new? Circulating Heathrow seems to be a given these days.

The seatbelt sign is on but as usual some idiot stands up around row three to retrieve his coat from the overhead bin. There's always one . . .

I march up authoritatively, and inform the young man to obey the captain's wishes.

As he does so, somebody else grabs my skirt. I swing

around in surprise and my surprise turns to shock as I notice the familiar face. Good grief, it's Oliver Kane!

'Oliver!' I exclaim in astonishment. 'I mean, Mr Kane. How are you?'

'I'm fine. How are you, more to the point?'

'Never been better,' I say feeling myself blush. Why oh why am I betraying myself like this? So what if I think he's gorgeous? He's not meant to know it! 'Listen, thank you so much for the sandals. They are amazing, really, you shouldn't have.' I feel all flustered now, having been taken completely unawares. Oliver is even better looking than I remembered. It's funny that I've never seen him on a flight before. Maybe it's one of those unexplained things. Like, you know, sometimes when you're walking down the street and thinking of somebody you haven't seen in years and you suddenly bump into them.

'Nonsense, it was the least I could do. Do they fit?'

'Like gloves.' I smile. I notice other passengers are beginning to take an interest in our somewhat bizarre conversation. I look up to the front of the cabin and see Sylvie glaring at me. She looks as though she's just swallowed a bitter lemon. She's craning her neck to try to make out what's going on.

I hear the wheels of the plane go down.

'I'd better go back to my seat, Mr Kane. I hope you enjoy London. Is it business or pleasure?'

'Business, I'm afraid. I fly to London at least three times a week. Listen, I'll catch up with you when we land.'

'Oh sure,' I say quickly feeling the plane drop suddenly. 'Take care.'

I shoot down the back of the plane and strap myself in

before the aircraft hits the runway with an almighty thud.

'Jesus Christ,' I mutter to myself. What kind of flight school did our pilots train at? Huh?

As soon as we reach our parking slot, all the passengers stand up, frantically putting on coats and scarves, and trying to jump over each other to get out. At least I'm at the back this morning so I don't have to utter the words 'thank you', 'good-bye', 'take care' and 'cheerio' hundreds of times. I busy myself by making the tea for the crew which we can drink during the turnaround if anybody's interested. Unfortunately I realise there isn't a chance in hell of squeezing my way past all the passengers to get to the front to say good-bye to the charming Mr Kane. Oh well . . . what a nice man though. What a distinguished, handsome man he is, too. I can't believe he sent me a pair of Jimmy Choos. What a fabulous guy. What a pity I can't say thanks properly. Hell, I can barely string a sentence when I'm near him. He must think I'm a gibbering idiot!

'Annie!' Sorcha, the pretty petite blonde next to me rushes to the hot-water tap that's overfilling the tea pot. 'Come back to planet Earth, Missus. You're in another world there!'

'Sorry.' I snap back to reality. 'Can you get me the bag of biscuits there to go with the tea, if anyone wants them?'

'Sure. And an extra spoonful of sugar for Sylvie. I think she needs some sweetening up. By the way, who was the man you were talking to? He was divine.'

'You said it,' I giggle.

'I think I recognise him. He must fly a lot. So do you fancy him?'

'He's married,' I say resolutely.

'You didn't answer my question,' she probes.

'Even if I did, it wouldn't matter because he's not mine and never will be.'

'So, I take it that's a yes then.'

'Zip it, Sorcha,' I warn her, trying my best not to go red again.

During the turnaround Sylvie is busy making an embarrassing fuss over the pilots, fawning over them, making sure they have hot breakfasts with fruit and real milk with their coffee, as well as all the papers. She completely ignores me and the other cabin crew as we're obviously not worthy of conversation.

I don't care. I flick through the tabloids which passengers have considerately left behind, and gossip with the rest of the cabin crew.

'How was your holiday?' Kerry, an easy-going dark-skinned brunette asks me. 'You've a fantastic tan.'

'Shhh.' I put my middle finger to my lips. 'Keep your voice down. I had a blast in Spain but I don't want that old battleaxe to find out where I was considering I was suspended and then on sick leave.'

'Oh, OK. Lucky you, though. I wish somebody would suspend me.'

'It's easy. Just look at Sylvie sideways and she'll give you a month off. I don't know what her problem is.'

'Neither do I. Her son is apparently a bit of a ride though. Have you met him? He's a pilot.'

I feel myself bristle immediately. 'Is he?' I respond like a robot. 'Have you flown with him before?'

'No I haven't, but he's gorgeous, even if he does have a bit of a reputation, if you know what I mean.'

I look at her curiously. 'What *do* you mean? Is he a womaniser?'

'A womaniser?' She frowns. 'Well, I don't know about that. But I have heard he's a party animal all right. Apparently he's always the one holding up the bar at the end of the night. I even heard that—' She suddenly halts mid-sentence as Sylvie stands up and claps her hands loudly. 'Now, girls,' she shrills. 'We've a full load for the return flight. So I want all hands on deck and no slackers,' she adds, shooting a warning look at me for some unknown reason. 'Let's do a full thorough security check, and make sure that all the seat backs are checked for any foreign-looking objects. Any suspicious items found should be reported immediately.'

I slink down the back to reapply my lipstick and lash on a coat of mascara to make myself look more alive. Kerry has gone up to the front to help Sylvie welcome the new passengers on board. I wonder what she'd been about to say about Danny?

The return flight goes without a hitch, thank God. It only takes just over forty minutes because the wind is behind us. When we land back in Dublin airport, I'm just thinking about getting back into my bed, pulling over the curtains and falling into a deep sleep dreaming about where I'm going to be wearing my Jimmy Choos next. If only I was going on a hot date somewhere soon. If only Niall hadn't dumped me. If only Danny's ex hadn't got herself up the duff. If only Mr Kane wasn't married. Hey, why am I even thinking about Mr Kane again? Now, that's just weird. I'll have to start training myself not to imagine what my life would be like with somebody who's clearly off limits.

Sylvie doesn't even say good-bye to me as she marches down the aircraft steps and totters across the windy ramp in her high heels, pulling her wheels behind her. I notice Kerry is chatting away to her. I wonder what they're talking about.

I slack behind, not wishing to catch up. Anyway, my bag is heavy, full of the sixteen passenger sausages I crammed in to it during my break. It's shameful the amount of food that's thrown out at the end of the flights, and my elderly neighbour, Mrs O'Neill, has a hungry little Jack Russell who's always grateful for any little titbits. He starts barking excitedly every time he sees me with my goody bag.

Thankfully the taxi doesn't take too long to come and collect us. Kerry lives near me in Mount Joy Square so we're sharing the ride home. Good. I've always liked Kerry; she's very easy company and doesn't go on about a husband and kids all the time (yawn), and how exclusive the airline used to be during the good old days, like some of the more senior crew.

'That morning was fairly painless, wasn't it?' remarks Kerry cheerfully as we pull out of the airport and on to the motorway.

'It would have been even less painful without Savage. She practically ignored me, not that I was complaining too much though.'

'What's your schedule like for the rest of the week?'

'Chicago tomorrow. Hell!' I groan.

'Still, there's some great shopping in Chicago when you get there. I've an overnight to Paris. I'm bringing my mum with me. She's never been and has always wanted a picture of herself in front of the Eiffel Tower. Do you ever bring your mum on trips?'

'No,' I say truthfully. Not that I haven't tried my best to persuade her. But my mum is only a shell of herself since Emily died and although I often invite her along on trips, she's never up for it. Neither is Dad. I wish there was something I could do to cheer them up. Maybe I should phone home more often. Perhaps I should suggest a spa break away with my mum so that we can catch up and do some mother/daughter bonding. Maybe I should offer to help Dad out in the garden more often. Andrea, my younger sister, lives in Australia with her boyfriend and Mum isn't really close to any of her own siblings. Sometimes I feel the terrible burden of trying to make her happy rests all on my shoulders. The problem is that Emily was always my mother's favourite daughter, the girl who ticked all the boxes and could do no wrong. When she departed from this life she left a cruel void in all of our hearts, especially Mum's. The only thing that really keeps her going these days is watching little Ben grow up to be a darling young boy. He has her huge kind brown eyes and looking into them is hauntingly like looking into Emily's soul. I wonder if I even suggested a spa break away, would she go for it or would she just dismiss it as a waste of good money. Even though Mum works part-time in a local boutique, she doesn't spend much. She's always putting money away for that rainy day. But even when it does rain, she's loathe to part with her hard-earned cash. Her frugal ways stem from when she was a child, I think. Her own father had a drink problem and didn't have the money to send her to college. He sent her brothers, but not her.

She's never really forgiven him for that, and to this day never touches a drop herself, except for Christmas Day when she opens the sherry bottle and makes the one glass last the entire day. My dad, on the other hand, often enjoys a pint in his local in Swords, although he's not exactly what you'd call a heavy drinker either. In fact, I've never actually seen him drunk. The closest I've even seen him to being merry was the day I became an air hostess. He cracked open two expensive bottles of champagne that day and we all had at least one glass. That was the happiest I'd ever seen my parents. To see me in my full uniform with my wings pinned to my collar was a big deal for them. The neighbours had called around to admire me and lots of photos were taken. But after that everything went downhill. After the doctor confirmed Emily's cancer, no more champagne was ever opened in the Anderson home again. In fact, barely a smile was ever raised. And who could blame them really?

'Oh by the way,' Kerry says suddenly, 'in case I forget to tell you, an extraordinary thing happened at the end of our first leg this morning.'

'Really? What?'

'Well, you know that man you were talking to in the aisle just before we landed at Heathrow?'

'Ye . . . es?'

'The good-looking, well-dressed man . . . in his early forties I'd say? Fabulous blue eyes to rival Paul Newman's?'

'I know the one you're talking about,' I answer anxiously. What does she know that I don't?

'Is he a friend of yours?'

'Eh . . . kind of.' Well, he knocked me down if that counts for anything. Oh, and of course I had sex in his yacht with Savage's son last week, which is an interesting titbit but one I'd rather not share with Kerry at this present time. I think it's probably best to keep all these little incidents to myself so as not to shock the eavesdropping taxi driver.

'I was thinking you must know him,' says Kerry, 'because after everybody else disembarked, he asked Sylvie to give you his phone number.'

My jaw practically hits the floor of the car. 'And did he write it down?'

'No, he just produced a business card and gave it to her. I saw her putting it in her bag. Oh how annoying! She must've forgotten to pass it on to you.'

My ass, she forgot, I think, but say nothing.

'Do you think he wanted to ask you out?'

'Of course not,' I say hurriedly as if the very idea was out of the question. 'He's married.'

'That wouldn't stop some people,' says Kerry, and the taxi driver, delighted at the chance to give his opinion suddenly chips in in agreement.

'Indeed. When you've been driving around the city as long as I have,' he mutters, looking from Kerry to myself in his mirror, 'you'd be surprised at nothing. Absolutely nothing. I've seen it all and more.'

Rule Nine: Never put sausages in your suitcase.

'Hello, you little mutt.' I pat the neighbours' yapping little Jack Russell who is leaping with joy at the sight of me. 'I suppose you're hungry as always. You're like a canine dustbin so you are.'

I open the door of my apartment, and to my pleasant surprise I see it's been left spotlessly clean with fresh flowers sprouting from a vase on the window sill. The heating has also been left on to make the place feel snug. Bless Edel for thinking of me. No matter how far I travel and no matter how fabulous my hotel rooms are, nothing beats coming back to my little flat. My very own place. Well, mine and the bank's.

'I've a lovely little surprise for you this afternoon,' I tell the yapping dog who is now bizarrely trying to hump my right leg. 'Patience, fella.'

I zip open my little wheelie case as the dog sniffs frantically in excited anticipation. But to my surprise when I open it, there isn't a sausage in sight. Oh shit, I've brought home the wrong flipping case. I don't bloody believe this. The dog glares at me, his pointed face a mixture of disgust and disbelief.

I rummage through the stranger's case. Was it Kerry's? Or could it be Sorcha's? There's no name tag on it. Inside there's just a spare pair of tights. And a pair of pristine-clean cabin shoes, and an apron, and the heavy safety manual in a red leather folder which all cabin crew are supposed to carry at all times in case of emergencies. Oh sod it; perhaps crew control would phone later with the identity of the rightful owner.

I shake my hair loose from the tight bun, slip off my high-heeled shoes, sink my feet into my fluffy pink slippers, and take a make-up wipe from my bedroom and scrub every last scrap of make-up from my tired face. I'm too tired to pack for America tomorrow. I think I'll just go to bed and hopefully wake up in a few hours feeling somewhat normal again. I put the yapping Jack Russell outside my flat with a bowl of slightly off milk which he laps eagerly. I'm so tired I feel if I lie down now I'll never be able to get up again.

I'm just about to drift off, half immersed in a dream where I'm back on the yacht, only this time Mr Kane is the host, serving champagne in Waterford Crystal flutes. Colin Farrell is also on the yacht which is pretty amazing because I've never socialised with a real celebrity, although I have served everyone who's anyone on board at some stage. Everyone from the members of U2 to Daniel Day Lewis and Posh and Becks. Daniel is very quiet and low key, while Bono and the gang are very polite and Adam Clayton usually orders a vegetarian meal. Beckham is as gorgeous as he is in reality and I don't know much about Posh, only that she didn't bother with the passenger breakfast I served her. People always ask me about the celebrities we have on board but to be honest when they're sitting in front of you and strapped into their seats they seem much smaller than they do on the big screens or smiling out of the papers at you. Anyway, we try not to give them preferential treatment and asking for autographs is considered to be a professional no-no.

Suddenly my phone blasts me back to reality. It's crew control. Oh God, what do they want with me now? They inform me that Sylvie has my bag containing all the sausages and she wants her own bag back immediately. Oh shit! Of all the people to take my damn case home, why did it have to be her? Now I have to drag myself out of the bed again, and pull on a tracksuit and trainers.

The door bell rings ten minutes later and rubbing my eyes I drag Sylvie's case to the door and press the Intercom.

'Do you have the case for me?'

'Annie, it's me, Danny. Can I come up?

Danny! What on earth is he doing at my door? How can he suddenly arrive back in my life without any notice? How will I cope with seeing him again? Will all my old feelings of lust be resurrected? My heart is beating faster than I'd ever have thought possible, I race around the flat looking for make-up to plaster all over my face. I whip off the manky tracksuit that I got in a sale last January because the zip was broken and struggle into a pair of jeans and a black polo neck since all my other clothes are in a basket well overdue for a trip to the launderette.

I take a deep breath, get the lift downstairs and open the main front door. Danny is standing there in his pilot's uniform looking stunning, like a romantic hero in a film.

I stand looking at him, baffled. 'What are you doing here, Danny?'

'You took my mother's case home and she's complaining that the one she's got stinks of rotting meat.'

'Oh Mother of God, I am so, so sorry,' I tell him. 'I don't know how that happened.'

'Are times so tough?' he asks me looking at me straight in the eye. 'Were you planning on having sausage sandwiches later?'

'No, it's not like that,' I explain, feeling more flustered than I'd like. My emotions are all over the place. 'Anyway, I'm a vegetarian. But my neighbour has this dog who . . .'

I realise Danny is laughing.

'You're winding me up, aren't you? As if I'm stealing my own dinner. Times aren't that hard yet, thankfully!'

'I see the funny side of it.' He grins. 'Don't worry!'

'And does your mum see the funny side too?'

'Eh . . . no. No, I don't think she does.'

An awkward silence hangs in the air between us. I bite my lower lip uneasily.

'Did she say anything about me?' I ask, knowing full well that the old biddy wouldn't have been able to help herself but to have a go.

'She described you as a very difficult girl.'

'Did she now? And did you stick up for me?'

I can't believe we're trading such an easy-going banter, as if nothing has happened.

'I said I'd met you briefly and that I thought you were nice. So are you going to be a nice girl now and let me into your place?'

'Hmm, you're not backwards about coming for-wards, are you?' I tease, secretly pleased that he's called. He didn't have to. I mean crew control could have easily sent a regular delivery van to switch the bags. God knows the airline has enough cars on the road at any given time, full of bags that have been mislaid or simply picked up by the wrong person. I must put a red ribbon on mine so that nobody else ever picks it up again by mistake. Thank God, there's only sausages in it this time. I mean, I could have packed a racy diary, full of the escapades enjoyed on the Costa Del Sol with Sylvie's son, or a case full of duty-free booze, which isn't rare. Still, I'm wary of Danny's presence. I can't forget what's happened between us.

'Come on in then,' I open the door wide, 'but do excuse the state of me. I certainly wasn't expecting visitors!'

He sits down and I offer him tea. He asks whether I have coffee.

'Are you in a rush?'

'I'm on reserve,' he explains. 'They haven't called me yet but I've my own case packed, ready to go.'

I sit down on the sofa beside him. 'So any news?' I ask in a more serious tone of voice. I haven't forgotten that the last time I spoke to Danny he'd just found out that he was to become a dad. I feel weird even talking to him. Does he still have feelings for me? Do I have any left for him? My head's a mess. I can't seem to think straight.

'About what? Oh, about that other thing?' he adds, his face darkening.

'Yes, that *thing*,' I answer with a frown. Surely he hasn't forgotten, I think sarcastically.

'Well, we had a big talk the other night. It didn't go very well. Fiona's not even sure the baby's mine.'

'How's that?'

'Apparently she had a one-night stand with another ex of hers a couple of days after we broke up. She says she was so upset after our split that she called him up, they got drunk, and one thing led to another . . .'

'So it's a big old mess?'

'You can say that again. Annie, I don't know what to do. I'm too young to be tied down. I'm a broken man.'

Danny looks so glum my heart goes out to him. I want to wrap my arms around him and comfort him but I'm not sure that's really appropriate at this time. I don't want to lead him on and yet I can't help the attraction I still feel towards him.

The kettle snaps off and I stand up to make two instant coffees, nicking some of Edel's Jaffa cakes in the process and placing them on a saucer.

'Thanks, doll. I appreciate it.'

'So have you told anyone else about the situation?'

'No, who can I tell? My parents wouldn't exactly be opening a bottle of champagne to celebrate the happy news with me.'

'But you'll have to break the news at some stage,' I point out. 'They've a right to know if they're going to be grandparents.'

'Yeah, but I'm not sure that this baby is even mine. We'll have to wait until it's born. I feel like I've got a sentence hanging over me. Hey, let's not talk about my problems. I'm sure you've got enough on your mind. What's your schedule like for the week?'

'I'm off to Chicago tomorrow,' I say. 'I'm looking forward to it. Just hope I can sleep tonight. I'm not sure whether I should go to bed now in case I can't sleep later on.'

Danny's face seems to brighten. 'I think you should go to bed all right, and lie down. I'll keep you company, if you like.'

I can't tell whether he's being serious or not. But knowing Danny, he probably is serious.

We're interrupted by the key sounding in the door. Edel lets herself into the flat, stopping dead in her tracks when she sees Danny.

'Oh, I'm sorry,' she says pausing at the door and looking from Danny to me. 'I didn't know you had company.'

'I was just going,' says Danny like lightning, standing up and putting his cap back on his head. I feel a little disappointed. I would have liked him to have stayed a bit longer, although I probably wouldn't have taken up his bedroom offer.

When he leaves, Edel turns to me, her eyes wide open. 'Who the fuck was that?'

'That was Danny,' I answer putting our empty cups in the sink and turning on the hot water to rinse them out. 'Why?'

'Why? Are you crazy? He's a total ride. Is he a friend of yours?'

'He works for the same company as me. I met him on holidays.'

'You did?' Edel's eyes widen even more in astonishment. 'I can't believe you met such a fine specimen on holidays and failed to tell me anything about him.'

'There's nothing to tell,' I answer matter-of-factly.

'Bullshit.'

'What do you mean?'

'Did anything happen between you two?'

'What do you think?'

'Jesus, it's so bloody obvious, Annie! Do you think I came down in the last shower?'

Rule Ten: Remember, you're the boss. Don't negotiate with disruptive passengers.

I arrive at the airport a good half-hour before my flight which is miraculous. I take the lift up to the mirrored dressing room on the third floor and pull up a stool so I can put my hair back in a bun like a nun and paint my face properly. Once I look suitably made up with my blusher cleverly done to give the illusion of cheekbones, I head up another floor to the check-in area and root around in my cubby hole to see if anybody has left me anything interesting.

There's a note from Kerry telling me about her twenty-third birthday party that she's having in her parents' home in Leopardstown, followed by mayhem and madness in Club '92 (God, I think I'm a bit old for that place now), and a request from a girl I don't know looking to swap a flight. Hmm, I'll have to think about that one. There's also a circular reminding people that the interviews for senior cabin crew members are being held next month. I draw a sharp intake of breath on reading that. I applied for the very position in a moment of madness but I'm not even sure if I want the responsibility.

The problem with being a senior air hostess is that you can't doss down the back when you're having an off day and you always have to be a shining example to the rest of the impressionable crew. Being a senior cabin crew member also means that you must make nearly all the announcements and if anything goes wrong, you're the one that has to shoulder the blame. Mind you, is there even any point in me putting myself forward for such a position of responsibility? I mean, I was only just suspended just the other week. Surely that must mean I'm already disqualified! I just don't know if it's worth all the stress. I mean, as a senior you must always look perfect with your nails immaculate and your shoes always polished. It's your job to notice if somebody falls below standards by doing things like wearing the wrong colour ponytail holder – a crime by cabin-crew standards, and to either pull them up on it, or write a report to their supervisor behind their backs. I'm not the type of girl who likes confrontation at work so I don't know if I even want this position. I mean, it's not like you're even paid that much more for the privilege. Still, maybe I should even pretend to show a bit of interest. I know if I was promoted I would make my folks proud, so maybe I should do it for their sake.

I put my hand back into my cubby hole in the vain hope that somebody may have left me a surprise present but no such luck. However, I do happen to fish out a pretty little pink envelope which is stamped, sealed and addressed to me, c/o the airport. How bizarre! I'm so late that I shove it in my handbag without opening it and go into the briefing room to meet my crew. Everyone seems to be in good form and there isn't a single bitchy face around the table, which is a blessing. Good. A nice crew will make a difference on a long flight to Chicago.

Today I'm going to be working in the middle of the cabin, along with two others, the cabin manager informs us. We all introduce ourselves and write down the important flight details in our company diaries including the captain's name, the number of passengers on board, the number of infants, VIPs, politicians, kosher meals and pre-ordered vegetarian meals. Once the paperwork is completed, we make our way up to the airport.

The lady passenger at the over-wing exit is refusing to stow her handbag away in the overhead locker. I tell her she must do it as a security precaution. The floor area around emergency exits must be clear of all hand baggage during take-off and landings. But the cross-faced woman is having none of it.

'I'm not putting my bag up there, I've got all my money in it.'

'If you need your money for any reason during the flight, madam, you are quite welcome to retrieve it. Don't worry; nobody's going to steal your bag.'

She's not budging on the issue and I feel myself in danger of getting high blood pressure.

'You'll have to change seats, then, with somebody who is indeed willing to obey by airline security measures,' I insist.

'But I want to sit here for the extra leg room,' the woman whines like a spoilt kid asking to be parted with her favourite teddy bear. I feel like snatching the damn bag off her and hitting her over the head with it. We haven't even left Dublin airport and already I can feel this is going to be a long, tedious flight judging by the uncooperative passengers already on board.

'Now listen here,' I say firmly. 'You have two choices; you either let me put up your handbag or you move. The offer is non-negotiable.'

The woman stares at me blankly as if everything I've told her has gone completely over her head. 'But, honey,' she says slowly and deliberately, 'you can keep telling me to put my bag away, but if this plane goes down and hits the water, how the hell am I going to get my passport?'

I can't believe my ears. I search her face for traces of sarcasm but fail to find any. Oh Jesus, didn't I just say it? This bloody flight is no doubt going to be never ending. I wish I was working first class. First-class passengers are ace because they give you no trouble and don't bother with the five million courses, various liquors, hot towels and all the other services that we try to force on them during every waking hour of their flights. Usually they just ask you not to bother them for the duration of the flight, which is great. They just go to sleep and wake before landing, refreshed and ready to go to their business meetings, having put blankets over their heads and conked out on the reclining leather seats for the whole flight.

Also, the brilliant thing about working first class is that any uncorked bottles of wine (and believe me, the wine we serve in first class is the absolute tops) is recorked by us and put in our bags to enjoy later, along with the luxurious discarded wash bags full of expensive moisturisers and body oils, in the privacy of our hotel rooms. I can't believe people just abandon them on the seats. I can never even leave a hotel room without nicking the soaps and I could set up a shower-cap shop with all the different ones I've collected over the years. Don't ask me why – I don't even use them. Anyway, as I said, collecting free stuff in first class is definitely one of the perks of the job, whereas down the back, all you ever get is a well-thumbed, dog-eared copy of *Heat* or *Now* magazine if you're lucky, or a book written in Spanish which you can't understand.

But today, as I explained earlier, I'm not up front with all the sleeping (rich) beauties but am stuck down the back here, very much behind the curtain with the riff-raff and it's going to be a long old day. I don't know any of the crew on the flight except Bernie, unfortunately dubbed the airline bike by a few cruel crew members. Word has it that she earned herself this nickname after giving one of the few air stewards a blow job down the back of the plane as passengers were boarding a flight to Lourdes of all places. Of course I don't know if it's actually true because the rumours that fly around an airline are outrageous at the best of times.

At last everybody is seated, the required handbags are safely stowed overhead, and the airbus A330 roars down the runway at terrific speed for take-off. Fifteen minutes later we're loading the lasagnes, chicken and vegetarian options (a few pasta spirals with spicy tomato sauce and congealed cheese on top) down the back and push the carts into the aisle. The proffered meals are met by the usual lack of enthusiasm as we dole them out. After everybody has been fed, they expect to be watered, so we head out with the bar carts. We used to give out free drink on this airline all the way to America and back but now we charge the customers for it. This has led to less enthusiasm for getting totally legless-drunk on flights (not difficult, as consuming alcohol at such a high altitude means the alcohol goes straight to your head), and has thankfully made our lives slightly easier. But of course there's always one or two who are happy to pay for the unpleasant experience of falling out of their seats after too many whiskies. Thankfully today they are not in my section, so not my problem. There a few seats free at the back which we have blocked off for ourselves so during my hour-and-a-half break, I skip the meal, and lie down with a blanket over my head. When I wake the girls are getting the carts ready for the tea-and-chocolate-muffin service. I quickly comb my hair, brush down my uniform and join the tea-and-coffee-pot brigade.

Seven hours later we land with a thump at Chicago O'Hare airport, gateway to the world in airline terms. As we proceed through customs, a burly-looking security guy with a gun strapped to his belt asks me if I am carrying $10,000 or more in my possessions.

'More,' I joke. For God's sake, I work for an airline. What is he like?

He stares at me with a blank expression and in a monotone voice says, 'I'll ask you one more time, ma'am. Are you carrying $10,000 or more?'

He obviously doesn't get my sense of humour. And he has a gun.

'No,' I say sombrely and he lets me pass.

A jolly porter loads our cases on to a trolley and follows us out into the nippy airport car park where half the crew are standing behind the little black crew bus sucking on cigarettes as if their lives depend on it. Soon we're all bundled into the small automobile and heading for town. The jet lag is already setting in and although all the girls are talking excitedly about hitting stores like Macy's and Carson Pirie Scott to pick up some Christmas bargains, and the pilots are discussing hitting the nearest Irish pub for some post-flight bevvies, I am simply dreaming about my hotel bed.

We zip through the busy streets of Chicago, home of my absolute icon Oprah (one of these days I'm definitely going to apply for tickets for her show like some of the other stewardesses have done), past the glass skyscrapers piercing the clouds, and arrive at our stunning hotel right in the heart of the city.

As we walk into the hotel along with the pilots, people stop in their tracks and stare. Children point in delight. It's always the same. The reaction we get to our uniforms is mind boggling. People treat us like celebrities. If you've seen the scenes in *Catch Me If You Can* with the drop-dead gorgeous and totally suave Leonardo di Caprio, you'll see exactly what I mean. Even when I'm on my own and walking somewhere in my uniform, people will smile and say 'Hello' as if they know you, as if they're your friend. It's kind of cute.

We queue at reception to collect our spending money and like most of my colleagues I plan to spend just $20 on food and the rest shopping. I don't care what I buy as long as I buy something. You can't possibly come back from America without anything in your case. Even if it's just non-breakable Christmas decorations purchased at

Wal-Mart! It's imperative that I fill my case if only to have something to talk about on the journey home to the rest of the crew. I mean, what else can I talk about? I'm not engaged (so no knuckle-dazzler to show off while taking people's eyes out), not newly married (so no wedding plans to discuss and photos to show around to polite colleagues in the galley while they suppress yawns), and I don't have any kids.

I'm just at that awkward age (29) where I find talking about getting locked every night, falling out of taxis, taking a year off to go backpacking, and fancying pop stars with the younger just-out-of-college-and-as-yet-undecided hosties, is as tedious as talking about what are the best schools to send kids to these days. Or maybe I'm just unsociable. Maybe I'm in danger of becoming one of those horrible people who just show interest when talking about themselves and nod off whenever the subject changes. Oh dear God. I hope not.

Okay, I'm going to set myself a challenge. The next time I get roped into a conversation with somebody I'm going to encourage them to talk all about themselves and not interrupt once. My older sister Emily always said that if I did that all the time, any man would love me, and find me very interesting and want to marry me. I wonder did she have a point. Emily was always wise beyond her years. I wish she was still alive and I could have brought her on trips like this one to Chicago and we could have gone shopping together. I never did get to bring Emily on any of my trips, unfortunately, because she was in and out of hospital so much during the last couple of years. I would always send her postcards, though, even if they did often arrive home after me. She'd always stick them on her mantelpiece.

'When I get better we'll go on a round-the-world trip together,' she would tell me brightly.

Immediately I feel the tears fill my eyes and I walk quickly over to the Christmas tree in the corner and pretend to admire it, in case anybody sees me crying. I hate when people notice that I'm sad because they always put their arms around me, which makes me bawl or else they tell me they know how I feel, which they don't. They really don't. They never met my sister, so how could they possibly know how I was coping without her?

'Do you want to join us for something to eat?' asks Klara, a nice girl with a kind smile. She has been working in first class all day so I haven't really had the chance to talk to her, but I've flown with her before and she's a good kid.

'I'm going to lie down for a little while I think, Klara. But thanks for the offer,' I say, fighting back the tears and hoping she won't notice the pained look on my face.

'Sure. But let me know if you change your mind.' She smiles thoughtfully.

It really means a lot to me to be invited out even if I don't take up the offer. Sometimes it can be just so lonely on overnights. I remember my first overnight ever was to Zurich. The three much older air hostesses I worked with were great friends and on the minibus on our way to the hotel they loudly made plans to have dinner in the centre of Zurich, completely excluding me as if I wasn't even there. They invited the captain, who agreed to join them and left out the co-pilot, too. Feeling sorry for the co-pilot as he seemed quite shy, I asked him when we were alone in the hotel lift, if he'd like to do something with me later.

He just stared at me blankly before telling me that he couldn't because he had a girlfriend. I was too shocked to answer back and tell him that he'd totally got the wrong end of the stick, and when the door opened at his floor he shot out of it like there was a firelighter with a flame stuck to his ass.

So that's why, even if I don't take Klara up on her offer, I'm still very grateful for her kindness because there's no feeling worse than feeling unwanted when you're so far away from home. I throw open the door of my bedroom and let it slam behind me. I rush to the window and pull the heavy lined curtains wide open to let in the light. You can practically see the whole of Chicago from here.

I take off my uniform and throw it recklessly over a chair. I know that by tomorrow I'll be kicking myself for not hanging it up properly in the closet, when I'm dragging out the iron and ironing board, but the jet lag has just hit me smack in between the eyes and my head feels light, and my body feels as though I've just completed a marathon. Barefoot and naked except for my underwear I pull the bedcover off the bed and throw it in a heap on the carpet. I always do this because you don't know who or what has been messing with the bedcover. They change the sheets in these places, but not the dark blankets or bedcovers and with my lively imagination I don't like to take chances. There's a nice slim hardcover guide book on Chicago by my bedside, complete with glossy photos and ads for expensive boutiques and jewellery shops. I grab it and slip between the bed sheets. I might just have a flick through, before I fall asleep, I think to myself, fighting the urge to close my eyes. But sleep wins and within minutes I'm pleasantly floating towards the land of nod.

I wake up at exactly 3 a.m. American time with my stomach rumbling like a steam engine. Oh God, it always happens to me. They say you should try to stay awake for as long as possible after a transatlantic trip but I never seem to manage it.

I switch on the TV and keep the sound down low, conscious of the person or people next door. If there's one thing that drives me mad about hotels, it's when your bedroom neighbours keep you awake with the drone of their blasted television. There doesn't seem to be very much on at this time of night, apart from annoying, drawn-out infomercials with fading belles telling you how to look twenty years younger or how to achieve washboard stomachs without even trying by calling some low-cost telephone line, or how to get your teeth unnaturally white by supplying your credit card details over the phone. It's all so nauseating I have to switch it off. I'm wide awake now and I'm bored. Looking out the window I see lights on in offices in skyscrapers, and lone figures bent over their computers. Don't those people ever go to sleep? I mean, what kind of life is that?

Tentatively I open the mini-bar to see what's on offer. Well, there are Snickers and crisps, peanuts and peanut butter chocolate bars, but a quick look at the accompanying price list forces me to close the door firmly shut again. How can they justify charging almost four dollars for a chocolate bar?

I take my old tracksuit from my case, get dressed quickly and wrap myself up warmly in a duffle coat and woolly hat and scarf, before taking the lift down to the lobby and heading out to the street to a deli on the corner. In the empty corner store I buy myself a large slice of carrot cake and a litre of mineral water. Then I hurry back to the comfort of my hotel and my big-enough-to-fit-four-comfortably double bed.

Back in my room, I snuggle under the bedclothes again, pick greedily at my kind of stale carrot cake (I don't want to eat it all as I reckon it contains a good eight hundred calories), sip my water and flick through my book on Chicago. There are so many upmarket department stores in this city that I momentarily wish I was rich, didn't have a mortgage, and ponder on increasing my weekly purchase of one lottery ticket a week to two.

Then suddenly I remember the envelope that I found in my cubby hole earlier on. I don't know why I forgot to open it on the flight but it just seemed to have slipped my mind. I put the half-eaten carrot cake in the bin to ensure that I don't finish it off in the morning, and reach down for my bag. I rumble through all the make-up to find the envelope which is now soiled in lipstick and eyeshadow. I can't remember how long it is since somebody wrote me a real letter. Years ago when I was in boarding school, Emily would write long letters full of news. Now everybody sends text and emails.

I lie back on the mound of pillows and rip open the

envelope. Inside is a matching pink sheet of notepaper with neat handwriting. The message is very simple:

Dear Annie, enjoy your flight to Chicago, from your biggest fan.

I stare at the note, completely baffled. What the hell is that all about?

Rule Eleven: The captain's always right – even when he's wrong.

A loud, ignorant knock on my door startles me from my coma-like sleep. For a moment I don't know where I am as I open my eyes to my unfamiliar surroundings. My bedroom is twice the size of my tiny room back in Gardiner Street (although you should see poor Edel's boxroom – I don't know how she manages to fit Greg into it).

The door flings open and the rotund Hispanic maid looks fairly pissed off to see me still in bed. What's her problem? I mean I'm not checking out till five-thirty this evening. Didn't she read the PLEASE DO NOT DISTURB sign firmly placed on the knob outside the door? Like, I could have been having mad passionate sex or something. I wish, I think, sinking back under the bedclothes again.

I wonder what on earth I'll do with the rest of my day, besides skipping breakfast. I read in the hotel brochure last night that there's a gym and sauna on the fourth floor. Well, I'll probably skip the flab-busting machines and soak in the sauna instead. I wonder whether you lose weight in a sauna. In any case, I'd better leave this hotel room at some stage before I die of claustrophobia. I have a quick flick through *USA Today* which has kindly been pushed through the door for me, and then I take a long, hot shower and get dressed. I've made a decision. I'm not going to give in to peer pressure just because everybody else always buys things. I'm going to bring my few dollars home, and then on my next trip I'll be able to buy a truly decent piece of clothing instead of filling my case with junk. On that positive frugal note, I leave the hotel and drop into the same deli where I was last night to buy an orange. The same Chinese guy who served me the carrot cake sells me my fruit this morning. With a smile, too. Crikey, and I thought my working life was tough!

I leave the hotel and turn right. I know where I'm heading – Lake Michigan. Even though I've passed it often on the crew bus I've never actually gone down to it on foot. I look up at the menacing grey clouds and hope it doesn't rain. It's cold enough for snow, anyway, I reckon as the icy wind nips at my cheeks. Hey, they don't call this the windy city for nothing. I'm glad I'm wearing my warm tracksuit instead of a skirt. I walk briskly along the busy road and eventually I cross it via an underground tunnel. When I come out the other end I'm practically on the sandy beach. Lake Michigan is enormous with more than one thousand, six hundred miles of coastline and twelve million people living along its shores. I'm not going to walk the whole perimeter today, obviously, but I am going to give my legs a well-deserved stretch. Above, seagulls circle and screech. It seems to be just them and me here this morning on this vast stretch of sand. I don't spot another human being. During the summer months I imagine this place is heaving with eager sun worshippers anxious to cool down in the water's edge. But today it seems like I'm the only lost soul feeling at one with nature.

I walk right up to the lapping water. The lake is calm and I pick up a couple of pebbles and send them skimming over the surface. Suddenly I feel at peace with the world. I feel almost happy. Chicago is the third biggest city in the United States with a population of eight million. Today, however, that population seems to be occupied elsewhere and the beach is peaceful and thought-provoking. I could spend hours here, lost in my own little world. I take a bit of time to reflect what's going on in my life. Things have been getting better recently and I'm more at ease with myself. I haven't thought about Niall in ages, which is a good thing, because he's not worthy enough to even be in my thoughts. God knows, he managed to waste enough of my time, as it is. I hope that I find the right man soon so that I can truly move on. But who is the right man for me? I fancy Danny, of course, but I don't want to take on anything that could lead to trouble and Danny has trouble written all over him. Oliver, on the other hand, is another man I've been thinking about recently, but I really wish that I could get him out of my head. There must be something wrong with me if I keep wishing that I could be with men who are simply out of bounds. I look out to the horizon of the lake. There's a whole world out there and I want to be part of it. Maybe I'll meet somebody brand new, my soulmate. That would be nice, wouldn't it? Yes, that would be very nice indeed. But who is he and where is he? Come to think of it, maybe

I have a secret admirer. Whoever sent me that little anonymous note obviously thinks a lot of me. But who is he? And why didn't he identify himself? I mean, what's that all about? It's baffling. I look at my watch. It's late. I really should be heading back to the hotel now, I think reluctantly. If only I could spend a bit of time here rather than have to fly back to Dublin tonight, knowing that I won't land until tomorrow. Night flights are a killer and when I go back to the hotel I know I'll be looking at the clock until pick-up time like I've a dreaded death sentence hanging over me.

After a couple of hours of walking I feel my feet beginning to freeze and soon I can't even feel my toes at all. I make my way back to the hotel, content in the knowledge that I've got myself enough fresh air now to probably last me a week. Still, the time in the fresh wintry air has done me a lot of good. My head feels clearer now and I'm in a positive state of mind. When I get back to Dublin I'm going to make more of an effort to see my mum and dad, and I'm going to email my sister in Australia, or maybe even send her a cute little card. She's always loved animals so I might send her a picture of a cute little puppy or kitten to make her smile. I should get in contact with Robert, Emily's widower too. He must get lonely sometimes. It must be hard for him looking after Ben all the time, who can also be a bit of a handful sometimes, albeit a fairly lovable handful. Maybe I'll offer to take Ben to the park on my next day off. I can bring him to Stephen's Green to feed the ducks. I think he'd like that. With that thought in my head I head towards the busy road, and back to reality again.

Later that day, as we check out at reception, I find out that most of the crew went out for dinner and then on to an Irish pub before retreating to one of the rooms for a further drinking session. There are still a few sore heads all around and I thank my lucky stars that I didn't join them. OK, I didn't get much sleep, but at least my head isn't packing in. Then of course, as we pile on to the bus, the girls start describing their purchases in great detail. I have to admit that I didn't buy anything, as if that's some kind of sin, and that I didn't go out at all (another cabin-crew sin), and I begin to feel embarrassed, like I'm some boring old Scrooge or something. Oh well . . . they don't know me so it doesn't matter what they think really. I close my eyes and try to relax before we reach the airport, drowning out the sound of chitter chatter from the rest of the crew.

As soon as we board, I get a horrible feeling that tonight's flight isn't going to be all plain sailing. Call me psychic or whatever but I can always feel it in my bones if there's going to be trouble ahead. For a start, it's Friday and weekend travellers, for some reason, always seem more troublesome than mid-week passengers. And the flight is full, which is a pain. This means we cannot move people around so they can sit together and those who have checked in late often get very narky about this. Also, usually if the flight is half empty we can reserve ourselves some seats at the back for a lie down or offer them to mothers and toddlers to give them more space. Sitting with a baby on your lap for seven hours must be hell, I reckon, and we only have a limited number of bassinettes on board.

We're at our stations ready for the onslaught. The

redcap has already advised me about a young brother and sister who are coming home to attend their mother's funeral. Her death was totally unexpected, apparently, and I'm told to be as sympathetic as possible. My heart sinks. I often go to pieces when I have bereaved passengers on board. Just one look at their pained, tear-stained faces makes me want to dissolve into tears. That's the thing, you see, about being an airhostess. People always imagine that you're flying with happy people going off on their holidays but we have everything to deportees, prisoners, and those flying home to funerals, as well as the unaccompanied minors. During the holidays, especially around Easter and Christmas, we get hordes of unaccompanied minors from broken homes being transported from Mum to Dad. Despite all the (guilt-related) presents, when you see them crying into their teddies, it would make anyone think twice about the implications of divorce.

The families arrive on board first with all their gear, having left their buggies at the gate to be deposited in the hold. They seem frustrated as families often are when flying. God, I don't know how they do it. I mean, I find it so much hassle even packing for myself, what with sorting out passports and visas and tickets, never mind packing for five, and remembering baby bottles and diapers! Once they're all seated and ready the rest of the passengers pour into the plane full of chat, and the usual '*The Quiet Man* is my favourite film of all time, have you seen it?' banter. One elderly American man is dressed head to toe in garish green. 'That's some outfit,' I tell him and he mistakes my comment for a compliment.

'Well gee, thanks.' He grins. 'I searched high and low

for this suit. I reckoned if I was coming to Ireland, I didn't want to stand out.'

I rest my case.

The rest of the passengers take their seats in dribs and drabs and the process of boarding seems like an endless task. Maybe it's because I feel tired and ropey but it just seems as though we'll never get off the ground. My aisle looks particularly dodgy. The young bereaved siblings are in front, sitting in silence. There are no tears so I reckon they're still in shock. I'm at a loss what to say to them. They probably feel numb and I can relate to that. When Emily died, the mere thought that I would never see her again, never phone her for a chat or hear the sound of her laughter was just too much to take in. For days and even weeks it seemed like a particularly awful nightmare that I might wake up from. Only I never did wake up. And in some ways I'm still stuck living that horrendous dream. I tell them that if they need anything, just to ask me, and they politely acknowledge my gesture. I get the feeling that they just want to be left alone. I can relate to that.

Three seats behind them is a young mother, probably only in her twenties, with an overweight baby on her lap. He has a shock of red hair and his cheeks are just as red, as though he might have a high temperature. She looks distressed and harassed and I feel sorry for her. I fetch her a baby belt and ask if she'd like me to heat up a baby bottle of milk for her. She hands one over gratefully and I disappear into the mid galley to fill an empty tea pot full of boiling water. I immerse the baby bottle inside. Five minutes should heat the milk up nicely and with any luck, it will send the baby into a deep sleep. The person sitting directly next to the woman and infant is a thin woman, probably in her early eighties, with a purple-rinse in her hair. She keeps barking orders at me.

'Lady, check and see if my camel coat is in the overhead locker.'

I know for a fact that it is because I put it there myself. Obviously the woman, being five foot nothing couldn't reach and I being five foot four can barely reach it myself. But in order to keep the old dame happy I open up the overhead locker and reassure her that indeed her coat is still there. When she asks me for the third time, I realise the poor thing has Alzheimer's. That's just my misfortune. By the time we land in Dublin tomorrow she'll probably have asked me three thousand times. Two seats down from her, across the aisle, is a very large woman with thick glasses and curly mousey-brown hair. When I say very large, I'm probably talking twenty stone. Discreetly I present her with an extension belt (after she asks for it, of course). As I show her how it works, I become aware of a very strong whiff of alcohol from an equally large man sitting right behind her. He has a three- or four-day old stubble, a greasy ponytail of hair, a menacing smile and a gold chain around his fat neck. He catches my eye and winks. I feel a chill running down my spine. I really don't like the look of him at all.

I look away. He seems keen to chat. 'How you doin'?' he bellows in an unnaturally loud voice and I can smell the stale whiskey stench from his breath, even from where I'm standing.

I turn around warily. 'I'm fine.'

'What's your name?'

'Annie,' I answer, remaining cool and polite but not overly friendly. If there's one thing I can't stand, it's a drunk, over-familiar passenger. I wish the ground staff would be more vigilant when letting these people through. I mean, if somebody like this walked into a pub, the likelihood is that the barman would refuse to serve them. If he happened to be abusive, the door security would swiftly remove them. Halfway across the Atlantic, though, we have no security and there's no point calling 999.

'You're the sexiest broad on this plane, Annie. I'm not kidding.'

I feel desperately uneasy about this individual and his over-familiar comments so I walk up to the first-class cabin to have a word with the cabin manager and to express my concerns.

She listens attentively and then goes into the cockpit to relay my fears to the captain. She then comes out and says the captain would like to talk to me himself. Once again I repeat myself, saying I feel uneasy about the guy with the ponytail. He bites his lip anxiously. I'm well aware that he won't want to miss his slot. O'Hare airport is the airline hub of the world and any delay could mean hours on the ground. All my instincts tell me that this passenger is a wrong one, but I don't want to be the one who has to make the call either. I've already been suspended once this month and the last thing I want to do is draw attention to myself again. The redcap (who, for those of you unfamiliar with airline terms, is the go-between between landside and aircraft) is called for and he goes down the cabin to have a word with the ponytail-haired one. He returns with a half-empty litre bottle of whiskey which he has now confiscated.

'The passenger in question promises that he has no more alcohol in his possession and that he will not be a threat to the safety of the other passengers or disrupt the on-board service in anyway,' 'the redcap reassures us. Well, he would, wouldn't he? He just wants us to get out of here.

'Do you think you'll be able to cope, Annie?' The captain looks at me questioningly.

I nod, obviously looking more confident than I feel. My instincts still strongly tell me that any potentially disruptive passenger should be removed, and that we shouldn't take any chances, but I'm being pressurised here.

I go back to my station as we get the all-clear to leave the stand. Shaking slightly, I stand hidden from view in the galley and pour myself a glass of cool water as the screens come down automatically to show the safety video. I sip the water and allow myself time to calm down. I know I'm tired, so maybe I'm worrying too much. There's no point always assuming the worst and acting all diva-like. Anyway, what harm can the guy do? He doesn't have a gun or any weapons on him. Sure, he's had a few drinks but haven't we all at some stage? Maybe he's a nervous flier. You'd be surprised at the number of people who are absolutely terrified of flying and make up for it by knocking back alcohol before their flight. He'll probably fall asleep after take-off and sleep right through. And if he does become boisterous I won't have to deal with him on my own, will I? I have all the support of the crew, and the captain, who, luckily for him, is safely tucked away in the cockpit with the door locked. Lucky him. Lucky pilots who don't have to deal with passengers and get paid five times as much as us. Now, why did I never think of learning to drive a plane?

Feeling more assured now, I take a deep breath and wander down my section of the cabin to ensure that all the seat backs are straight, the table trays are stowed away and that everybody is safely strapped in. As I pass the overweight ponytailed man he grins, flashing a gold front tooth.

'Hey, you haven't checked my seatbelt properly,' he sneers, pointing lewdly to his crotch. Before I can answer the purple-rinse woman wants me to check one more time that nobody has run off with her camel coat. Oh God. It's going to be a night from hell.

Rule Twelve: Never flirt with passengers, especially alcohol-fuelled ones.

'Annie, you're wanted by one of the passengers.' One of my colleagues tugs anxiously at my arm as I'm halfway up the cabin with my meal cart.

'Woman with purple-rinse hair?'

'That's the one. She says you stole her coat.'

'It's in the overhead bin. Take it down and show it to her and then stow it away again. Thanks, petal.'

'And there's a man sitting quite near her who asked me if you were single.'

'And what did you tell him?' I asked mildly alarmed, knowing of course that it had to be Ponytail. Of course it had to be him. People always ask if we're ever chatted up by passengers. Well, yes, we are. By lunatics.

'I said I didn't know.'

'Well, will you do me a huge favour? When you're on your way down to Purple-rinse, will you tell Ponytail that I'm unavailable and soon to be married?'

Immediately she looks down at my fingers to spot the sparkler.

'Tell him a lie,' I urge before she has the chance to ask me any tricky questions.

Despairingly I look at my watch. We're only one hour into the flight and already it's showing all the signs of being hellish. That's it, I vow to myself, next week I'm going to go back to my PR studies to learn some skills that will see my safely into a nine-to-five job where I won't have to work through the night and avoid drunken thugs and paranoid old ladies who think I'm a thief. I'm going to send out my CV to companies around town. With any luck, this time next year, I'll be in a job where I can wear my own clothes, and talk business with clients over lunch in fancy restaurants and spend my evenings attending glamorous soirées with people in the media. Now wouldn't that be a goal worth working for? The only downside to leaving the airline, and believe me it's quite a big negative, would be having to forfeit my ridiculously cheap flights which I live for. Oh well, with the Internet now, can't you get bargains to everywhere? I have to be positive.

Now that everybody has been fed and watered some people are looking to be watered for a second time. But before that we obviously have to try to sober them up with cups of tea and coffee. I'm busy in the middle galley waiting for the tea to brew and pretending to make decaf tea for some American passengers (like, as if we stock such a thing on an Irish flight) when a blood-curling scream startles me from somewhere in the cabin. It seems to be coming from my row of passengers. Typical!

Like lightning I pop my head around to see who's causing the trouble. Purple-rinse is yelling at the redheaded baby who has just started to bawl uncontrollably because he has dropped his rattler.

'Shut up,' the old dear is screeching. 'Just shut the hell up, goddamn you!'

I'm appalled and so is the baby's mother, by the looks of things. She looks absolutely terrorised by the forgetful old woman. I rush down the aisle to sort out the problem. Down on my hands and knees I retrieve the rattler from under some passenger's smelly socks and hand it to the mother. Now, for a bit of peace, I pray silently as I rush back to the safety of the middle galley before the tea gets cold. But just as I'm getting the jiggers and sugars ready on a little plastic tray another yell from the cabin forces me out again without my pot. What is it now?

I race back down the cabin with my best stern face on me, like a sergeant major. This time it's not Purple-rinse. She's too busy taking in the extraordinary scene behind her, as are the majority of dumbstruck passengers.

The large lady with the extension belt and the glasses is in floods of tears. Behind her, Ponytail looks like he's got smoke coming out of his ears. I'm just in time to witness him roll up his newspaper and whack the large lady over the head with it. Nobody is as stunned as me.

'What on earth is going on here?' I demand in astonishment.

'He called me a beached whale,' the large woman wails and a few of her neighbouring passengers testify to the fact. 'He told me to lose some weight.'

I glare at the culprit who himself seems to be the proud owner of at least four bellies. He's certainly one to talk!

'She put her seat back and I can't breathe,' he snarled self-righteously.

I put my hand on my hips in my best attempt to look cross and authoritarian. 'This woman is quite entitled to put her seat back now that the service has finished,' I say in a loud, clear voice.

He leers at me. 'Hey, relax, baby. Y'know you're kinda sexy when you do your angry woman impersonation. Wanna go on a date when we get to Dublin?'

Everybody looks at me expectantly to see how I'll react. I feel myself blush furiously. I hadn't seen this coming at all.

'Don't you be cheeky,' I say, trying to placate him.

'I mean it, you've got a great ass.'

With that, one of the more senior cabin crew members appears on the scene. 'What on earth is going on here?'

'I'm sure Annie here can manage her own love life without you getting involved,' Ponytail says brazenly, leering at the name badge pinned to my right breast.

I stand rooted to the spot, too shocked to speak. 'This man is causing a lot of problems for his fellow passengers, ma'am,' a respectable-looking middle-aged man with a grey moustache pipes up.

'You mind your own business, Fuckface,' retorts Ponytail. I want the ground to open and for me to be sucked outside to die peacefully on one of the clouds. This is a greater nightmare than I'd originally anticipated and here I am stuck in the middle of it. The star of the show, so to speak.

'Annie should be flattered that I'm asking her out. I wouldn't ask you out, 'cos you're too old.'

The large woman with the glasses swings around furiously. 'Who do you think you are, insulting everybody like this?'

He grips the back of her chair with both hands and starts shaking it violently. 'I thought I told you to shut up, bitch.'

Soon Klara has joined our trio and I realise that everybody has taken off their head phones and nobody is watching the film. We, our bizarre little group standing in the aisle, have suddenly become the in-flight entertainment.

'If you annoy that woman one more time, I'll deal with you,' the man with the moustache threatens angrily.

Ponytail leaps from his seat in a flash, his face purple with rage. He throws himself at Moustache Man with all his weight and screams can be heard from various members of the audience, sorry, passengers.

He puts his hands around Moustache Man's neck and starts choking him. His wife or partner, a thin woman with a beak nose, starts yelling at the top of her lungs. 'Stop him, somebody. He's trying to kill my husband.'

The cabin manager is now here and while some people have scrambled out of their seats to move to the back of the plane, others have moved up towards us, anxious not to miss out on the action. Ponytail shows no sign of lessening his grip on Moustache Man's neck which is turning purple at this stage.

I push past the crowd, race up the cabin, through first class where the rich and gentile are sipping champagne blissfully unaware of the chaos down the back. I key in the secret code to let me into the cockpit and burst in.

The captain looks startled. 'Is everything OK, Annie?'

'No. It. Is. Not. OK,' I say, fumbling on the ground for the security bag with the handcuffs. I've never had to use them before. 'We have a lunatic on board.'

'You mean the same . . .'

'Yes, the same,' I interrupt him, my blood boiling. If somebody could have just listened to me back in Chicago none of this would be happening.

'Are you going to use the handcuffs on him?'

'May I have your permission?' I ask in a tone that indicates I'm going to use them whether he likes it or not. He nods and I tear back down the cabin, hiding the handcuffs under my apron. When I get back two male passengers have managed to wrangle Ponytail off Moustache Man, who falls back into his seat breathlessly.

Ponytail eyeballs me. 'Hi, honey, where have you been? Get these assholes away from me.'

'OK, just give me your hand,' I ask him in a quiet tone of voice. He obeys like a puppy dog and, taking my opportunity, I grab his arm, wrench it behind his back and slap on the handcuffs. 'Now put your other hand behind your back, mister,' I demand in a not-such-a-nice tone of voice.

Everybody is stunned into silence, including Ponytail, who finally seems to have accepted defeat. His head is bent and he's no longer struggling. The relief that the whole sorry episode is coming to a close is overwhelming. Breathing heavily, I'm suddenly overcome with exhaustion. I feel dizzy. Holding on to the nearest seat backs, I try to balance myself. The last thing I need is a fainting episode to add to the drama.

And then, from nowhere, a shrill voice pierces the air. 'Does anybody know where my coat is, dammit?'

Rule Thirteen: Never mix business passengers with pleasure.

'Hey, what a surprise, Mr Kane!' I greet our first passenger on the red-eye to Brussels. 'My goodness, but we're seeing a lot of you these days.'

It's more of a shock than a surprise, bumping into Oliver Kane again. Every time I see him I feel strangely attracted to him and I wish to God I didn't harbour those feelings. I mean, in an ideal world somebody like Oliver would be my dream man but because he's so obviously unavailable I'm always a bit of a mess when I'm in his presence. It almost feels like he's flirting with me and a perfectly happily married man shouldn't do that. But is he coming on to me or is my imagination in overdrive? If he was flirting with me, would that make him a sleazebag? He doesn't seem sleazy, but if he's hitting on me, then that couldn't be right, could it?

'Well think of all the air miles I'm clocking up,' he answers me with a twinkle in his eye. 'Anyway, it's good to see you too. Was that your face I saw on the news the other night?'

'Oh, would you stop,' I say, waving him away playfully. I don't want to encourage him or lead him on in any way so I try to deal with him in a professional manner and treat him like I would any regular passenger. Only he isn't just any old passenger and I don't go weak at the knees when I chat to everybody else. I wish I felt more in control.

'I thought you handled the situation really well. That guy got what he deserved anyway.'

He was right, I think to myself. That bully we had on the flight did get what he deserved when the judge sent him to jail. After all, he put all our safety at risk and to be honest I found the whole incident terrifying. In fact, the episode has kind of put me off flying altogether. It's made me fear for my safety every time I step on a plane. It's no longer fun for me any more.

'Yes, well, some people thought that three months was a hefty sentence but personally I think there should be more of them handed out. That guy was so scary. Anyway, it turned out he was high as well as drunk. And he was a convicted criminal. They should never have let him on the flight in the first place.'

Mr Kane becomes aware of the queue of people behind him anxious to come on board, takes his seat in row one, and seems to watch in amusement as the pompous politicians embark, drowning each other out with their self-important declarations. I glimpse at him between all the 'hello's and 'good-morning's'. He's flicking through the *Irish Times* with a bemused look on his face and I can't help but notice how attractive he is. And not for the first time either.

It turns out to be a busy flight – Brussels always is, but

thankfully it's a morning flight and not the dreaded afternoon flight where our taxes are poured down the thirsty throats of our various, er, upstanding government members.

An hour and fifteen minutes later we're saying good-bye again, but instead of shooting out the door first like front-row passengers normally do, Mr Kane holds back.

'Did you get my message the last time, Annie?'

'No, why?'

'Well . . .' he hesitates slightly. 'I had given my business card to one of your colleagues.'

'Really?' I feign surprise. 'I never got it.'

'Would you have any interest in joining me for dinner one evening?' he says, offering me his card. 'No pressure, Annie, I'm sure your diary is already full to the brim. So I'll leave it up to you.'

With that he turns and makes his way down the steps of the aircraft with me staring at his back in bewilderment.

'What was that all about?' the other air hostess asks me.

'I honestly have no idea,' I mutter. I put his card in my bag. I'm pretty stunned by his gesture to be honest. Flattered, but a bit shell-shocked all the same. Oliver giving me his card is a really big deal. It must mean he likes me. Or does it? Does he want me to contact him, and where does he think all this will lead? Although I've given up denying that I'm deeply attracted to him, it's just not right that I should have these feelings towards him. Does he think we might have an affair? Would I even contemplate such a thing? I try to banish all thoughts of the desirable Mr Kane by sticking his card in the zip pocket of my handbag alongside the second anonymous letter I received yesterday before my flight to Milan. That one had simply read, 'Enjoy Milan.'

I wonder what kind of sicko would find that an idea of a joke! I mean, it's not even remotely funny. But maybe it's not supposed to be funny. Maybe it's supposed to be romantic? During our turnaround break I decide to show it to one of the other crew members.

'Did you ever get anything like this?' I show her the neatly written note.

'God, no,' she says scrutinising it. 'How bizarre. Who would be sending you these cute little notes? Someone must have a crush on you. How exciting!'

Exciting? I'm not sure if that's the word I'm looking for. It is intriguing though. Could it have been from Danny? I haven't heard from him in a while, although I have been looking out for him on flights, to no avail, unfortunately. The guy just seems to have disappeared out of my life again without explanation. I thought he would have kept in contact but there hasn't been even a peep from him. I'm almost disappointed that I haven't heard from him. Surely he hasn't forgotten me altogether? Then again, maybe this little note is just Danny's way of keeping in touch? It's very odd, all the same. Why doesn't he just phone? It's not like he doesn't have my phone number. Then again, maybe the anonymous note is from Oliver? Nah. On second thoughts, Oliver doesn't seem like the type of man who would send a note without his name on it. It's got to be from somebody else, but who? And more to the point, why?

'I don't know about that. It could be just one of my friends having a laugh.'

'Very funny, not!'

I happen to agree. But back to more important things, like why does Mr Kane want to ask me out for dinner? True, he's a dish, but he's supposed to be married, for Chrissakes. He's still wearing a wedding ring because I checked earlier. And there was me thinking he was one of the nice guys!

Back in the apartment that afternoon Edel pops home for a bite of lunch. She's all excited because Greg has an interview for a job.

'Great,' I say trying to muster up some enthusiasm for the fact that her good-for-nothing boyfriend has finally got off his lazy arse in a bid to do something with his life besides eat my food all day long, listen to alternative music and roll foul-smelling joints.

She looks at me, puzzled, as she pops a couple of pieces of bread in the toaster. 'You don't seem yourself,' she says sounding concerned. 'Do you want me to get you anything in the shops to cheer you up? *Irish Tatler*, *Closer*, *Heat*, *B* magazine, a bar of Cadbury's Turkish delight, perhaps?'

Although sorely tempted, I smile, shaking my head. I don't really feel like anything just at the moment. I have no energy left. Chicago's flight left me completely drained. Even though crew control gave me an extra two days off to recover and even offered counselling sessions to deal with my trauma, I just feel like I need another holiday right now. Sun, sea, sand, plenty of money to go shopping, and a perfect body (or a perfect one beside me, at least). At the moment I just feel old and weary. Of course, never in a million years did I think the events of that one flight would spark so much media interest! I was on both TV3 and RTE news talking about the consequences of air rage, then the

Evening Herald came round to my flat with a photographer to get my story and the following day I was invited on the *Seoige and O'Shea* show. I unwillingly became a media whore in a couple of days for doing something that I wasn't even particularly proud of. I mean, anyone would have done the same thing in that situation, wouldn't they?

Of course Edel thinks all the hoo-ha is the most exciting thing ever and is telling anybody who rings her that she's sharing a flat with a celebrity. Purlease! But the truth is I'm so drained from all the fuss that I just want to curl up on the sofa and hope that it all blows over as soon as possible. I still haven't heard a word from that old wench Sylvie and I don't know if that's a good or a bad thing. I mean, now I definitely don't think I'll be considered for the position of senior cabin crew. After all, if I had been a capable employee and in control, chaos wouldn't have erupted on my side of the cabin in the first place, would it? In a way, I think that all the mess was partly due to me.

I decide to tell Edel about meeting Mr Kane on the flight.

Her eyes widen in excitement. 'Mr Jimmy Choo?'

'The same man who sent the sandals, yes.'

'The ones with the steel-bar heels, 115mm high?'

'The same one, yes, but the thing is, Edel . . . the thing is I shouldn't have accepted them. Emily always said to me that there was no such thing as a free lunch. And now I'm beginning to think that there's no such thing as a free pair of Jimmy's either.'

'Nonsense,' scoffs Edel. 'Sure didn't the very same man nearly kill you? Imagine if you'd ended up in a wheelchair after he knocked you down? That would have cost him millions in insurance money. In my humble opinion he got off lightly.'

'It was an accident. Besides, you could look at it another way . . . his car stopped, another one might not have been able to stop in time. So in a way, maybe he even saved my life.'

'Oh Lord, whatever . . .'

'He wants to take me out for dinner.'

'Anywhere nice?'

'Oh stop being flippant, Edel. Please, I'm serious. I need your advice on this one.'

'Go out with him for dinner, then. It'll save you cooking.'

'But he's married.'

'He asked you for dinner, right? Not to go to bed with him. God, Annie, you have a one-track mind. He probably just wants to thank you for not suing him.'

'So you don't think he has any ulterior motives?'

Edel throws her hands to the ceiling in mock exasperation. 'For God's sake, child, I don't know the man, do I? He probably finds you very attractive, which you undoubtedly are, but that doesn't mean he's going to jump your bones before you get a chance to order dessert. I'd take him up on his offer if I were you. You need a pick-me-up if anybody needed one.'

'Where would we go?'

'Oh choose somewhere nice. He can well afford it. Chapter One, perhaps, or L'Ecrivain or that place Venu on Anne's Lane. That place is very hip from what I hear.'

'OK, I'll ring him,' I say, fishing out his card from my bag. 'Actually, no, I'll email; it's easier.'

I think of that weird handwritten note again. Should I tell Edel about that too? On second thoughts, maybe I won't. It's probably just some crank. I'll just put it out of my head.

Edel goes back off to work after finishing her microwaved soup and I open my laptop. First of all I check my bebo page to see if anyone has sent me any scandal and then I check my emails. I freeze when I see the first message. It's from Robert, my dead sister Emily's husband. He wants to meet me as soon as possible.

Rule Fourteen: Expect the unexpected.

'Hi, Mum, just ringing to see what the plans are for Christmas?' I ask breezily.

I hear my mother sigh at the other end of the phone. She always sounds worn out whenever I call her.

'I haven't even thought about Christmas this year, darling.'

'But Mum, I was thinking we need to start celebrating again. I know it's tough without Emily being here, but I honestly think she would want us to be together and remember her. Maybe we could all go to Mass together on Christmas day and light a candle for her at the crib.'

'Yes, maybe. How are you, anyway? Travelling anywhere exotic this week?'

'No, but I have an overnight in Limerick,' I giggle. 'No chance of getting a tan there anyway. But I've put in a request for a trip to Dubai. If I get it, would you come with me? I believe the shopping there is out of this world!'

My mother pauses. 'Sure don't they have everything I need at the Pavillions shopping centre? I don't know if I could handle a long-distance flight and I don't know the language.'

'But everyone speaks English these days, Mum. It's not like you'd have to go to Arabic classes in advance.'

'Well, I'll have to think about it. I've a lot to do. I need to buy a present for Ben. Poor little Ben.'

'Me too. He's still at an age where he's expecting Santa. I'm going to get him something fabulous this year. Speaking of Ben, Mum, I got an email from Robert. I wonder what he wants.'

The silence from my mother is deafening. Even bringing up Robert's name is difficult for me. I barely slept last night wondering what on earth could be so urgent that he needs to meet me. I mean, if Ben was ill or anything he would have phoned straight away.

Eventually my mother speaks. 'I have no idea, Annie. I suppose you'd better go and meet him and find out.'

'I suppose so. I'll phone you afterwards and let you know what it's all about.'

'OK, you do that. When are you going to call over and see us? Your dad's a bit down with his arthritis. I blame the rotten weather we've been having. By the way, Deirdre from down the road says she saw you on TV. Is that true? That silly woman always seems so confused I thought she might have imagined it.'

'No, it's true, Mum. There was an incident on the plane and I was interviewed about it, that's all.'

'Still, that must have been exciting, did you tape it?'

'Yes, I did. I'll bring it over next time I call around.'

'Right. See you then. Any other news? Any men?'

Immediately images of both Danny and Oliver pop into

my head, but there's no point telling Mum about either of them. What's there to tell anyway? Nothing. If I told mum that the two men who occupied my mind most were a) a toyboy with a pregnant girlfriend and b) a married man who presented me with his business card, I don't think she'd understand. I don't even understand any of it myself. God, why can't I just fancy men who are young, free, and single like I'm supposed to?

'No, Mum,' I mutter. 'No men at all.'

'And Niall hasn't been in touch?'

'No.'

Trust Mum to bring up Niall of all people. Suddenly it hits me that I haven't thought about Niall in ages. Well, that can only be a good thing, can't it? In fact, I couldn't care less what Niall is up to these days. At least I'm over him completely now. Even if the same fellow begged me to go back with him at this stage, I believe I would turn him down flat. Oh yes, I am so over that deadbeat now.

'That's a pity. So who will you bring to the cabin crew ball this year?'

'Oh, God only knows.'

To be honest, the annual cabin crew ball had completely escaped my mind. A veritable fashion show for all the air hostesses, where they get that long-awaited opportunity to compare their stunning evening wear finds from every city from Boston to Paris, it has got to be the most glamorous event on our work social calendar. Normally I'm counting down the days to the event, which is like our Christmas party if you like. But this year, being single, I'm not exactly jumping for joy in anticipation of the soirée.

'I'll say a prayer that you meet somebody nice soon.'

'Thanks, Mum. Bye.'

I email back Robert and ask him can he meet me the following evening in the bar in the Clarence hotel. Always on his Blackberry, Robert replies immediately and agrees a time. He still doesn't say what the meeting is about, though. Hmm. Strange.

I decide to get a taxi to Dundrum Town Centre in a bid to buy at least two Christmas presents. I really want to have a proper Christmas this year. Last year we all went to Lanzarote and spent the day on the beach eating ice cream as though it was any other day, and the year before we went to Florida and ended up having our Christmas Dinner at McDonalds. But I think enough time has passed now, and although I don't for a minute ever think Christmas will be the same now Emily has gone from our lives, I honestly believe we've got to start being a family again.

The taxi deposits me outside the shopping centre which reminds me of the super-size American malls. It's so sparkly clean you could almost eat off the floors. And they've got everything here including my favourites, House of Fraser, Coast, and BT2 as well as Easons for reading fixes and Toni & Guy on the top floor for my regular hair appointments. There's nothing I like to do more on my day off than spend the afternoon browsing around this place.

I wander into a toy store and pick out a big red fire engine for Ben. I really think he'd love it and I can imagine him whizzing it around the place beeping its horn. It's sad that he's never going to have his mummy for Christmas. Of course he doesn't remember her but . . . oh my God, I think I'm going to cry again. I pick up a Barbie doll dressed in disco gear and pretend to concentrate on it while willing the tears to go away. It's just so difficult not to think of Emily at Christmas time. Even when I'd been in Boots earlier, I'd spotted Emily's favourite perfume and spritzed it on my wrists, thinking that I should definitely get my sister a bottle for Christmas before realising suddenly that she wouldn't be here. I keep doing that. For years I've been picking up the phone to dial Emily's number and if I hear any funny jokes, I still think I must tell Emily . . .

I leave the shop, the fire engine in my arms as it doesn't fit in a brown paper shop bag. I think I should buy somebody else another present, but instead I go down to Marks and Spencer's food hall on the ground floor and buy myself a bottle of champagne. Well, a girl has to indulge sometime . . .

Back in the apartment Edel is sitting watching an old episode of *Sex and the City* with her swollen feet in a bowl of soapy water.

'Never work in a shoe shop,' she advises.

'I won't,' I promise.

'So did you email your man?'

'What man?' I say vaguely, admiring Carrie Bradshaw's baby-pink coat. It's so delicate and cute and expensive-looking. Just how does she run around the streets of New York without getting it dirty? Why do the four girls in the show always look immaculate? Especially Kim Cattrall. Would you believe she's only three years younger than my mum? Anyway, after a day's trawling through New York stores, I always need a good scrub to wash away the dirt and grime, especially if I've been using the subway. I love

New York to visit but I don't know how people actually live there. So bitterly cold in the winters and sweltering hot in the summers. I know everybody in Ireland complains about the rain but at least nobody dies of extreme weather conditions.

'The Jimmy Choo man.'

'No, not yet.'

'Do it now.'

'I will, later. In the meantime, do you want to join me for a glass of champers?'

Edel's eyes open wide in admiration. 'On a week night? How decadent!'

'Every night is a week night for me, even weekends. The joys of working for an airline, huh?'

'At least you don't have to look at smelly feet all day.'

'Wanna bet? You wouldn't believe the stink when some passengers remove their shoes during flights. Thank goodness for smelling salts!'

I expertly pop open the champagne, careful not to let any fizz escape. Being a flight stewardess may not qualify me for a job in an accountancy firm or to set up my own plumbing business, but I sure know how to open bottles swiftly and without fuss.

'So what are we toasting? Greg's new job?'

As if! Why on earth would I waste my hard-earned cash buying champagne to toast the good fortune of that loser? Mind you, I should have realised he'd got the job as I haven't seen his unshaven face around the place for a while.

'He's got the job? Well, I'm absolutely delighted,' I say with a big false smile on my face. 'I gather we won't be seeing as much of him in the future then?' I comment, maybe a bit too eagerly.

'No, I suppose not. He's working as security in the bank just round the corner from the shop I'm working in which is brilliant because now I can arrange my lunch break to coincide with his.'

'Fantastic.'

'But obviously he's still going to pursue his dream of breaking into the music industry.'

'Of course.' I nod, not even aware that Greg had a musical note in his head. I'd also like to toast that it's almost two years since myself and the bank bought my apartment but I refrain because I don't want Edel to feel bad that she hasn't got her foot on the property ladder yet. God knows, it's bad enough with everybody else in Dublin banging on about property and making everybody else feel that they missed out on the building boom, without me sticking my oar in as well.

I pour a glass for Edel and one for myself and then fetch two strawberries from the fridge and slice them for added effect. I then snuggle into the couch beside Edel and raise my glass.

'To Christmas,' I say.

'And the New Year.'

'Yes, well, let's not get too much ahead of ourselves,' I say hurriedly. 'Sure isn't Halloween just finished? We've got to live in the moment, Edel.'

'Speaking of living in the moment, you should contact that man and go out for dinner.'

'Hmm.' I grimace.

'Why put it off?'

'Because he has a wife and I don't even want to go there. Besides, I've a lot on my mind. The cabin crew ball is in three weeks' time and I haven't even got a man to bring along, never mind a dress.'

I feel guilty for lying about my feelings about Oliver to Edel, but I'm wary of pouring my heart out. Edel might naïvely encourage me to get involved with Oliver and that would just be a disaster. If I was to have an affair, how many people would get hurt? Whatever about me, Oliver has a wife to think about. He might not care about hurting her but could I really do that to another woman? Could I wine and dine another woman's husband, knowing that she was at home worried about him? Maybe he had kids. Would I feel comfortable about potentially breaking up a family home? I don't think so. At the back of my mind, I would always feel guilty. Anyway, being somebody's mistress never seemed like fun to me. Dinner and drinks on week nights while he pretended to be at business meetings, and spending weekends at home alone because he always spent those days doing family things. Could I really spend Christmas at home while he tried to sneak out into the garden to spend two minutes on the phone with me while his wife, the woman he once made his vows to, slaved over the family turkey? No. I never would. And I'd never understand women who accepted to be 'the other woman'. Why would any self-respecting female settle for being second best? The bit on the side? It was a line I wasn't willing to cross. I decided not to tell Edel how strongly I felt for the man who could never be mine.

'Why don't you bring that hunk Danny, who called here the other day?'

'Well, I'd love to, but he's unavailable.' I grimace.

'Has he got a girlfriend?'

'Yeah, something like that.'

'But you still fancy him?'

'Well yes and no, Edel. I'm still very much attracted to him but I don't know if there's anything more. I'm at an age where I'd like to be involved with somebody a little more stable. Danny is more than capable of breaking my heart again and I don't know if I could cope with that. I have to protect myself from getting hurt again.'

'I know what you mean, but there's nothing to stop you having a bit of fun with him as long as you accept that he's not for keeps. You could bring him along as a platonic friend? At least he'd know everybody at the ball and you wouldn't have to mind him for the night.'

'Actually,' I sip my champagne thoughtfully, 'that's not a bad idea, Edel. Not a bad idea at all!'

I give it some serious thought. Why not bring Danny indeed? He and I get along really well, and despite the fact that we had a drunken one-night – sorry, one-afternoon – stand, it's not like we've fallen out or anything. In fact, we'd probably be an item if there wasn't that small matter of another woman's child on the way. I paid for my tickets months ago so if I didn't bring somebody they would both go to waste as I sure as hell wouldn't be going along on my own. The more champagne I drink the more it makes sense. If I could only trust myself not to fall for his charms again, then maybe Danny would be the perfect date after all. I should be able to handle him and make sure that I don't ever get too involved again. I'm not a schoolgirl any more and I'm older and wiser than Danny so there shouldn't be too much of a problem guarding my poor fragile heart. It's under lock and key for the moment, and nobody, and I mean, nobody, is going to get the chance to trample on it again.

I take out my mobile phone and text him before I change my mind. He doesn't text back immediately and after an hour when the champagne bottle has been emptied I still haven't heard from him. Oh well, I think, anxious not to jump to immediate conclusions. He could be flying with his phone switched off. But the next morning when he still hasn't replied to my message, I have the distinct feeling that I've been snubbed.

I make my way to the Clarence Hotel to meet Robert. I'm a little anxious about seeing him. I haven't a clue what all of this is about, and the worst-case scenario is running through my head. Like, what if he has decided to move to the other side of the world to take up a new job and is bringing Ben with him. That would cause many tears for our family as Ben, although we don't see him half as often as we'd like, is the closest link we have to our dear Emily.

The uniformed doorman welcomes me with a smile at the U2-owned boutique hotel overlooking the River Liffey and I make my way to the trendy Octagon Bar. There are no other customers at the bar due to the early hour but no doubt by lunchtime the place will be hopping. I sit on a dark green stool up at the bar and order a cappuccino.

Robert arrives before the cappuccino, looking very smart in a navy suit, crisp white shirt and silver tie. His shoes are so polished they gleam, and under his arm he carries a smart leather tan-coloured briefcase. He looks well and handsome and happy. He certainly looks far too well to be a young widower and the father of a boisterous young toddler.

He bends over and kisses my cheek before taking the stool beside me, then orders a cappuccino for himself.

'You look great,' he says, smiling, although I hear in his voice that he's strained.

'As do you. Are they keeping you busy at work?'

'Don't even talk to me,' he says looking at his watch. 'I've a meeting at 12. There's never a dull moment for a stockbroker in this city.'

'I don't know how anybody does it. God, all that pressure . . . I couldn't handle it at all.'

'Well, I'm glad to be busy. If I hadn't been kept busy over the last couple of years I don't know how I . . .'

The barman interrupts us with our cappuccinos.

'So, how's life with you?' he asks breezily, dropping a spoonful of sugar into his cup.

'Oh fine, fine.' I keep the grin plastered on to my face, anxious to know where all this is going. I know he didn't request me for a chit-chat about the weather and I'm anxious to get to the point.

'Did I see you on the news the other night?'

'Yes, that was me. It was nothing, really. You know the way the media blows these things out of proportion.'

'But it must have been pretty terrifying all the same. I saw a picture of the guy. He's the type of man you'd cross the street to avoid; I can't even imagine what it was like having him cooped up on a plane.'

'It wasn't pleasant, I have to admit. But that's just the way things go. The majority of passengers are cool. It's just that one per cent that makes the job difficult for all of us. So how's Ben?'

'Oh fine, he's great. He looks more like Emily every day. Even my mother says so. Hang on' – he roots in his pocket for his mobile phone and shows me a photo of Ben sitting on Santa's lap – 'That was taken a few days ago.'

I scrutinise the grainy photo. He does indeed look like Emily. His little face is a bundle of joy. How sad that my sister will never get to see him looking so happy.

'Annie,' my brother-in-law's voice takes on a more serious tone, 'there's something I need to tell you. I wanted to tell you before you heard it from somebody else. You know what a village Dublin can be like.'

I nod feeling slightly alarmed and wait for the bombshell.

'The thing is that I've . . . I've met somebody, Annie. I mean, in a romantic way. She's a primary school teacher originally from Cork and now living in Dublin. We've been dating for ten months now, and it's become serious.'

I open my mouth to speak but all the right words simply elude me.

'Listen, I know it must come as a shock to you, but I've fallen for her, and she adores Ben. We didn't rush into things, we really didn't, but—' he breaks off.

I sit rooted to the stool my head spinning. It never even occurred to me that Robert would ever start dating again. I don't know why. I mean, it was fairly obvious that he wasn't going to remain single all his life but it's still a shock.

'Emily will always be the love of my life and Julie, that's her name, knows that it's been difficult for me, and has given me time to grieve . . . God, I don't know,' he falters, putting his elbows on the counter and his head in his hands, 'I was dreading even telling you, but I knew it had to be done.' He looks up at me again. 'We've been talking about getting married.'

'When?' I ask directly, suddenly finding my voice.

'Next year.'

'So Ben will have a stepmother?'

'I suppose so. I think it will be good for him.'

I take a deep breath, close my eyes for a few seconds, and think of Emily. Good, kind, selfless Emily who loved this man with all her heart, who fell for his good looks and charms the minute she laid eyes on him.

'There'll never be another man for me, Annie,' she would say.

And there never was. Robert was the light of her life. And now he had somebody else.

I open my eyes and look straight at Robert's concerned face, waiting anxiously for a response.

'So do I, Robert. I think it will be good for Ben. And I think it will be good for you too. I know all my sister wanted was for you and Ben to be happy. I . . .'

But I can't continue. I feel a sharp pain in my breast and for a moment I can't breathe. This is totally unexpected.

'I'm sorry, Annie. I didn't want to shock you.' Robert puts a hand over mine as my face crumples and I burst into loud uncontrollable sobs.

The bartender offers me some tissues which I gratefully accept. Poor Robert looks deeply distressed.

'You don't have to pretend to be pleased for me, Annie. I understand if you're angry because yourself and Emily were so close.'

'I'm sorry,' I sniff, dabbing my streaked mascara with the tissues. 'I don't know what came over me. I had a couple of glasses of champagne last night so maybe I'm feeling extra fragile this morning. Honestly, I don't want to give you a guilt trip. I am pleased for you, Robert, you're a young man, after all; Emily was terribly young when she died, too. But I miss her so much.'

'So do I. Sometimes the grief is still unbearable but having Julie around has eased the pain somewhat. We were hoping to go away on a holiday soon and I didn't think it would be fair to bring Ben on a long flight so we'll probably leave him?'

'Are you asking me to mind him?'

'I was going to. I really don't want to leave him with the nanny for the week, and your mum might not be able to cope very well.'

'My dad's arthritis is back and this time it's bad, I gather. I was talking to Mum yesterday.'

'And how is she?'

'Not brilliant, to tell you the truth. But I'm determined that this year we'll all spend Christmas at home. If it comes to it, I'll even cook the dinner myself!' I manage a laugh. 'Actually, Robert, why don't you come along with Ben?'

'I'd love to.' He breaks into a genuine smile and suddenly I feel guilty for never having including him in any family social outing since the funeral. Not that there have been too many celebratory occasions, I must admit. My parents have given up on me giving them a big day out, and Dad ended up donating his only black tie suit to the bin last year after it had been attacked by opportunistic moths.

He looks at his watch apologetically.

'I know, you have to go, I understand. Listen, when do you need me to take Ben?'

'Next month?'

'Early December, then. Right, there shouldn't be any trouble getting the time off work. Actually, I'm kind of looking forward to spending time with my adorable little nephew. By the time you get back, he won't want to leave me.'

'Don't tell me you're getting broody yourself, Missus.'

'Jesus, that'll be the day. I don't even have a man.'

'Well, I wouldn't say there's a shortage of admirers. Listen, I'll give you a bell about arrangements over the next few days. I'm going to tell Ben now so that he'll get used to the idea of staying with Auntie Annie for a while.'

'You do that,' I say, giving him a hug. We part company just as the bar is filling up with lunchtime punters. I wave Robert good-bye and watch him head right at the door on his way towards Westmoreland Street to his business meeting. Blinking in the sunlight I take a deep breath of fresh air before heading back inside the hotel to see if I can grab some lunch. I feel like treating myself, and I need to sit down and think about everything. As I walk into the elegant restaurant that is the Tea Room, my mouth watering as the heavenly aromas drift from the area of the kitchens, my phone starts ringing in my bag. I fish it out to check what number is flashing. It's Danny's. I answer immediately.

'Babes?'

'Is that you, Danny?'

'Yeah, where are you?'

'At the Clarence Hotel. I'm just about to sit down to lunch. Why? Where are you?'

'At your apartment block,' he says breathlessly. 'But there's no answer from your bell.'

'That's because I'm not there.' I point out the obvious.

'Don't order yet. Go back into the bar and order a drink. And order one for me. You choose. Don't worry, I'll pay. How long do you think it would take me to run from here to the Clarence?'

'About fifteen minutes?'

'I'm on my way.'

Rule Fifteen: Never knock on a hotel room door in only your underwear.

'I think I'm in love with you, Annie.' Danny takes both of my hands in his and looks at me beseechingly. He looks as though he hasn't shaved in days.

'Well, this is a surprise . . .'

I feel the bartender eavesdropping into the conversation, albeit very discreetly. I hope he doesn't think this is a date and that Robert was a date too. Or that, God forbid, I'm a working girl discussing fees with clients. Maybe I shouldn't have worn a short skirt!

'Look at me, Annie. I know you don't take me seriously after all I've put you through . . .'

'That's right,' I answer back immediately. 'I don't!'

'I've been talking to Fiona.'

'Listen,' I say firmly, raising my Sex on the Beach (that's our drink, by the way, as we don't have a song); 'I don't think your relationship with Fiona is any of my business.'

He grabs my hand urgently. 'You don't understand,' he says. 'It's all off between us. That's what we were talking about. When I got your text I was so happy because I always thought we had a really strong connection.'

I stare at him in amazement. He really is the most unpredictable person I have ever met in my life. How could it all be over with Fiona? What about their child?

'She says it's definitely not mine. She rechecked the dates.'

My mind is spinning. Is there ever a moment in my life not filled with drama? 'God, this is all very sudden, isn't it?'

'Yes, I'm so relieved. Of course, I would like to be a father one day, but there's so much I need to do first. But I've learned my lesson. I'll be a lot more careful from now on. I want us to make a go of things.'

My heart does an unexpected flip. I can't rush in to this, though. First of all, his mother hates me, and, second of all, he's younger than me and not terribly mature for his age. And last but not least, he's not the most stable of individuals. One moment he's here, and the next minute he's gone. I don't know if I could deal with that kind of messing on an ongoing basis.

On the plus side, though, there's never a dull moment when Danny's around; he has a good job which he enjoys and he's drop-dead gorgeous, which in Dublin (there's a depressing man-drought at the moment) is a rare find. What the hell? Maybe I should date him. Or have a fling at least.

'Do you want to come to the cabin crew ball with me?' I ask him flirtatiously, crossing my legs on the stool.

'As boyfriend and girlfriend?'

'As friends with a view to seeing how things progress.'

'Sounds good,' he says breaking into a smile. 'You hungry?'

'I'm bloody starving,' I say, conscious that my tummy has been grumbling loudly for over an hour.

'Well, this could be your lucky day, then. Lunch is on me.'

'They say there's no such thing as a free lunch.' I take his proffered arm, glad of the distraction after Robert's impromptu news early on.

'And do you know something?' They're right. I'll expect a return on my investment for this.' He laughs as he leads me out of the bar.

Edel eyes Danny and myself suspiciously when we arrive back in the apartment hours later, having finished our long leisurely lunch with Irish coffees in the fabulously cool Morgan Hotel (just a quick walk across the Ha'penny Bridge over the Liffey).

I give nothing away and after a few pleasantries Edel says something about promising to take the neighbour's yapping Jack Russel for a walk, and makes herself scarce. Not wasting a minute Danny pulls me into the bedroom and throws me down on the bed where we kiss passionately before ripping off each other's clothes.

Our lovemaking is passionate and intense and I lose myself in his touch, letting myself go in reckless abandonment. I no longer feel wary around Danny, or have a sense that I need to make myself feel fun around him. It's like I've known him for ever. The fact that he has almost confessed his undying love for me, makes him all the more appealing. When you know a gorgeous man is mad about you suddenly they seem to become even more attractive.

'You're hot,' says Danny rolling over and breathing heavily after we've both climaxed.

'Shut up, you sound like Paris Hilton.'

'I do? Thanks. Speaking of Hiltons, how do you fancy a dirty night away in a luxury hotel?'

I sit up in bed, the sheets sticking to my damp, sweaty body, smoothing my bed hair over to one side.

'I'll have to check my roster,' I tell him. 'I'm busy for the next fortnight, starting with a Shannon overnight tomorrow night.'

Danny looks startled. 'You're kidding?'

'Why would I joke about something as boring as that?' I ask him.

'It's just that I'm going to be in the same crew hotel in Limerick tomorrow night as I'm flying out of Shannon the next day to London.'

He looks genuinely pleased at the chance of meeting me again tomorrow night.

'We get in late, though; it's the last flight from Dublin to Shannon and by the time we drive into Limerick it could be well after eleven.'

'Never mind, I'll probably go to Nancy Blakes for a pint and meet you there, and then who knows? We could hit a nightclub maybe? Have you been to the Trinity Rooms before?'

'I have, yeah, but God, I don't know if I'll be in the mood for dancing after pushing and pulling carts in the cabin all day.'

I ruffle his dark hair and wonder where he gets his energy from. Then again, he's a good couple of years younger than me. I prefer my comfy bed with a nice glass of wine and a riveting romance. I wonder if I'm slowing down. Am I really becoming like a mother who never likes to take off her slippers and go out, always opting for a night in with a blazing fire and the cast of *Corrie* instead? When I first joined the airline I used to pity cabin crew who were around the same age as my mother. There would never be any question of them attending wild room parties. No, they would scarper to their rooms to unwind in a hot bath with the evening paper and a bottle of vino they'd swiped from the plane or bought in the duty free. Now I can totally, totally see their point. Almost worryingly so.

Still, it's pretty cool that Danny will be staying in the same hotel as me. We've never had an overnight together so it's something to look forward to. Hopefully he will behave himself. And it's nice that I have such a good-looking escort to come to the ball with me. Heaven knows I've been on my own every other year pretending that it was brilliant having another night out with the girls while the smug couples glanced over sympathetically at us. This year I'll have a partner, I smile contentedly to myself. This year it won't be just another lonely ticket for one. It will be Annie and guest. Annie x2. Annie plus one. I'd be lying if I said I wasn't over the moon. The only problem now is sourcing a dress.

'OK, I'll meet you tomorrow night, then,' I say, giving him a friendly hug. He smells of Armani aftershave. 'I'll look forward to it.'

'Not as much as I will.' He grins as I open the door for him to leave.

*

When Edel comes home she plonks herself on the sofa while putting a plaster on yet another burst blister. Why oh why doesn't she leave that job which requires her to stand all day in a shop wearing uncomfortable high heels that dig into her skin? Soon the dreaded inquisition starts up again. Edel has to know *everything*.

'So are you an official couple then?' she quizzes, eyeing my dressing gown and slippers. 'It's a bit early for bed, isn't it?'

'We were having a lie-down,' I answer, trying unsuccessfully not to blush.

'Oh, so that's what you call it now? I thought you said nothing was happening between you guys?'

'Well, nothing *was* happening. That's the infuriating thing about Danny. I never know where I stand with him. Every time I vow to myself not to get involved with him, he turns up in my life looking amazing and suddenly I am overcome with desire to rip the clothes off him!'

'Gosh, this is very exciting. So are you boyfriend and girlfriend now then?'

'I wouldn't go that far, but you could say we're some sort of an item anyway. Danny is full of surprises so I'm not holding out for marriage just yet but he is exciting and charming, and secretly I think he likes me a lot more than he lets on. In fact, you know those little romantic notes I've been getting at work?'

'From your secret stalker?'

'Yeah. I've come to the conclusion that they're from Danny. I mean, I can't think who else could have sent them to me. Isn't he sweet?'

'Will you ask him if he sent them?'

'I don't think so. I don't want to embarrass him. Anyway, I think Danny would rather die than admit to being my secret admirer, macho man that he is.'

'Yeah, you're probably right. Still, it's all good though, isn't it? You, me, Danny and Greg will have to double-date soon.'

Er, God, I don't think so somehow! I can't imagine Danny sitting around the flat discussing the merits of The Frames' latest offering while sucking pensively on a Marlboro Red.

'I've invited him to the cabin crew ball, which is a relief. Now that I've the man sorted, all I have to do is go hunting for the dress. Perish the thought.'

'God, it sounds as stressful as going to your debs' dance. At least you've the shoes sorted. You will wear the Jimmy Choos, won't you?'

'Of course.'

'But you haven't taken Mr Jimmy Choo up on his dinner offer yet, have you?'

'Not yet,' I admit. 'But I will. I might see him on my London flight tomorrow.'

'I thought you said you were going to Shannon.'

'I am, but I've got to go to London first, unfortunately. The airline makes you work for your overnight allowance,' I moan.

'I don't feel a bit sorry for you,' she says folding her arms. 'Yes, your hours may be long, but you spend most of them eating lunch at airports and lounging around in some fancy hotel swimming pool. I, on the other hand, watch Cinderella types try to squeeze their swollen feet into tiny shoes just because they're half-price and seem to blame me when it doesn't work. Not to mention the headaches I get from those fluorescent lights.'

'Yes, but apart from the swollen ankles and the inevitable blisters . . .'

'And the smell of feet,' she interrupts grumpily.

'Yes, that too. But it is kind of exciting working in town, though.'

'Maybe, if you could afford to go out for lunch; a luxury I don't really have. All we have in our canteen is a kettle, a fridge that's far too small for all our stuff, and a daily loaf of bread for which we all have to pay fifteen cents a slice.'

'You're kidding!'

'Do you see a smile on my face?'

Er, that would be a no.

'That's why I usually come home for my lunch. I can't afford to eat in town, and if you bring in your own sandwiches everyone thinks you're a misery guts.'

'You'll have to get another job.'

'I know. I'll get a job as soon as you phone Jimmy Choo. I think you're rude not to. What does he do for a living?'

'He's a company director. I don't know anything about the company, though, except that they seem to have offices all over the place that he's always travelling to.'

'Maybe he'd give me a job,' says Edel wistfully and I don't think she's joking.

'Anyway, Edel,' I say, wishing to wrap up this conversation sooner rather than later, 'I think Oliver is great, amazing even. If we lived in an ideal world, he would be the man for me, but unfortunately we don't live in such a world and Oliver is very much off the market. So although he's perfect, he's married, and although I'm very flattered by his pursuing me, it's not a route I'm prepared to go down. And that's the matter closed. Anyway, I'm in a relationship now with Danny, remember?'

I decide to have an early night in preparation for my long day in the air tomorrow. I pack my little case in five minutes – I have it down to an art now:

Tracksuit – tick.

Slip nightie that doesn't take up any room – tick.

iPod – tick.

Mobile – tick.

Clean blouse, scarf, knickers and tights – tick.

Apron – tick.

Cabin shoes – tick.

Safety manual – tick.

Jeans, boots and cashmere polo neck in case I get dragged along to a pub – tick.

Make-up, toothpaste, toothbrush and shampoo (because hotel shampoos always make my hair feel like cotton wool) – tick.

There. I'm all set now. I think I'll have a little at-home spa now. Unfortunately on my wages as an airhostess, going on a real proper spa holiday is out of my budget. I mean, why pay for two days in an Irish spa hotel when I could have a fortnight in Lanzarote instead? Granted, I might end up staying in a two-star complex with a pool so cold you can almost see floating icicles on the top, and it might be so near the airport that you can regularly hear planes thundering by during the night, but you still might come home with a tan? Besides, everyone else will be so envious that it's worth it.

My at-home spa consists of a cinnamon-scented candle (€5 from the local supermarket), fluffy towel, slippers that I nicked from the hotel on my last overnight (free!), a treatment bought from Toni & Guy – much cheaper than asking them to put it in my hair for me (€11), soothing music (from a giveaway disc that came with last Sunday's newspaper), baby oil from Tesco (just a few quid), and body moisturiser from a sachet that came glued to a magazine page.

All in all, my at-home spa comes to about a twentieth of what I would have had to spend in a spa (including a tip). Somehow that makes my little treat all the more enjoyable, I think as I start running the hot bath until the steam deliciously fills the room.

The following morning I appreciate the chance of a proper lie-in. It's so nice being able to wake in the natural light of day without being blasted out of it by the annoying screech of my alarm clock. I sit up in the bed in my comfy jim-jams and stretch like a cat among the pillows. The sun is shining through a crack in the curtains, filling the room with a hazy light. I glance out on to Gardiner Street which is still bumper-to-bumper traffic. Sometimes when I look at those bored faces behind the wheels, I thank my lucky stars I'm not part of the commuter circus.

I potter around the empty flat in my bare feet with *Ireland AM* on the television in the background. Somebody is on talking about the most popular toys to get for kids for Christmas. God, why does it always seem to creep up so fast every year? I listen with interest in case they recommend anything else I could get Ben. What do little boys like these days? Suddenly it dawns on me that I know absolutely nothing about children. How am I going to look after my little nephew for one week on my own?

Ireland AM finishes with three skinny models with flawless faces showing us the upcoming party dresses that we should be wearing during the party season. It only depresses me as the prices are astronomically high and I'm so damn broke as usual. I wonder how I can make more money for myself? I suppose I could always move home to Swords to live with Mum and Dad, and rent out my room, but how unbearable would that be? Could I honestly revert to being somebody's child again? Mind you, I'm not even sure how welcome I'd be. Mum has certainly never suggested it.

It's ten o'clock now and time to put on my uniform and make myself look smart. An hour later, all coiffed and made-up, I make my way down to Busaras. People smile at me in the street. Some even say hello. Like I said, people do that when you're an air hostess. I think I must remind them of happier times in their lives when they were going on holidays or something. At the terminal I pop into Easons and buy myself *Closer* magazine and a bottle of Diet Coke, which I drink while waiting for the Airport Express to whisk me to the airport. It arrives promptly. Good. If the traffic isn't too heavy, I'll be there in forty minutes.

There's a postcard waiting for me in my cubby hole. It's pink with a simple flower on it. Scribbled on it are the words: *Enjoy Limerick.*

Weird, I think. Weird and most disconcerting. I mean, who is this creature who keeps sending me these messages? And what's more, how does he know my timetable? Nevertheless, there isn't much time to waste. I'm due on board in twenty minutes. I meet my crew and we head off en route to our plane. Predictably, it's a busy flight there and back. There's no sign of Mr handsome Jimmy Choo. Pity, really. I've got used to looking out for him and am almost disappointed he's not on board. An ex-boyfriend of mine is sitting at the emergency exit reading the *Financial Times* and I get very embarrassed doing my safety demonstration in front of him as he smirks up at me. I notice he's wearing a wedding ring and still has all his hair. Smug bastard.

After we get back from London, we have to hang around the terminal at Dublin airport for what seems like an age before the flight to Shannon. Being naughty and not caring about calories today I make my way up to McDonalds on the third floor and order myself a large fries. As I stand in the queue I get a text from Danny telling me he's looking forward to some mischief and mayhem once we get to Limerick. I giggle at the text.

Then I go back down to the Arrivals area where the other two girls who are on the same Shannon flight as me are having coffee and watching the flight screens to make sure our flight isn't delayed. I ask them whether they have any intentions of heading out on the tiles later in Limerick.

'Not me,' says the older of the two, a woman in her early fifties who's been with the company for about thirty years and looks like an old boot. I bet she's one of the ones who they let in years ago because she speaks German or something. Apparently the credentials years ago were that you either had to be stunningly beautiful or speak a foreign language. Well, no surprises there. I hardly expected somebody who's lived as long as Anya to be donning her dancing shoes. 'But I might go down to the bar for one,' she adds.

Sheena, a young thing with platinum-blonde hair and pink cheeks suggests that she might be on for a night out. 'I suppose it depends on the cockpit crew,' she says with a throaty laugh.

I feel a cold hard knot form in my stomach. If she thinks she's going to flutter those pale eyelashes anywhere in Danny's direction she can forget it. Then I chide myself for being so possessive.

Soon it's time to board our flight. Miraculously it's not delayed this evening. The last Shannon flight is often delayed as it's so late at night and often the aircraft is stuck in a UK airport due to weather conditions. I'm tired now and I can feel my contact lenses clinging to my eyes, but at least there's no bar service down to Shannon except glasses of orange juice and water which we put on trays and whiz through the cabin. As soon as we're up we seem to be down again. The captain on our flight seems a quiet enough man. I hear him arranging to meet Anya down in the hotel lobby for a drink. Well, I'll be damned if I'll join them in some boring hotel bar where some eejit is usually playing Oirish songs for tourists on the piano, and the beer is flat and overpriced. I ask Sheena whether she has made up her mind about going out. She says she has decided to stay in her room because she's seen in the paper that there's a good film on RTE later. Hmm. Methinks it has something to do with the co-pilot being a woman. If one of the cockpit crew is a female, the cabin crew usually feign exhaustion or headaches. And if, God forbid, in the rare case that both the captain and the co-pilot are of the fairer sex it's almost 100 per cent that you won't see anybody until the following day at pick-up time.

The mini-bus pulls into our city-centre hotel. I quickly check my mobile phone to see if Danny has left me a message, but there's nothing except a message from Mum reminding me to phone my little sister in Australia tomorrow as it's her birthday.

I wonder where he is. I hope he's not in town getting drunk. If he is, I'll have a hell of a lot of catching up to do. At reception I say good-bye to the others and tell Anya and the captain that I won't be joining them for a drink down in the piano bar on this occasion. The other co-pilot, a young fellow of about twenty-two, looks disappointed. Before joining the airline people probably told him that all overnights were a blast, and that the cabin crew were all gagging for it. Unfortunately, though, if you're ginger with traces of teenage acne, as Seamus is, the overnights tend to be rather quiet. He agrees to meet Anya and the captain for one. But probably only because he's afraid of the captain and can't say no.

I get out at the fourth floor, turn the key in the door of the hotel room and push it open. It's a large, comfortable, pristine-clean room with a couple of chocolates on the pillow case and a complimentary bottle of wine along with a bowl of fruit on a table. Now, who says cabin crew aren't well looked after? I smile, taking off my coat and hanging it up. I then kick off my shoes, jump on the bed and greedily unwrap the sweets. I'm starving. I pick up the room service card and study it. Luckily this hotel provides soup and fresh sandwiches twenty-four hours a day so I pick up the phone and dial 0 for reception. After placing my order I then boil the kettle in my room for a cup of tea. Where the hell has Danny got to? I wonder. At this stage I'm so wrecked I don't think I could possibly face a night bopping around a Limerick nightclub, no matter how trendy it is.

Just as I'm about to give up on him and tuck into my soup and delicious cheese sandwiches, my phone rings.

'Are you in Limerick yet?' shouts Danny. It sounds like he's in a particularly noisy pub. 'Are you coming into town?'

'I don't know,' I say, my mouth half full of bread. 'I'm just having something to eat. How much have you had to drink?'

I sound like his mother. I think of Sylvie and shudder. Well, no actually, you could never really compare me to her.

'Just one or two.'

'Are you sure that wouldn't be five or six?' I quiz him, not believing him for a second. It sort of sounds like Danny's had a lot more than two drinks.

'Stop giving me grief and come on in and meet me for a drink.'

'Where are you?'

'Nancy Blakes in town.'

'I should have guessed. OK, then, but we won't stay long. I'm tired.'

'How long will you be?'

'Give me twenty minutes. I need to change first and order a taxi.'

'Great. I'm just inside the door. You can't miss me.'

'I'll bet,' I giggle and then hang up.

I struggle into my skinny jeans, knee-high leather boots and a simple black polo neck. I spritz some Dior Addict behind my ears and am ready to go. Opening the door of my hotel room I take a furtive glance up and down the corridor just to make sure none of the crew are hanging about. The coast seems clear. Good. I pop my room key in my bag and take the lift down to the ground floor. Immediately I spot the cockpit crew chatting to Anya over a beer beside the open fire in the lobby and my heart sinks. Should I just pretend I don't see them and try to sneak out? No. Too obvious. I'll just have to go over and make up some hair-brained excuse. Eagle-eyed Anya spots me immediately and beckons me over. I pretend to be surprised to see the trio and wave as I approach their table.

'Hi, guys!'

'Are you joining us?' asks the captain eagerly. 'What can I get you?'

'Actually,' I struggle, 'I'm not having anything to drink, if you don't mind. I'm not feeling great so I was thinking I'd go outside for a bout of fresh air.'

'It's cold out there.' Anya looks concerned. 'And you have no coat. Do you need an aspirin or anything? I've a packet in my room. I can nip upstairs and get you one.'

'No, honestly, thanks,' I insist, wishing they'd stop making a fuss. There's no way I can walk over to the concierge now and ask him to order me a cab. 'I'm sure if I have a little walk, I'll be fine.'

'Do you want me to go with you?' the co-pilot offers hopefully, obviously dying to be rescued from Mammy and Daddy. 'It might not be safe walking around Limerick at this time of night.'

'No, honestly, thanks a million, but I'm sure I'll be fine. I won't venture too far. Anyway, I'll see you later, guys.'

And with that I make a beeline for the revolving doors before they can say anything else to me.

I walk briskly through the car park. Anya was right. It's bloody cold. Standing out on the road, I look up and down hoping to flag a passing taxi. Why in the name of God am I putting myself through this? I ask myself. For Danny of all people? I hope he bloody well appreciates my efforts! Fortunately a taxi pulls up pretty promptly and I hop in. Within minutes we're outside Nancy Blakes. I pay the driver and hop out.

Danny is exactly where he said he would be. Just inside the door. However, he's not alone. Sitting with him are three American backpackers who are 'doing Europe' at the moment. They are very friendly, even if a bit put out, perhaps, that Danny has a date they probably didn't know about. As I settle in they make to leave. They've an early start in the morning to take the bus to Galway. They thank him profusely for the drinks and his email address and make themselves scarce. Danny and I are alone.

'Where are the other lads on the training course?' I ask him.

'Don't I get a kiss?' He gives me a mournful look. I reach over and plant a smacker on his lips.

'They left earlier,' he said. 'Boring bastards.'

'Sensible guys, more like. When did you get here?'

'About four.'

I look at my watch incredulously. 'Four? You mean you've been here all this time and expect me to believe you've only had one or two?'

'I can handle my drink, Annie,' he says with a slur and bloodshot eyes that beg to differ. 'Stop lecturing me. It's not attractive. You weren't like this in Spain.'

'Spain was different. We were on holiday then.'

'And we're in Limerick now.'

'Yeah, but not on holidays. This is work. I'm surprised your liver is still intact.'

'So what'll you have?'

'I'll get it. It's easier.' I jump to my feet. I don't trust Danny to be able to walk to the bar. It would be highly embarrassing if we were both thrown out. I reach the bar just before last orders are called and buy a glass of Carlsberg. The last thing I want to do is endure a sleepless night due to excessive alcohol consumption.

'You're being very good,' says Danny noticing my glass. 'No shots for you then?'

'Not on a week night,' I laugh.

He places a clammy hand over mine. 'I'm glad you're here.'

'I'm glad I'm here too,' I reply, not exactly truthfully. I can think of places I'd rather be. Like my bed.

'Do you know something?' he slurs as my heart sinks. I really feel it's pointless having a conversation with somebody on a different wavelength. Namely, when they're pissed and you're as sober as cold water.

'What's that?'

'I think I love you.'

'No you don't. You don't even know me.'

'I've known you long enough to know that I've fallen for you.'

'Well, thanks.'

'And you musht like me too if you're bringing me to the ball.'

I look at him levelly. 'Yes, it's true, Danny. I like you a lot but love is a very strong word. It just doesn't roll off my tongue easily.'

'I've mished you.'

'Have you? But there's Fiona, your ex, to think about. She could be expecting your child.'

I thought I'd remind him just in case he'd forgotten.

'Lesh not talk about that now.'

'OK.'

That's fine by me. It's not as if it's my favourite subject, anyway. Nevertheless, it's not easy to brush the matter under the carpet. There's a baby on the way and somebody is the father. Very possibly Danny.

It doesn't take me long to drain my glass. Danny is nearly finished his, too. Thank God. It means we can get out of here soon.

'Do you want another?'

'Even if I did, it doesn't matter 'cos they've stopped serving,' I point out matter-of-factly.

'Already? Thash ridiculous.'

'It's not, Danny. Time's up. I'm sure the people who work here have homes to go to.'

'We can order more drinksh at the reshidensh bar back at the hotel then,' he says brightening somewhat.

I suddenly remember Anya and the cockpit crew back

at the hotel and am certain that stumbling towards the residents' bar after we finish up here would be a very bad idea indeed.

'Come on, Mister, let's get ourselves a taxi and head back.'

'Are you not shtarving?'

'No, I had something to eat back at the hotel.'

'I'm shtarving.'

Oh God! This is like being out with a spoiled child.

'We can order something from room service at the hotel,' I suggest hopefully.

'Nah, I don't feel like ham shandwishesh at thish time of night. There'sh a chipper round the corner.'

Five minutes later we're standing in a queue waiting for Danny's chicken burger and curry chips. The smell of grease is overwhelming and the fluorescent lights are unforgiving. Danny looks a hell of a lot less attractive than when I met him back in Malaga. Back then he seemed fun and sexy. Now I'm beginning to wonder whether he has a drink problem. I mean, he hasn't exactly built up a very good case for himself. The first night I ever met him he got completely locked, but at the time I just put it down to holiday madness, but then he continued to drink solidly for the entire Spain trip. The thought of him knocking back the champagne on Oliver Kane's yacht also springs to mind – he just didn't seem to know when to stop! And when people talk about Danny, it seems that they can't even mention the guy's name without referring to the fact that he can drink anyone under the table. Is this really a man I can honestly see myself getting serious with? I know I like to down quite a few myself on occasion but I'm also well capable of enjoying myself without the gargle. Danny, on the other hand, seems to be a veritable Peter Pan type, with a staunch refusal to grow up and face the music of real life. If I'm to be totally honest with myself, what kind of a life can I see myself having with somebody so immature? Our future together would appear to be anything but rosy right now.

We stand outside the chipper as Danny scoffs his chicken burger, mayonnaise escaping from his mouth and dribbling down the side of his chin.

'You sure you don't want shome?' he says, his mouth full.

'I'm positive.'

I manage to hail a taxi but the driver says he won't take Danny while he's still eating his food. Another couple gratefully jump in instead. My feet are slowly beginning to freeze. Danny finally finishes his grub but it takes another bitterly cold fifteen minutes before another cab pulls up. At this stage I feel numb and I'm bursting to go to the loo. I wasn't able to use the ones in the take-away as there was no toilet paper. Nice.

As we walk into reception I gently persuade Danny that sitting in the residents' bar would be depressing and that he should freshen up and come along to my room in about ten minutes. Luckily he seems to think this is a great idea. He tells me that he's got new silk boxers with little love hearts especially for the occasion. I can't tell whether he's joking or not.

'What room are you in?'

'Four oh four. Don't be too long, OK?'

'Promish,' he says as he almost staggers out of the third floor.

I shake my head in disbelief. God, what have I got myself into now? There won't exactly be a whole lot of loving going on between Danny and myself tonight by the looks of things. Still, it will be nice to wake up in his arms in the morning. Let's just hope he doesn't snore.

I get out on the fourth floor, make my way to room 404, and carefully take off my make-up with cotton wool pads before splashing my cheeks with warm water. Then fresh-faced, I brush my teeth, gargle with mouthwash and then slip into my nightie. I check the time on the radio clock. It's been over ten minutes since I said good-bye to Danny in the lift. Hopefully he hasn't fallen asleep or anything. In the state he was in, he could very well have passed out on his bed. While I'm waiting I decide I may as well lie on the floor and do some tummy crunches. Hotel rooms are ideal for these types of exercises because of the thick-carpeted floors. At home in my flat, it's all wooden floors and therefore not very comfortable. After sixty I'm flattened. God, I really must start getting fit. If only I didn't hate gyms so much. It's now a good twenty minutes since I last saw Danny. Where the hell is he? If he'd changed his mind about coming up, the least he could have done was inform me and not have me waiting around like an eejit.

Then I hear a commotion out in the corridor. It's very loud. As if somebody is thumping their fists against a door. What on earth could be going on? Tiptoeing to the door I open it surreptitiously and to my shock I see Danny, five doors up, and, sure enough, he is wearing his boxers – only his boxers – with the little red love hearts. Oh my God, what on earth is he playing at? He's at room 414. The wrong room. Anya's room! I'm about to call out to him to tell him he's at the wrong door when I hear a very sharp, very cross female voice.

'Danny Savage, what the hell do you think you are doing?'

Rule Sixteen: Don't be like Cinderella and go to the cabin crew ball on your own.

The phone rings bright and early. It's Danny. He sounds wretched.

'That Anya one gave me a right bollocking.'

'Danny, I'm still furious with you. What happened last night was unforgivable. Can you blame poor Anya for losing her rag? Talk about giving the old dear a fright! Let's hope she's not going to report you.'

'She says she won't, on the understanding that it never happens again. I'm more worried about her telling my mother.'

'Does she know her?'

'They're old friends. They joined the airline the same year. Anya was at my christening, apparently.'

I try to stifle a laugh. I just can't help seeing the funny side to it. Danny isn't laughing, though. 'Can I come up to your room?'

'No, Danny. Imagine if Anya caught you. How could you explain that away?'

'I suppose. What are your plans for this morning. When

are you being picked up?'

'At 11.30. I can meet you down at the pool, if you like. A swim might do your head good.'

'You're right. See you down there in a while.'

I make sure neither Anya nor either of the cockpit crew are in the vicinity before I join a forlorn-looking Danny in the Jacuzzi.

'Of all the doors to go banging on!' He sighs.

'Tell me about it. Did she explain that she wasn't into toyboys?'

'Don't start. Maybe I'll look back on the incident and laugh, but at the moment I'm just cringing.'

'What was she wearing?'

'Don't even go there.' He gives my upper arm a playful slap. 'I was too busy staring at her angry face to notice.'

'Just think of what she could have been missing!'

'Listen, I've been thinking,' Danny says, sounding very far away.

I lower myself further down into the bubbles. It kind of reminds me of those glorious few days I spent with Danny on the Costa del Sol. Things seemed a lot less complicated back then.

'About what?'

'About the cabin crew ball. I'm thinking it's maybe not a good idea if I go with you.'

I feel my heart sink like a stone. I'd had a niggling feeling that he was going to let me down on this one. Danny's word seems to count for nothing. Now, I'm more confused than I ever was. On the one hand, I think maybe I'd be better off attending the ball without Danny, especially because of his recent erratic behaviour, but on the other hand, the thought of turning up at the dinner dance alone, is almost too difficult to bear.

'Why?' I ask in a small, dejected voice. 'What has brought on this sudden change of heart?'

'Nothing's changed between you and me,' he assures me, 'but, given the circumstances . . . and what happened last night . . . I just think it's best for the two of us to have a cooling-off period.'

'But what has last night got to do with the cabin crew ball?'

'My mum goes every year. Herself and Anya and all her other cronies sit at the same table and make a night of if. If they saw us together they'd put two and two together and then I'd be in big trouble.'

He has a point, I grudgingly admit. After all, the last thing I want is another meeting with Sylvie about my behaviour. Of course Anya would realise that Danny had been trying to get into my room instead of hers. Damn. It was all Danny's fault. If he hadn't gone and got wasted then we wouldn't be in this mess.

'OK, Danny. If that's how you feel.'

'I'm trying to save your ass here as well as my own.'

Gee, thanks for being so understanding. Who on earth am I going to bring now? I've already gone and bought two tickets and I'm not going alone. I'm not going to bring a female friend along, either, as women always outnumber men at these things as it is. I give a deep sigh. Honest to God, this is the last thing I need to be worrying about.

The hot water is now too hot for me and I can feel my blood beginning to boil. I step out of the Jacuzzi.

'Where are you going?'

'For a dip in the pool,' I answer. 'I need to cool off.'

'I hope this isn't the end for us.'

'Of course not,' I tell him, and at that point both he and I give each other a look that probably means it really is the end.

I spend the next few days fretting about the upcoming ball. I'm sitting at a table of couples and I can't face the pitiful smiles I know I'm guaranteed to get being the token singleton. I'd rather chew off my own arm than go through that. I desperately start racking my brains to come up with a solution. It's not like I know a whole gang of eligible single lads and most of my exes are married or have new partners. Besides, I think I would rather go alone than with any of them.

Of course I do know some males. Friends of friends and men that I've known for years but don't fancy. None of them would make particularly fine escorts. Harry is hilarious but heavy so I don't think he would fit in with the skinny minnies at the table. Bart has a brilliant mind but is unfortunately prone to BO and I'd be a bit worried that every time he put up his hand to bid at the charity auction, one of the cabin crew at my table might faint. Derek is decent but dull, and Nigel is nice but nothing to natter about. Finbar has a funny habit of becoming frisky on whiskies and I didn't like to take a chance on his wandering hands. Geoffrey is a golf bore, Pat only ever talks about property, Duncan sweats like hell if you let him near a dance floor and Arthur has always been awfully argumentative.

In the end I decide I might as well try Jake. He is safe

enough, I reckon. A friend of my brother-in-law Robert, he works in insurance and always has a twinkle in his eye. I haven't seen him since my sister's wedding, and even then I wasn't talking to him for very long, but somebody told me that Jake is still single for a fact and is always up for a laugh which is good. At least he won't send the table to sleep. And with any luck he'll manage to keep my mind off Danny for the night.

When I ring him he sounds positively thrilled to hear from me, as if he can't quite believe his luck. This scares me a little bit. I hope he's aware that this is just a date and not a marriage proposal. Still, it's better for a date to be wildly excited than to be only mildly interested. And it takes the pressure off knowing I won't have an empty seat as an escort for the night. Now all I have to do is get the dress. I'd love to go to the Design Centre in the Powerscourt shopping centre and splash out a small fortune for a once-off showstopper but the remaining balance on my credit card unfortunately won't allow it. I'll have to make do with a dress from Whistles or Monsoon. As it's my day off I decide a trip around the shops is in order. The sooner I get this blasted dress sorted the better. God, I just hate when I have to buy something formal that I'll probably only end up wearing a few times. Can you imagine what I'd be like trying to find a wedding dress?

I find the perfect dress in neither Whistles nor Monsoon. There's quite a nice choice in Pamela Scott but not exactly what I'm looking for. On and on I trundle through the stores, in and out of crowded changing rooms until I feel a headache coming on. To cheer myself up I pop into the Reverie café in Marks and Spencer and treat myself to a scone and a piping-hot cup of tea. My feet are grateful for the break. Feeling a little more energised now, I pick myself up again to do battle with the shops. Finally, in Coast, I spot the dress of my dreams. It's fitted pink satin with a side bow and gives me a perfect hourglass figure. I love it. I twirl around to admire the back. I just hope it doesn't look too much like a bridesmaid's dress.

At the checkout desk the friendly shop assistant admires my choice. 'It's lovely, isn't it?' She beams, taking it from me to wrap in light paper.

'Well, I've spent all day wandering around town looking for something and nothing measures up.'

'I'm not surprised. They've been selling like hot cakes.'

My heart hits the floor with a thud. This is exactly what I was not hoping to hear.

'Really?' I ask, disillusioned.

She obviously doesn't notice the disappointment in my face. 'Yes, in fact, they've been selling so much I've just put in an order for another batch.'

'How about the blue ones?' I ask quickly, having noticed that the dress came in quite a few colours.

She frowns slightly. 'Well now, funny that you should mention it, but the blue one is proving much harder to shift for some reason. I don't know why. I think the blue is lovely too.'

'I'll put this back and take the blue,' I decide in an instant. I can honestly think of nothing worse than turning up to the ball only to discover that half my colleagues are wearing the same dress. It's bad enough having to wear the same clothes as them every day as it is.

I hand over my credit card all smiles when the card

actually goes through and isn't rejected like I always fear it will be. With a skip in my step I leave the shop and head for home.

At home my answerphone is flashing furiously on top of my bedside table. I pick it up in the vague hope that it might be Danny. I've long since accepted that Niall won't be phoning again. Oh well, maybe Jake and I will hit it off and live happily ever after. As far as I remember he's a pretty attractive guy. I just wish I could get some advice from my sister about him. Emily would be able to put me straight.

The message is from Robert reminding me that they will be dropping Ben over to me on Sunday, along with enough clothes and toys to do him for the week.

I ring Robert at once at his office to tell him I got the message and that I'm looking forward to having Ben for a week. I have taken a week's annual leave to look after him.

'I can't wait for him to come to stay. I've all kinds of exciting things planned for him including a trip to the zoo and a trip to see Santa's grotto. It'll be a novelty having him around.'

'You're saying that now,' my brother-in-law laughs, 'let's see if you're still as enthusiastic after a week in the company of the little rascal!'

'I might not want to give him back.'

'Oh believe you me, I'd bet my house and my car that you will. Anyway, he'll be in pre-school in the mornings so you'll have a bit of time to yourself then. He keeps talking about his holiday with Annie Annie. He can't wait.'

Aahh. I can feel my heart melting. Ben has always

called me Annie Annie because when he was younger he couldn't quite get his tongue around the 'aunty' bit.

'By the way, Robert, since I have you on the phone, I need your advice about something. The annual cabin crew ball is on Saturday night and not being able to think of anybody else, I invited your friend Jake to it. Do you think that's a good idea?'

Robert sounds amazed. 'Have you already invited him?'

'Well, yeah. Why? You don't sound too keen. He's an alright bloke, isn't he?'

'Yeah, Jake's great. He's a real lad's lad, though. I wouldn't have put him with you.'

'I'm not putting him with me either,' I'm quick to point out. 'It's just for a dinner dance. It's not like we'll even be anywhere alone as I'll know half the people in the room. Oh God. You don't think it's a great idea, do you, Robert? Maybe I should have got your advice first.'

'You'll be fine. He's a laugh. A little unpredictable, though.'

'How do you mean?'

'I dunno. With Jake you never know what's going to happen next. That's probably why I like him. At least he isn't boring. He was always the joker in school.'

'Well, it's a long time since either of you were in school. Hopefully he'll have grown up a bit in the meantime.'

'I wouldn't bet on it,' Robert says with an air of caution. 'But good luck anyway.'

Hmm. I'm not sure if I like the way he emphasised the word *luck*.

*

That evening I take a taxi home to see my parents. A long-overdue visit has been called for. I take a taxi because the buses to Swords always take for ever and I can't be doing sitting beside people yapping loudly into their mobile phones or blasting me out of it by the tinny sound of the earphones on their iPods. Anyway, who says you can't be extravagant now and again? Besides, the kindly shop assistant gave me €20 off my blue dress because there was a tiny mark on the back and it was the only one in my size, so it all evens out when you think about it. As I'm going to be spending the night out in Swords anyway, I arrange to meet my cabin crew colleague Cathy for a drink. She had suggested Wrights but if I go to Wrights I know I'll end up staying till the early hours and dancing. So I suggest The Slaughtered Lamb as a much safer bet.

My mother is in good spirits and seems glad to see me, as does my dad. Mum hasn't taken the fact that Robert is remarrying as badly as I'd feared she might.

'It was bound to happen,' she said expressionlessly, while my dad agreed that it didn't mean he didn't love Emily, but that life had a habit of going on regardless. Mum asks if I have heard from Niall at all. I think she asks me these kinds of questions just to annoy me.

'No.' I look at her blankly and refuse to be drawn into a discussion about my ex. After a fairly pleasant homecooked meal (believe me, I'm not used to them!), I kiss them goodnight and tell them I'm going to meet Cathy.

'Well, have a nice time,' my mother says grudgingly. 'And if you meet any nice men, don't be rude to them and encourage them to talk all about themselves. Emily always did that and she was very popular with the boys.'

I bite my lip to refrain from answering, grab my coat, and go.

The trouble with Swords is that, due to its close proximity to the airport, half the airline employees live here. To make it twice as bad, because I grew up here, I always bump into people from my past that I want no future with.

As soon as I walk into the pub, I spot the glamorous Cathy sitting at the bar, nursing some kind of exotic-looking cocktail, her lightly streaked blonde hair falling sexily around her bare shoulders. She's wearing a flimsy black camisole that she bought on an LA trip despite the fact that it's November and minus something outside.

We both do the obligatory air-kissing thing before I grab a stool of my own and perch myself up at the bar too. But of course, Swords being Swords, I spot Michael, an old ex of mine whom I dated in school and ditched when he snogged another girl at my deb's dance. I pretend not to see him. I'm not being childish, I'm just . . . OK, then, I am just being childish. And rude. But I've never forgiven him.

I order the same cocktail as Cathy and she excuses herself to go to the Ladies'. I'm just about to pay for my drink when a tap on my shoulder nearly makes me jump out of my skin.

It's Rory, a guy I went to school with. Now there's a real blast from the past.

'Well, if it isn't old Annie.' He breaks into a smile. 'How are you?'

'Oh fine, thanks. And yourself?'

'Couldn't be better.' He beams.

I see him checking out my wedding-ring finger. He couldn't be any less subtle if he tried.

'If you don't mind me asking, are you, er, settled?'

It's funny the way people don't really ask any more whether you are married. I suppose it's because so many people have partners these days instead of spouses.

'No, are you?'

He looks aghast. 'Of course not, Annie. I've been waiting all my life for you to come back into it.'

I can't tell whether he is serious or not.

'Good one,' I laugh. 'Anyway, fancy seeing you here. It's a small world.'

'It is but I wouldn't like to walk it, haha. Besides, I'm always here,' he said, 'which is more than I can say for you.'

'Oh well, I like to try out different places, you know. I no longer live in Swords so it's a pain socialising here and having to get taxis back into town afterwards.'

Rory suddenly spots Michael out of the corner of his eye. 'Speak of the devil,' he says loudly, 'isn't that your ex over there?'

'Oh yes, so it is,' I say uncomfortably.

'Have you two fallen out?' Rory asks.

I look at him oddly. 'Actually, I haven't seen Michael in over a decade.'

'So you've split up then?'

'Obviously.'

'You used to be mad about him.'

'Yeah.'

'Do you remember when he snogged somebody else at your debs?'

'Remember? How could I ever forget?'

'You never come to any of the school reunions.'

'Well, I'll come along to the next one. Who organises them?'

'Me, I'm the only person around here who seems to bother. And I organise the college reunions, too. Everybody else seems to be too busy buying property.'

'So what are you doing?'

'I'm still in UCD. I'm a mature student.'

'Really?'

Mature? Ancient, more like. Who stays in college for ten years?

'It's not the same, though, without the old gang. Remember the laughs we had in the UCD bar?'

'Yeah.'

'And do you remember the Freshers' ball when you fell into the lake?'

God, this chap was stuck in a time warp.

'And do you remember when Michael was two-timing you with Caroline, the school bike and nobody told you?'

I stare at him, stunned. Was that true? Then I glance surreptitiously over at Michael who finally raises his glass at me in recognition.

'And do you remember college?'

'Of course I do.'

'I've loads of pictures of us back them. Remember when your hair went orange when you tried to dye it yourself? That was so funny. And remember when you were stood up by the captain of the UCD rugby team and . . .'

He drones on and on, not even seeming to realise that he's mostly having a conversation by himself. Cathy has even rejoined us but Rory hasn't even noticed, so intent is he on reminiscing about the glory days.

'And how's your sexy sister Emily? I always kind of fancied her. Not that she ever would have considered me. Now, don't you go telling her what I said or anything.'

I feel my smile freeze on my face. Cathy's jaw has dropped southwards.

'I won't,' I assure him.

'How can I believe you? I know what you girls are like when you get together.'

'Emily's dead,' I deliver dully.

Rory looks like somebody has hit him.

'Oh, I'm sorry. I hadn't heard.'

'It's OK. Anyway, nice seeing you,' I lie. 'Hopefully it won't be another ten years until we meet again. Come on, Cathy, let's go to Wright's.'

The music in Wright's is pumping and it feels like a Saturday night even though it's only Wednesday.

'Are you OK?' Cathy pats my arm gently.

'Yeah, I am.'

'Does that happen to you often?'

'What?'

'People asking about Emily.'

'Yeah, it does. It's not their fault, though. I never get used to people asking. It kind of unnerves me. That's probably why I tend to avoid Swords on a night out. I just see too many people. Like ex-boyfriends of Emily's or kids she used to hang around with in school or girls she went away on holidays with. That kind of thing.'

'It must be tough,' Cathy says sympathetically.

'I think it's worse for Mum and Dad because they live here so they see the hairdresser where she worked, and they see the shops she used to visit, and they bump into her old school teachers on the street and other friends and neighbours who rather than say the wrong thing about Emily, choose to say nothing at all. As if she never existed.'

I fight back the oncoming tears. Dear God, but a day doesn't go by without my missing Emily. Our other sister is in Australia so at least she isn't constantly bombarded with reminders. I'm sure she misses Emily just as much as I do. People deal with grief in different ways. Her way was simply to leave the country altogether.

I plaster a fake smile on my face as a couple of cabin crew make their way over in our direction. It's impossible not to bump into at least several familiar faces in this place. Still, it'd be kind of boring if we didn't know anyone at all. Inevitably the conversation becomes focused on the cabin crew ball. The other girls discuss their dresses and their partners and I tell them I'm bringing an old friend called Jake. I ask them whose table they're sitting at, just to be polite really. At this stage I don't give two hoots about the ball and wouldn't be bothered if it was cancelled altogether.

'We're sitting at Fiona's table,' one of them explains. 'Fiona McFay.'

The name doesn't ring any bells. Then again, there are so many cabin crew it's hard to keep track.

'Oh, I know her,' Cathy says. 'Very pretty girl. She's a part-time model also, isn't she?'

'That's right. So we're sitting with her and her boyfriend Danny and . . .' she goes on to mention several other people but I don't hear her. Fiona and Danny. Danny and Fiona. The penny drops with a thud. I feel like the walls of my head are caving in on me. I can hardly breathe.

'Is that Danny whose mother is an air hostess?' I croak as I somehow finally find my voice.

'That's right,' the girl yaps on happily. 'Her mother flies with us.'

'She's my supervisor,' I say in a monotone voice.

'He must get his looks from his dad,' Cathy adds cattily.

'Is he, I mean Danny, a bit of a player?' I ask.

'Well, he did have a bit of a reputation for a while when he first joined the airline. Then again, with all the cabin crew throwing themselves shamelessly at his feet, who could blame him? But I believe Fiona has tamed him now, the lucky cow.'

'Now, this is probably just a rumour,' Cathy tells us all with a mischievous glint in her eye, 'but apparently our Danny has a liking for older women.'

My heart sinks even further into my shoes. That would be me. Danny's younger than me. So it's a game he plays, is it? Something he gets off on? Suddenly I feel ill. That homecooked meal my mother made me earlier is now churning in my stomach.

'Get away,' says one of the cabin crew, wide-eyed. You can tell she's only thrilled to have a juicy bit of gossip to spread around. 'How much older are we talking?'

Cathy speaks quietly so they all have to lean forward to hear the rest. 'Much older. I'm talking ancient here. I swear to God. You know Sheena Flynn?'

Everybody nods. Sheena is a notorious gossip and always prides herself on being first with all the scandal.

'Well, she was on an overnight recently in Limerick, and she heard this terrible commotion outside her hotel room in the middle of the night. At first she thought it might have been a robber trying to break into somebody's room and was about to call security . . .'

Oh my God. I know exactly where this story is heading. The girls wait eagerly for Cathy to continue. As far as they're concerned this beats an episode from *Coronation Street* any day. I feel dizzy. The room is spinning furiously.

'Anyway, she didn't even know Danny was supposed to have been on the overnight so it came as a huge surprise when she saw him in his Y-fronts banging like a madman on, wait for it, the door of Anya Moloney's room.'

To say that I'm feeling stunned would be an understatement. In fact, I'm so unbalanced I almost correct Cathy over the fact that Danny had been wearing boxers, not Y-fronts, but fortunately I stop myself in time. Anyway, the girls probably wouldn't even have heard me they were so busy squealing with delight mixed with disbelief.

'Anya Moloney of all people.' One girl shakes her head incredulously.

'If I'd known he was that unfussy, I would have given him my room number,' another one cackles. 'I haven't had any action for months.'

'Jaysus, she's old enough to be his mother. Who would have thought it? I wonder does he have a fetish for older birds like some men have for fat birds?'

The girls all start cackling again and suddenly I'm just too overwhelmed. Today has been a very bad day for me, and now all my energy has vanished. I feel very much alone in a crowded bar. Everyone seems to be having a good time, except me. And to top it all Danny has been lying to me. He didn't even have the guts to tell me he was going to the ball.

'Hey, are you OK, Annie?' Cathy suddenly enquires. 'You've got a bad colour on you.'

'Um, yeah, I'll be fine. I'm just thinking about poor Emily. We were both at the opening of this place. It just holds too many memories for me.'

And with that I burst into tears and sob until I fear my heart will break.

Rule Seventeen: Behave with dignity at all times, even when there's no dignity left to behave with.

'You look stunning,' Edel says with open admiration. It's the night of the dreaded cabin crew ball and I'm parading up and down the sitting room to show off my new dress. This should be a happy occasion for me but in fact I'm feeling so low I can barely muster a smile.

'Do you think so?' I ask, unsure of myself.

'Absolutely. You'll turn heads at the ball tonight, so you will,' she adds, 'in fact, wait there till I get my digital camera.'

She comes back within seconds and happily clicks away as I pose in my best model-type position – sideways with one leg in front of the other and a hand on my hip with attitude. Showing me the results there and then I have to admit I look better than I have in months. I've lost four pounds in the last fortnight without even trying. Stress, I reckon.

'Danny will be proud.' She grins as I grimace. 'What time is he calling for you?'

'He's not,' I admit in a small voice.

'Why not?'

'It's a long story. Do you mind if we don't talk about it now? I'll tell you later, I promise, but tonight I just want to try and not talk about Danny Savage.'

'Really? What's happened now then?'

'What hasn't happened, more like? Oh Edel, he's just been giving me the run around. I feel like such a fool for putting my faith in him when every bone in my body was telling me to just cut my losses. Anyway, I'll fill you in later. If I talk about him now, it'll just put me in a bad mood.'

'I know what you mean. You poor thing, I have to say, Annie Anderson, you really attract them, though, don't you? Come on, cheer up now. Put a smile back on that pretty face of yours. Let's talk about your fabulous Jimmy Choos instead. They're spectacular. It's as if they were made for that dress.'

'Thanks. They are pretty amazing, aren't they?'

'Absolutely. And don't worry about going to the ball alone. Cinderella did it and look how well that turned out for her.'

'You're right. Only Cinderella was make-believe. Unfortunately, real life doesn't have so many happy endings. Still, all's not completely lost. I do have an escort tonight in the form of a chap called Jake, a friend of a friend. Don't even ask.'

Edel gives me a reassuring hug. 'I won't then. But don't be so downbeat. You never know, this Jake might turn out to be the man of your dreams. Now don't drink too much. Remember to have one non-alcoholic drink for every alcoholic one and try to remember everything because I want to hear all about it in the morning.'

'Well, I can't have a hangover, anyway,' I tell her, 'because Ben is coming tomorrow, remember? And little boys and hangovers don't mix. I'll be home early, don't worry. It's not like I'll have anyone to dance with.'

'Nonsense; those shoes were made for dancing. Now when is this fella picking you up?'

'He's not. I'm meeting him there.'

Although Edel does her best not to show it, I can tell she's not impressed.

'Right then,' she says brightly. 'We need to order you a taxi.'

The taxi driver drops me right outside the Conrad Hotel. People have already begun to arrive so at least I'm not too early. The porter with the top hat and coat tails gallantly opens the door for me. I wonder if he will turn into a dormouse at the stroke of midnight. Well, there's as much chance of that happening as there is of me being rescued by a handsome prince this evening. I know nearly everybody here so at least I'm not on my own for long. I clutch a glass of champagne like my life depends on it and wonder whether Danny has arrived yet. Thankfully I haven't spotted him which is good. I don't think I could face him dead sober. I feel like he has made a complete idiot out of me, and I was only too happy to go along with it. Now I'm back at square one with no man to speak of, dreading this ball when all I want to do is turn on my heel, go home, pull the curtains tightly, get into my warm bed and hide beneath the covers. But it's too late for that now. I'm here to face the music and get through the next couple of hours as best I can. I gulp down the contents of my glass and then reach for another.

The fashion here is truly to die for. Luckily I don't see anybody wearing the same Coast dress as myself and hopefully I won't either. However, just in case somebody does happen to show up as my twin, I've sensibly opted to keep a white fake fur bolero around my shoulders for the time being.

The chattering all around me hums at a high but not unpleasant level. 'I had my dress especially flown in from Paris,' quips one frightfully thin woman, definitely an American-size zero by the looks of things. 'Where's that photographer from?' whispers another. 'Is he from VIP?' asks another girl, anxiously patting the top of her hair. 'Do I look OK?'

Cathy joins me looking splendid in a gold number slashed daringly to the hip. Herself and her boyfriend Jack look like an achingly hip A-list couple. He tells me I look fantastic which is rather nice considering we've just met for the first time and he doesn't know what I normally look like. Then we're joined by a couple more of Cathy's friends and suddenly the place is thronged by men in monkey suits and women in shimmery dresses. The air is heavy with the whiff of expensive perfumes and aftershaves. There doesn't seem to be any sign of Jake, however. I begin to feel quite nervous. Where is he? Am I sure I gave him the right date? The right hotel even? Imagine if he doesn't show? What if I'm left sitting beside an empty seat for the evening like I was last year and the year before? With Danny grinning over at me, his arm around his real girl-friend, Fiona? I can feel myself break into a sweat. Great. That's all I need. I hope I don't dampen my lovely dress.

As the minutes tick on I become increasingly worried. Even the champagne isn't managing to dispel the butterflies in my stomach. Where the hell is he? Do people think that I've been stood up? Then I notice Cathy beginning to laugh. In fact, she's laughing so loudly that people begin to turn around and look at her. I throw her an odd look. She can't be drunk already, can she? Then Jack joins in and they both nudge each other in amusement. I wonder if they've some kind of private joke going on. Then one or two of her group also join in. Soon everybody's laughing and for the sake of it, I laugh too, although what's supposed to be so funny I have no idea.

'Who's yer man?' cackles one girl.

What man? Who are they all gawking at?

And then I see. Suddenly I feel all the colour drain from my face. I clutch the stem of my glass in horror. I too have spotted Jake now. Well, it would be very hard to miss him. One leg and arm of his tuxedo is white, the other leg and arm black. His battery-operated dickie bow is flashing with red, blue and yellow lights. He looks like something straight out of the travelling circus.

'I hadn't realised they were organising a comedian,' says one man in our group loudly. 'Bloody funny.'

I try to escape but the soles of my shoes are firmly stuck to the ground. It's like a dream where you can't run. He's coming at me with his arms outstretched and a wide grin on his face and I can't stop him. The people in our group stop chatting among themselves as it dawns on them that the lunatic is with me. The next thing I know Jake has wrapped me in a bear hug and is planting a smacker on my cheek. 'Introduce me to all your beautiful buddies, baby.'

Horrified, I make the introductions quickly, describing Jake as an old friend of a friend, just to assure him and everybody else that we aren't a proper couple. Thankfully, before my face can get any hotter, a young waiter comes around ringing a bell. It is time for everybody to go into the ballroom and be seated for dinner. As I walk over to the board to check the seating plan with Jake in tow, I spot him. The sight of him hits me like a punch in the stomach. Danny. Laughing and chatting to people with his arm around a svelte brunette in a stunning red backless dress. I've never seen her before because I would have remembered a figure like that. She doesn't look pregnant at all. Danny looks dashing in black tie, like a real Mr Bond. He hasn't seen me (and my accompanying clown) yet so I hope to reach my table and sit down unnoticed. With any luck I can leave before the after-dinner speeches and the raffle begins.

We make our way to the table where Jake cracks a few unfunny jokes and people smile politely and some look mildly repulsed. There's soup for starters and Jake tucks in appreciatively while I can hardly even look at mine. My appetite, along with my dignity, seems to have gone. The evening gets progressively worse.

'I didn't know you two were an item,' Cathy whispers to me during the main course as I half-heartedly pick at my plate with a fork.

'We're not.'

Obviously Jake has super-human hearing because he places a warm hand on my thigh. 'Not yet,' he guffaws as my heart sinks. God, how have I got myself into this? Obviously he has mistaken this for a romantic date. The minutes tick by slowly and everybody apart from myself seems to be having a whale of a time. I can't help but glance over at Danny's table. He has his back to me, and has taken off his dinner jacket. I notice him knocking back the wine. No surprises there then.

'Are you having a nice night?' I ask Jake to be polite. After all, I'm the one who invited him here and he doesn't know anybody, so the least I can do is make him feel welcome.

'Best night of my life, babes.' He winks cheerfully at me and it's hard to tell whether he's joking or not. As desserts arrive, I nip off to the Ladies' to touch up my make-up. When I go to wash my hands, I notice with shock that Fiona is washing her hands also, while admiring her face in the mirror.

'Nice dress,' I tell her truthfully. I wonder does she know anything about me? Nah, probably not. Danny has hardly filled her in, has he?

'Thanks.' She smiles, showing off the most beautiful-looking teeth. There's a few grand's worth of work gone into that mouth, I reckon. 'I like yours too,' she adds. 'Coast, isn't it? I actually tried the same dress on last week. It's lucky I didn't wear it tonight – we would have been twins!'

Yes, except she would have been the taller, skinnier twin.

'The problem is that this dress is a bit tight around the middle,' she says, patting her non-existent stomach. 'There'll be no dessert for me tonight, I'm afraid.'

'But sure you're not showing at all. Most pregnant women couldn't get away with such a tight-fitting dress. You're lucky.'

She looks at me as though I have suddenly grown a second head.

'You don't think I look preggers, do you?' she asks in a horrified voice.

'Of course not; as I said, you're not showing at all.'

'Showing? I'm not up the duff, you know.'

Oh Jesus. What have I said? 'I know you're not pregnant,' I laugh nervously, as I furiously backtrack. 'That was just a joke. I always say that to women who are thinner than me to freak them out!'

Suddenly I spot Cathy behind me in the mirror.

'Is this lipstick OK?' she muses.

'The lipstick's fine, but you look pregnant.'

'Feck off, weirdo,' she laughs.

And with that Fiona gives us both an odd look and makes a hasty exit.

'She's not pregnant at all,' I whisper to Cathy, still in a state of shock.

'Fiona? Of course she's not. Sure I was flying with her yesterday and you can't fly when you're pregnant. Why? Is there a rumour going around? Jesus, people are awful gossips.'

'Yes,' I say, And liars, I add mentally.

When Cathy and I return to our table Jake is entertaining everybody by sucking helium out of the balloons. I feel a headache coming on. This reminds me of a particularly awful debs dance.

The band starts playing after the remains of the pavlovas have been cleared away and against my will, Jake drags me on to the dance floor. This is really terrible. Any hopes of pretending that Jake isn't really with me vanish as people sitting around the dance floor drinking their coffees look on in amusement. Jake seems to think he's Elvis incarnate for some reason.

After one song, I feign exhaustion and leave Jake to make an exhibition of himself alone. I scurry back to the table, head bowed, in order to draw as little attention to myself as possible. Too late. As soon as I resume my seat, Danny joins me, pulling up Jake's empty chair.

'I saw you on the dance floor,' he gushes.

'Did you now?' I answer coldly. 'Good for you.'

'Is that your new boyfriend?'

'It's actually none of your business.'

'Don't be like that,' he says, looking wounded. Christ, he's definitely wasted as a pilot. The acting world is missing their true star. 'I've explained the situation with Fiona.'

'First of all, you never had the decency to tell me she was also an air hostess, and not only is she an air hostess, she actually works for the same airline as us. And secondly,' I pause for ultimate effect, 'I know Fiona isn't pregnant because she told me tonight. That is just a pathetic excuse for you to cheat on your girlfriend.'

Danny blanches. 'You two spoke?'

'We had a little heart-to-heart earlier this evening, Danny, and the air has been cleared. I found out all I need to know.'

Danny grabs my arm. 'What did she say to you? What did you tell her about us?' he asks frantically and, I must say, I'm enjoying watching him squirm.

'Oi, you're sitting in my seat, mate.' For the first time so far tonight, I'm relieved to see Jake, even if his forehead is dripping in sweat from all that jiving.

'It's fine,' I say with saccharine sweetness. 'Danny was just leaving, weren't you?'

Jake proceeds to get very drunk and irritatingly keeps calling me Anna instead of Annie. Then he tries to light up and is told off by waiting staff.

'You really pick 'em,' whispers Cathy at the end of the night as Jake is being escorted from the hotel by security after deliberately tripping up the 'novelty act', a man on stilts.

Rule Eighteen: Don't give your number to married passengers.

I wake in the morning with a heavy heart. I feel so depressed I don't know how I'm going to find the strength to haul myself out of bed. Last night was a complete and utter disaster. Of course, I had accepted long before yesterday that Danny and myself were history, and that I was better off without the cad, but I'd like to have thought that it was my decision for once. However, meeting Danny's very sweet, beautiful and very un-pregnant girlfriend, has left me without a shred of dignity.

And as for Jake? Far from turning up as my modern-day super hero in order to make everything all right, he has made me the laughing stock of all my colleagues. For as long as I live, I don't think I will ever, ever live this incident down.

A small knock on the door precedes Edel's timid entrance. She's holding a tray of buttered toast and fresh orange juice. Aw, bless her.

I sit up in the bed gratefully.

'I thought you might have a bit of a hangover this morning,' she says gently.

'Hangover? No, if only it was that simple, Edel.'

'So I take it last night wasn't the best night of your life.'

'Now that . . .' I say, pausing for effect, '. . . would have to be the understatement of the year.'

'Do you want to talk about it?' she asks as I dig into the toast hungrily.

'Not now, if you don't mind. One day I might look back on last night and laugh, but I'm sure that day is a long way away.'

'Fair enough. By the way,' she says, handing me a large white envelope, 'this arrived for you this morning. It was pushed in under the door.'

I tear it open. It's a card with a picture of a plane on the front. How odd. Inside the message reads, *Thinking of you.*

I frown as I flip it over. There's nothing written on the back. Would Danny have delivered this? Maybe as a way of apologising for last night? How pathetic!

With that, the front door sounds, making us both jump.

'That must be Ben,' I say, throwing the card on the ground. 'So much for my leisurely breakfast in bed!'

Robert is at the door holding Ben in his arms.

'Annie Annie,' the young lad reaches out to me excitedly and struggles to break free from his father's grasp. An attractive woman with chestnut-coloured hair in a sleek bob stands back awkwardly. She's holding a suitcase.

'These are Ben's things.' She smiles shyly. 'I'm Julie, by the way,' she adds, giving my hand a hearty shake. I smile back to put her at her ease, before introducing Edel. I initially had thought I wouldn't warm to this woman at all the woman who has replaced my Emily in Robert's and Ben's lives, but she has such an open, honest face it makes her instantly likeable. Anyway, coming to my flat with Robert can't be easy for Julie either. I'm glad the ice has been broken.

'I hope I haven't forgotten anything,' she says with a slight frown.

'Don't worry, if I need anything I can buy it. Listen, you two go on quickly. It will make it less painful for Ben if you do.'

'Oh, he'll be fine,' Robert assures me. 'It's been Annie this and Annie that all week. This is a big adventure for him.'

'He sometimes wets the bed, though, if he's scared, so maybe you can leave the hall light on?'

'Don't worry. I always do anyway, and if there are any unfortunate accidents . . . well, that's what washing machines are there for. Now leave,' I add jokingly.

After hugs, kisses and surprisingly no tears on Ben's part, Robert and Julie disappear.

Ben settles in well. We have the Barney CD on play and he's sitting contentedly in front of the television munching on a biscuit. I'm quite liking the idea of having the little cherub all to myself. I have a timetable mapped out for us for every day of the week. We're going to go to the cinema one day, the zoo the next, shopping for kiddies' clothes the next, plus a trip out to Swords to visit his grandparents. I think they'd like that. I've bought a couple of disposable cameras to picture all our moments on film. I've bought in a load of picture books, too, because I won't have it said that Annie Annie hampered Ben's educational process by sticking him in front of the box for a week. At some stage I have to return to the Conrad because in the rush to get home last night I forgot my bolero. I rang the hotel this morning and they say they're keeping it for me. Unlike Cinderella and her forgotten shoe, there's no prince making his way to Gardiner Street on horseback with my bolero on a satin cushion.

Pretty soon, Ben gets tired of Barney and wants to do something else. Oh well, I knew it was too good to last. What if I put Ben in his pushchair and make my way over to the hotel? The longer I leave it the more I'll put it off.

'Would you like to go for a walk, Ben?'

'Why?'

'Well, I think it would be good for us to get some fresh air,' I explain.

'Why?'

'Because it's not good to be indoors all the time.'

'Why?'

'That's why,' I say shortly and then berate myself for snapping, especially when Ben's only been here a mere couple of hours.

He looks up at me with those big brown innocent eyes, chocolate smeared over his mouth. 'OK,' he says resolutely.

Once he's strapped into his buggy we make off into town. It doesn't take us long to reach the Liffey and cross over O'Connell Street bridge.

'I want to go wee wee,' Ben suddenly announces.

My heart dips. Where can I bring him?

'Can't you hold on, Ben?'

'Kay.'

I up the pace and push frantically all the way to Grafton Street. The one good thing about having a buggy is that people get out of your way quickly in order to save their ankles getting a knock. In McDonalds, I bring Ben into the Ladies' with me. But suddenly he decides he doesn't want to go.

'I want some chips,' he orders.

'They're not good for you,' I tell him.

'Why?'

'Because they're cooked in fat.'

'Why?'

If I buy you an ice cream, Ben, will you for God's sake stop asking why? I'm tempted to scream but I refrain myself. Instead, I give in and buy chips for himself and myself. No wonder the little devil wanted to stay with Annie Annie. Obviously he intends making me into his personal slave for the week!

Halfway up Grafton Street Ben decides he wants to go wee wee after all.

'You'll just have to wait a few minutes now, Ben,' I say firmly, and push on resolutely. Until, that is, I notice the trickle falling from the bottom of the buggy and realise we're leaving a trail behind us all the way up Dublin's busiest shopping street.

'Oh Ben,' I groan. 'Didn't I tell you to wait?'

He looks full of remorse. 'Couldn't wait, Annie Annie. Sorry.'

So it's off to Dunnes to buy new underpants and trousers, and finally when we reach the Conrad, we head straight for the bathroom to clean Ben up. The very same bathroom where I had that encounter with Fiona last night. It doesn't seem like just hours ago, it seems years ago now.

I put the soiled garments in the bin as there's no way I'm carrying them around town with me all day with people thinking the funny smell is off me. I retrieve the bolero and am about to push Ben out of the hotel when I hear a voice calling my name.

I swing around expectantly and, to my surprise, I see Oliver Kane. My heart does a double flip. Well, there's a blast from the past. I haven't seen Mr Kane for weeks. I am genuinely thrilled to see him.

'This is a nice surprise, how are you?' He clasps my outstretched hand and the touch of his skin on mine is electric. Good God, I'd almost forgotten what an effect he always manages to have on me. 'And who's this?'

'This is Ben.' I grin, very thankful we didn't bump into Mr Kane ten minutes ago. He looks tanned and relaxed, like he's been on holidays.

'He's the image of you.'

'Thank you.' Then I suddenly realise he thinks Ben is mine. 'He's my nephew.' I feel so flustered about meeting him so unexpectedly, yet it's good to see him. I wonder if he can tell that I fancy him? Hopefully the expression on my face isn't too readable. 'Er, have you been away, Mr Kane?' I enquire politely.

'Please, call me Oliver. Yes, I've been in Barbados for ten days. The weather was very pleasant. But I'm back to business now. I've a meeting first thing in the morning.'

'Do you always stay in the Conrad?'

'Yes, it's my favourite hotel. A home from home, you

could say. The staff here all know me. Listen, you weren't leaving, were you?'

'Eh . . .'

I can't think of an excuse to leave. Not that I want to leave, of course. I'd love to stay and chat to Oliver, but I'm just worried about Ben becoming restless.

'Please join me for some tea.'

Oh Gosh, this is it, isn't it? My chance to actually spend some time with the gorgeous Oliver Kane. For a moment I almost wish Ben wasn't here with me, but that thought is immediately followed by guilt. How could I possibly wish my darling godchild away? What kind of a monster does that make me?

'Em . . .' I pretend to think about it. Is this me playing hard to get? I don't know. My head is spinning and I can't even think straight.

'Don't even think of turning me down, young woman.'

'OK, then, you've twisted my arm.'

For some miraculous reason, Ben is staying pretty quiet.

'I used to have a son just like you.' Oliver smiles at Ben as we find a table near the window.

'What happened to him?' I ask, wondering why he is talking about his child in the past tense. Hopefully nothing terrible happened. I hope I haven't gone and put my foot in it by being the usual nosy me. Suddenly I realise that I know very little about Oliver, apart from the fact that I fancy him like mad. Why oh why couldn't he have been the man to have accompanied me to the ball last night?

'He grew up into a teenager. He's in England now pretending to study for his A-levels. He says he doesn't want to be a pilot like me, he wants to be a rock star,' he laughs and I can't help but think what a handsome man he is, especially when he smiles and his eyes crinkle.

'I want to be a pilot,' shouts Ben before making the sound of an airplane.

'Shhh. Keep your voice down, Ben,' I say terrified that he might annoy the other hotel clients. Then I turn my attention to Oliver again. 'Did you say you were a pilot?'

'I still am. I make sure to renew my licence every year. It's not something I'd like to give up.'

'And you sail, too,' I add. 'I'm impressed.'

He looks surprised. 'Who told you that?'

I freeze momentarily. I haven't told him about being on his yacht in Spain. Maybe now's not a good time to do so. Can you imagine what he would think if he knew I'd made love to another man on his vessel of pride? I start to feel my cheeks redden at the naughtiness of it all.

'Somebody must have told me,' I say hurriedly. 'So what do you do now?'

'Oh, I'm still very much connected to the airline business. In fact, I'm executive of a cargo company in England at the moment and I've also been at the helm of various charter companies.'

'So that's why you're always flying. Think of the airline miles you're clocking up. I bet you get some fantastic trips.'

'Yes, I do, but I sometimes get tired of living in hotel rooms and out of a suitcase.'

A waitress comes along and we order tea and sandwiches and a sticky bun for Ben.

'Does your son not live with you, then?' I ask, hoping I'm not being too much of a pest by asking all these questions. Suddenly I want to know everything there is to know about Oliver. He seems like such a sexy, fascinating man. The more I know about him, the more I want to know.

'He's in boarding school. His mother wanted him to go to the same boarding school as her own father so I had to respect her wishes. At least they keep a good eye on him there. I can't say what he'll be like next year when he leaves and goes out into the big bad world. He's threatening to be a busker in tube stations in London.'

'It's probably just a phase,' I laugh. 'We all have our rebellious years.'

He sips thoughtfully from his tea. 'So what was your rebellious plan, Annie?'

I ponder the question. 'Do you know . . . all I ever wanted to be was an air hostess. At least, that was the dream. But now that I have the dream, and I'm living it, I don't think it's what I want any more.'

'So what do you want?'

'I'm not too sure. I always thought a nine-to-five job would be the undoing of me but now I'm thinking it wouldn't be so bad after all. I started a PR diploma course last year so I'd love to put it to good use, only I wouldn't even know where to start. In a way, I'd hate to leave the airline and give up all my travel concessions, but after that hairy incident on the Chicago flight I don't get the same thrill from flying as I used to.'

'It's not the same job that it used to be, I agree,' muses Oliver.

'The thing is, any nutter can board a flight and cause havoc on it. If you walked into a bar and started causing trouble, you'd be flung out. But on a plane, you can't exactly open the door and push out the unreasonable passengers. And there's no point barring alcohol from flights as some people suggest, because it's often the case that drugs are involved. You wouldn't believe the amount of times that needles have been found in the toilets after the plane has landed.'

'It's a problem, all right, and bound to get worse as air traffic increases. Have you thought about applying to head office? At least then you wouldn't have to give up the perks of the travel which you obviously love.'

'I did,' I sigh, 'but they said they'd let me know if a vacancy arose. So far none has. Anyway, they'd probably want somebody with a bit of experience.'

We continue to chat amiably until Ben starts getting a bit cranky.

'I'd better get this little man home,' I say, reluctant to leave. Oliver Kane is very easy company and I'm enjoying getting to know him. But I'm afraid if I walk away I might not hear from him again.

Oliver looks disappointed about my decision to make tracks, which is quite an ego boost for me. It means that he likes me.

'Well, hopefully we'll bump into one another on a flight soon,' I suggest, getting Ben ready so I can put him into his buggy.

He looks at me pointedly. 'Let's not leave it to chance,' he counters, whipping out his mobile phone. 'What's your number there, Annie?'

I give it to him without hesitation. Oh my God, he's so drop-dead gorgeous. He may be married, but he's not at all sleazy and I trust him. And he could be another friend. A really good friend. It's possible, isn't it?

I tell him that we'd better get going in case it rains but Oliver won't hear of us walking home, hails a taxi and prepays the driver. 'It's the least I can do.' He smiles, lifting Ben's buggy into the boot of the cab.

Before we speed away, I roll down the back window.

'Lovely to meet you again. Thanks for the tea.'

'We must do it again sometime. And you, young man,' he adds, addressing Ben, 'you look after your aunt, OK?'

Rule Nineteen: Keep calm, even in extreme emergencies.

'I've resigned!' Edel makes her announcement as I walk into the kitchen to prepare some breakfast for myself and Ben.

'You what?' I stare at her in disbelief.

Edel has been threatening to resign from the shoe shop ever since she moved in with me but I never actually thought she'd go through with it.

'Yep, I told them yesterday evening. I'm a free agent now. I can watch TV all day long if I want, and drink wine with my lunch.'

'So no more great discounts on shoes?'

'Nope.' She shrugs, sipping her hot chocolate. 'Oh well . . .'

'So are you going to start looking for a new job straight away?' I ask, mildly alarmed that she may not be in a position to pay me rent this month.

'I've put a bit by to keep me going for the next few weeks,' she says, putting my fears at rest. 'In the meantime I'm going to chill out a bit and be good to my poor swollen feet and give them a rest.'

'Then I reckon a trip to Dublin Zoo with Ben and myself would be out of the question?'

'I'll make an exception for the zoo so,' she smiles, 'but if I get tired you can put me in the buggy and Ben can walk.'

I'm delighted Edel is coming with us. Much and all as I adore my little nephew, all that baby talk can get to me after a while and I start craving adult company.

We get the number 10 bus from O'Connell Street. Ben is so excited about seeing elephants and giraffes in real life. He's never been to a zoo before.

'Will I be able to pet the animals?' he wants to know.

'No, love, you can look but you can't touch. But we have the camera so we can take lots of pictures.'

'Will there be zebras there?' he asks excitedly.

'Yes, there will, and there'll even be a baby zebra there, too.'

'Can we ride them?'

'No, we can't ride them, but we can wave to them, darling.'

Ben seems to think that he can ride all the animals because Robert and himself went on a donkey ride on a trip to Tramore last summer. God love him but it's wonderful to be that innocent.

We get off the bus at the Phoenix Park and Edel and myself are as excited at seeing all the animals as Ben is. We spend a couple of hours wandering around. It's quiet today, being a school day, and the animals are happy to show off for us. Ben takes a particular shine to a hairy orang-utan who sits glaring at him while munching a banana.

'Is there a baby orang-utan?' Ben wants to know.

'Not this year, I don't think,' Edel explains.

'Is that a mummy or a daddy orang-utan?'

'I think it must be a daddy because he's so hairy . . . and grumpy,' Edel laughs.

'I don't have a mummy 'cos she died,' Ben announces out of the blue and tears immediately fill my eyes. I look away so that he doesn't notice. I feel my heart is about to break.

'Oh yes you do have a mummy, pet,' Edel takes over, gently ruffling the top of his head. 'She's in Heaven now, but she's watching you all the time.'

'Do animals go to Heaven too?' he asks innocently.

Oh dear. It really is a day for difficult questions.

'I believe that they do, Ben. So your mummy is up there now playing with all the animals, and they all love her.'

Oh God, I hope I'm saying the right things here. It's just so difficult to know . . .

'In Heaven, can you ride the zebras?'

'I don't know . . .'

'I bet Mummy is riding the zebras and having a race,' he says sounding happy.

To change the subject I suggest getting ice-creams at the zoo cafe. Fortunately my suggestion does the trick.

At the café, my phone rings. At first I don't recognise the number or the male voice at the other end. But then I realise it's Oliver. My heart does a double flip. He sounds upbeat, having had a series of successful meetings in Dublin during the week. To celebrate he says he'd very much like to take me out for dinner somewhere next week.

I motion to Edel that I need to step outside to continue the call. She gives me an understanding nod.

'Oliver,' I begin hesitantly, 'I'd love to take you up on your generous offer, honestly. But I'm very busy at the moment.'

'That's a pity. I hope you're not just playing hard to get with me,' he says jokingly.

I take a deep breath. I don't want to be rude but I have to let him know straight that I don't date married men. Never have. Never will either.

'Oliver, you're a great guy and I think you're brilliant company, but . . .'

'. . . you don't find me attractive.'

'On the contrary,' I can feel myself blushing and I'm glad we're not having this conversation face to face, 'it's just that since you have a beautiful wife, would you not take her out for dinner?'

There, I've said it. My stance on the matter couldn't be any clearer.

'I'd love to,' he replies in a quiet voice and in a tone that's hard to decipher. 'But unfortunately that can't happen.'

I feel my throat constrict. I didn't realise Oliver was divorced.

'Charlotte died a couple of years ago.'

His words hit me like a slap in the face. This was the last thing I expected to hear.

'Oh . . .' I falter. 'Oh Oliver, I'm so sorry.'

'It's OK. You weren't to know. In fact, you're the first woman I've asked out since she passed away. I haven't a habit of chasing pretty women.'

I believe him. There doesn't seem to be a lecherous bone in that man's body.

'Please come to dinner,' he tries again. 'I promise if you hate me I'll release you before dessert.'

'OK then,' I relent, 'how about next week? Are you in town on Wednesday or Thursday, as they are my days off?'

'Sadly I won't be around until the following week. I'm flying to Frankfurt on Monday at 11 and I'll be stuck there for a few days.'

'Ah, Mr Kane, now I definitely believe that you're following me around,' I giggle. 'I'm flying to Frankfurt myself that Monday.'

'Well, I expect some first-class treatment from you, then.'

'As always, sir.'

We say good-bye and then I rejoin Edel and Ben who has managed to get ice-cream all over his face, neck and jumper.

'What am I going to do with you, young man?' I ask taking a few tissues from my bag and rubbing his face as he scrunches it up.

'Well, what was all that about?' asks Edel, curiosity getting the better of her.

'Now, that would be telling . . .'

'Not Danny?'

'Certainly not,' I scoff. 'As if! Somehow I don't think I'll be hearing from him in the near future.'

'Mr Jimmy Choo, then?'

I feel myself redden as I nod, not wishing to say much in front of the inquisitive Ben.

'Who's Jimmy Shoo?' he wants to know. 'Does he live in the zoo?'

'No, pet, now finish up your ice-cream.'

But for the rest of the afternoon Ben is convinced that Mr Shoo lives in the zoo and keeps pointing to strangers and asking them if they are the man himself. Luckily most people see the funny side of it.

The week that passes is extremely enjoyable with trips to McDonalds, Captain America's, visits to see three different Santas, and a shopping spree in Toymasters along with Ben's doting grandparents, and by the following Sunday evening, I'm shattered, albeit in a pleasant way. At least I have the date with Oliver to look forward to. I really can't wait to get that man all to myself. It's been too long since I actually met a decent bloke and now Lady Luck seems to have noticed me at long last. I'm just unloading Ben's clothes from the washing machine in order to iron them and pack them in his little case for tomorrow when the phone rings.

Edel answers it and then tells me I'm wanted. I take the handset from her.

'Hello?'

'Annie, it's Robert. A terrible thing has happened.'

I feel my heart leapfrog as I imagine the worst. A car crash? Maybe they've been mugged or something?

'We've missed our flight,' he says helplessly. 'There isn't another one out of here until tomorrow night.'

I feel a wave of relief washing over me. Thank God they're both safe.

'Well, there's nothing you can do about it; relax, Robert.'

'But what about Ben? I know you've had him for a week already so I hate asking you to look after him for another day. Anyway you're probably working tomorrow, are you?'

'Well, yes, I have a flight to Frankfurt in the morning . . . but I suppose I could ring in sick . . .'

'I'll look after him,' offers Edel from the kitchen. 'No problem at all.'

'Thanks,' I mouth in her direction. 'It's sorted, Robert. My utterly reliable Edel has agreed to look after Ben for the day. He loves her, so don't worry about anything. Now you two check into a nice hotel, order in some room service and a nice bottle of wine, do you hear me?'

'I can't thank you enough, Annie . . .'

'Now go before we change our minds,' I say jokingly.

I put down the phone and continue pulling Ben's clothes out of the machine.

'There's never a dull moment around here, is there?'

I wake bright and early on Monday morning. Or at least Ben wakes me at 6.30, playing with his Action Man under the bed clothes. I'm not hugely looking forward to flying to Frankfurt and back, but I'm not dreading it either, thanks to the fact that the irresistible Oliver Kane will be on board. I hop out of bed with a spring in my step and quickly shower, before dressing leisurely. Although there's frost on the ground, the weather reports that there will be sunny spells throughout the day. Not much use to me, of course, as I'll be up in the air for most of it. But at least Edel will be able to bring Ben for a nice walk somewhere without them both getting drenched.

The three of us enjoy a long, lazy breakfast with heated croissants as the rest of the world commutes to work. Edel assures me that she's looking forward to playing nanny to Ben for the day. I couldn't be more grateful.

Once I'm dressed and ready to go, I check the fridge to see if there's enough food to last Ben for the rest of the day. To my dismay I realise we're dangerously low on milk.

'I'll just pop around to the corner shop and get some,' I tell Edel. 'It won't take me long.'

Grabbing my coat and keys, I take the lift down to the ground floor and head out on to the street. It doesn't take me long to make my purchases and I'm back within ten minutes.

'Helllooo!' I call cheerfully, about to put my key in the front door when I discover the door hasn't been locked at all. That's funny, I think to myself, I could have sworn I locked it on my way out. I must be getting forgetful in my old age. Pushing open the door, I freeze. Caught in a moment of horror I take in the scene in front of me. A white-faced Edel is sitting on the sofa in front of me with a terrified-looking Ben on her lap. Beside them is a menacing-looking man with a shaven head. And a gun.

I'm too stunned to speak.

'Shut the door, Annie,' growls the man, waving the gun threateningly at me.

Edel nods her head frantically. 'Do as he says, Annie.'

I nudge the door closed. 'What's going on?' I ask in a trembling voice. I am shaking all over.

'Welcome home, Annie.' The man gives an eerie smile. 'Now don't try and do anything funny and everything will be all right,' he says in a thick Dublin accent. His eyes look mad, as if he's high on drugs, which he probably is.

'Do you want money?' I ask, reaching in my handbag. 'How much do you want?'

'Don't be rude, Annie. We haven't even been properly

introduced yet, although I have been fortunate enough to meet your lovely and indeed cooperative flatmate and your darling nephew Ben.'

The way he says Ben's name sends a freezing shiver down my spine.

'Who are you, then?' I ask warily. What on earth is this all about? I feel as though I'm trapped in a particularly awful nightmare. I just want the end credits to start rolling.

'My name is Anto. I'm your pen pal. Did you enjoy receiving my notes? You never wrote back.'

My blood starts to freeze on the spot. The walls of the room crush in on me and I feel the room spin. So this is the guy who's been writing to me? Oh God, so they weren't some kind of romantic gesture from an admirer after all? This guy has been stalking me, and I didn't even realise it. And now he's here in my flat, threatening the safety of me, my flatmate and my nephew. Christ, what have I done to deserve this?

'What do you want?'

'Now, now, what kind of way is that to treat a guest? Don't I even get a cup of tea?'

'I've got to go to work,' I say suddenly looking from the frantic look on Ben's face to Edel's petrified look.

'Ah yes, work. Is that what you call it? Flirting with passengers all the way to Frankfurt. Is that what you sluts call work these days? Don't make me sick.'

The room is spinning. This feels like a horror film. How does this psycho know so much about me? What have I ever done to him?

'You think you're so smart, don't you?' he continues menacingly. 'I know all about you. I saw you on the news thinking you were some kind of fucking Laura Croft pinning down the big guy on the flight. You were so brave then, weren't you? Surrounded by all your cronies. Bloody bitches, the lot of you. You think you're all so high and bleeding mighty. Well, you're not so brave now, are you? Where are your handcuffs now, Annie Anderson?'

'Look,' I say, trying to keep my voice steady. 'I don't know what your game is so you'd better tell me. Why are you here?'

'OK, then. I'll tell you exactly why I'm here. I have a little package for you here,' he says, motioning to a black leather bag at his feet. 'I want you to bring it on board your flight to Frankfurt.'

'Why me?'

'Well, Miss Cock-of-the-Hoop, I thought you'd be perfect for the job. I've seen you on TV, you're a natural, you love all the attention, acting like you're some bleeding kind of celebrity. Who do you think you are? Fucking Madonna?'

'What's in the package?' I ask, my voice quivering. I can see Ben out of the corner of my eye, playing with his favourite teddy bear and gurgling softly. This whole scene is surreal. My stomach is churning. I feel that I'm going to throw up any minute. This cannot be happening to me.

'Well, that's none of your concern, Missy. You just bring it on board, hide it, then make your excuses, get off the plane before it takes off, and—'

'And if I don't?'

'Oh, but you will, sweetheart. Because if you don't do as I say, by the time you get back home there will be two bullets in these two people's heads.'

At the mention of the word 'bullet' Edel screams and Ben begins to whimper. I'm gripped with terror. This guy is clearly a nut and capable of doing anything.

'I'll go,' I say automatically.

'Good girl. And you won't say anything to anybody about this little package, do you hear me?'

'I hear you.'

'And don't even think about phoning anybody en route to the airport or you'll never see your precious Ben again. And that goes for Edel too. Got it?'

'I've got it,' I say, fearing I will collapse.

I walk unsteadily towards the door, almost expecting a bullet in my back at any second. Shaking uncontrollably, I press for the lift. It seems to take an age to reach my floor. My face is perspiring and my clothes are wringing. I take the lift down, and stumble outside into the daylight, completely shell-shocked. I don't even remember hailing a cab and rushing to the airport. I don't even recall checking in with crew control. But suddenly I'm walking past the airline security guard with the small leather bag stuffed carefully into my wheelie bag, terrified that he might stop me for a rummage. In all my years flying I've never had my bag checked by security as we have a separate access to the ramp but today could be just the one day . . . thankfully he's busy chatting to somebody on his mobile as I rush past him with a wave. Safely on board, I greet the other crew members with huge difficulty. I can barely speak, my throat has constricted so much. I agree to do a full security check down the back and, with trembling hands, put the package in an overhead locker at row 20. Then I stumble to the loo, close the door behind me, and puke my guts out into the bowl. Tears streaming down my cheeks, I gargle out my mouth and freshen up as best I can. Why is this happening to me? Why couldn't he have just killed me and let everybody else live?

I don't know any of the other crew members I'm supposed to be working with today but they all seem like nice girls. One is older, perhaps a mother of a couple of children. Another is a young girl probably just barely out of her teens. The third girl is wearing an engagement ring. All of them have people at home, whether they be parents, fiancés, husbands or children. And I am about to kill them. Kill them? I feel the bile rising in my throat again. My stomach heaves. This cannot be happening to me. What do I do? If there's a bomb on board, I will be responsible for murdering over one hundred passengers including my colleagues and, oh my God . . . Oliver Kane. I'd completely forgotten about him. Do all these people deserve to die so that I can keep Ben and Edel alive? Suppose the gunman panics and just decides to kill them anyway before turning the gun on himself? He might even wait until I get home and kill me too for good measure. Who knows what he will do?

'Are you OK?' asks Tanya, the girl with the sparkler on her fourth finger and no idea that she is so close to possible death.

'I'm not that great,' I say, shaking.

'Were you out last night?' she asks.

'Yeah, silly me,' I answer, quite unable to believe I am having a somewhat normal conversation with somebody who could be killed. How will her fiancé cope? What a waste of a young life, I think, turning my head away. I can't bear to even look at her.

'Quick, here they are.'

'Who?' I almost screech.

'The passengers of course,' she says, giving me a very odd look. 'Who did you think?'

Swaying slightly, incapable of walking in a straight line, I make my way unsteadily to the top of the cabin where the first of the passengers are making their way on board. Passenger number five is Oliver Kane. Again, I feel like none of this is real. It's like a bad dream I've been caught up in. Any minute I'm going to wake up now and it will all be over.

Oliver gives me a broad grin but I'm unable to smile back. I remain rooted to the one spot, a million terrifying thoughts flying around my head. Will he be blown to pieces too? Will I be at his funeral? Who will tell his son?

I'm interrupted by a young German woman with an infant in her arms. He's only a couple of years younger than Ben. She's looking for a baby belt for him so that he can sit on her knee. A baby belt? I look at her blankly. The baby isn't going to need a baby belt because nothing will be able to save him when this plane bursts into flames 30,000 feet above sea level. The baby smiles at me innocently. Does he have a father? How will the father hear? On the news? Is all of this going to be on the news? Am I going to be famous as the air hostess who helped blow up all these people?

'Is everything OK?' the woman asks me in a voice full of concern.

I look once again at the baby and his cute little dimples. At least I have lived some of my life. This toddler has his whole life ahead of him. Does he deserve to die in order to let Ben live?

'Can I have a baby belt?' the woman repeats herself.

I look at her blankly. 'No.'

'What?'

'There are no baby belts left. I'm sorry.'

'Excuse me?'

'Get off this plane now,' I urge her.

She looks at me as if I'm insane. She's probably right. I am in fact losing my mind.

The baby looks at me too. I can't bear it any more. 'You must get off this plane,' I tell her frantically. 'Please do as I say. There's a bomb on board.'

The woman screams at the word 'bomb' and runs to the top of the cabin. I run after her, scrambling past bewildered passengers, in a bid to silence her. If she alerts the other passengers, then we're all fucked. When I reach the top of the cabin, she has gone, racing down the steps of the plane, ignoring the protests of the senior cabin crew member.

'What was that all about?' she asks me.

'I don't know.' I shrug. 'She seemed a bit odd.'

'Now we'll have to get the woman's bags offloaded,' the senior sighs, glancing at her watch. 'That means we'll be delayed and will miss our slot for take-off.'

'But we can't be delayed,' I say in loud alarm.

She shrugs. 'There's nothing we can do about it. What a strange woman. I mean, she seemed so normal coming on.'

I feel a tap on my shoulder. It's Oliver. He's looking at me full of concern. 'Are you all right, Annie? You seem a bit off. Did you not notice me earlier on?'

'I'm very busy, Mr Kane,' I address him as I would any ordinary passenger. 'I would ask you to kindly take your seat.'

'Annie, I . . .'

'I mean it!' I snap. I can't take it any more. I am asking the man I am crazy about to strap himself in so that I make sure he dies? Hang on a sec, did I just say I was crazy about the man? I don't even know him! I don't know any of these people. If they die, it's just fate, isn't it? I'm not responsible. Everybody has to go sometime. Just some people have to go early. Like Emily. These people mean nothing to me but Emily's son's life is at risk. She trusted me. Robert trusted me. At this moment there's a gun being held to his little head and I'm here fussing with passengers and talking about suitcases. I'm here alive. And they, Edel and Ben, could be . . . could be . . . my head is cracking. Suddenly I'm seeing stars. A million stars. Before I sink into a black nothingness.

I wake on a stretcher with an excruciating pain throbbing at the side of my head. I open my eyes and see the sky. Threatening black clouds. And I seem to be strapped into something. A stretcher. I'm on the middle of the ramp. A nurse is wiping my head with a damp cloth. And there is Oliver.

I sit up in a panic. To my right I see the plane with the senior cabin crew member at the top of the steps. She seems to be having a word with the airline engineer.

'I need to get off this thing,' I say, struggling with the straps.

'Now, Annie, just relax. You're going to be OK,' Oliver says in a soothing tone.

'I'm going to vomit. Quick, get me off this thing.'

Himself and the paramedics help me off and I rush towards the plane ignoring the cries of protest from behind me. I notice the senior cabin crew preparing to electronically bring up the steps. I shout for her to stop but she can't hear me as another plane is arriving nearby and the noise is deafening. But just as the steps are halfway up she spots me and a look of horror crosses her face.

'Annie, what are you doing? They're bringing you to the hospital.'

'Let down the steps!' I scream.

'What?'

'JESUS. Let down the fucking steps. There's a fucking bomb on that plane!'

'Annie.'

I turn around as Oliver Kane raises a hand and smartly slaps the side of my face.

I'm too stunned to speak. I notice blood on his hand and my cheek stings where he hit me.

'I'm sorry, Annie, but this isn't a time for hysterics. Now, what are you talking about? What's all this about a bomb?'

I explain where I left it as calmly as I can, and Oliver quickly boards the plane to tell the captain to inform air traffic control immediately concerning a red alert. Then he phones the airport police who in turn contact the army. How does he have their number on his phone? How does Oliver know exactly what to do? At this stage the yellow shoots have been deployed and people are frantically shoving each other to get out of the plane in a scramble. I watch in a daze as people spill out of the plane falling on top of one another, never moving from my spot, even when two screaming fire engines come roaring up the ramp. All I am thinking of is Ben and Edel who, at this stage, may very well be dead.

The next minute, Oliver is back at my side. 'Come on, Annie, you're in shock. We need to get you to a hospital.' As if in a trance, I tell him to ring the police. 'There's a gunman in my flat,' I tell him. 'He's going to kill Ben.'

'He has Ben?'

'My nephew,' I reply numbly, the tears escaping from my eyes now. 'My only nephew. My dead sister's only child.'

Before I know it, myself and Oliver are in a squad car racing out of the airport at full speed. We are being escorted by two policemen on motorbikes. The traffic parts to let us speed along the motorway towards Drumcondra. At this stage I am bawling my eyes out, the tears incessantly flowing down my cheeks. I don't even attempt to dry them. I have fucked everything up big time.

Even if Edel and Ben have remained unharmed, I have put their lives at risk. I have also done the one thing we as cabin crew have always been trained not to do. I let the passengers know there was a bomb on board, causing the ultimate chaos. No matter what the situation, we are to behave calmly and responsibly at all times. I should have quietly let the captain know my concerns so that we could have evacuated the passengers without alarm. I crossed all the wrong boxes. I will definitely get fired over this, and when I have no income coming in, the bank will repossess my home. At this stage I feel so suicidal I could open the side door of this car and throw myself out. Before we know it we're at Gardiner Street which has been blocked off by police causing traffic mayhem. Outside our apartment block, the road is black with curious bystanders, uniformed police on walkie talkies, photographers, journalists with notebooks, a fire engine and an ambulance. My heart quickens at the sight of the ambulance.

'Who's that for?' I scream. 'Has somebody been shot?'

'Calm down,' Oliver puts an arm around me. 'It's probably for you. You're in a state of shock.'

His phone rings and he quickly takes the call. Seconds later he assures me that the army disposal unit have deactivated the bomb and that everybody on the plane is now safe. But I'm barely listening. I don't care. I want to know about Ben and Edel.

We jump out of the car and Oliver takes my hand as we push through the crowd. Suddenly I see Anto being escorted from the building in handcuffs. My heart somersaults. How did they get him? Did he surrender? Where are the others? Was there a shoot-out? Has he killed them? I rush forward. At the front door of the building, a young guard denies us entry, explaining that the entire building has been cordoned off and that the official hostage negotiator is the only person who is allowed inside for the time being. I'm about to scratch his baby face in rage when Oliver calmly explains who I am. We're granted entry. We run up the stairs because I can't wait for the lift. I fling open the apartment door not sure what I'm expecting to find. The place is chaotic. Mirrors have been smashed, furniture upturned, curtains and cushions are piled on the floor. On the wall, just over the mantelpiece, are two fresh bullet holes and on the couch is Edel with Ben on her knee.

'You're safe!' I cry through my tears as I stagger towards them, arms outstretched.

'We're both fine.' She smiles as I cradle them both in my arms, shed the last of my tears, and then collapse in a heap to the ground.

Rule Twenty: The rule is there are no rules.

'Oh my God, please, no more interviews, Oliver,' I beg as another reporter leaves. 'People are going to start recognising me as the nut who constantly finds herself in the middle of all airline dramas.'

'But you're great at dealing with the press,' Oliver insists. 'You're in the wrong job!'

'You can say that again. So what's the story with Anto? Has he gone to court yet?'

'He should be going in about now. In fact,' he turns on the television in my hospital bedroom, 'we might get an update now.'

Sure enough, there is Anto with a jacket over his head being led into the central criminal court. He doesn't look too brave now, flanked by two burly officers.

I cringe as I watch myself on TV coming out of the apartment block with Edel and Ben. I look a mess whereas Edel has somehow managed to brush her hair despite the mayhem. A detective at the scene has a few words commending the police, and the hostage negotiator who managed to persuade Anto to give himself up after half an hour of trashing the place.

At first I had been confused about how the police managed to storm the block so quickly, but then I heard how Edel had begged to go to the bathroom and in there had made a secret call to the guards. God love her, it was such a brave thing to do. She must have been terrified.

It turns out that Anto is a loner with a history of mental illness, who was thrown out of the army a while ago and who had an in-depth knowledge of explosive making. He could have blown up that plane ten times over with what was in that small package, apparently. I still shudder when I think about it.

The reason he'd wanted to blow up that plane was because he had a lifelong ban from our airline after being convicted for being drunk and disorderly on a previous occasion. It also turns out he was jilted years ago at the altar by a former aircraft cleaner on our airline, who is apparently a dead ringer for me, and he never quite got over it. According to police he had singled me out after becoming obsessed with me after I refused to serve him any more alcohol on a flight to Birmingham about a year ago, and made a note of the name on my name badge, before I reported him to the airport police. Once he had my name he then hacked into the airline website to read my rosters and had been trailing me for quite some time. It unnerves me to even think about it. Then, apparently, he saw me on the news having restrained that guy on the Chicago flight and had gone fairly beserk.

When the guards raided his house they found lots of cuttings of me from the papers talking about the incident, as well as footage from the news. They also found scrapbook after scrapbook with various cuttings from 9/11, Northern Ireland bomb scares and terrorist threats, as well as numerous books on bomb making. And to think that I'd imagined his little notes were innocent scribblings from a love-struck admirer. God, even now I'm mortified when I remember how I thought Danny could have sent them in a bid for my affections!

The television flashes a clip of Oliver Kane. He speaks eloquently about the airline and how professional the staff were in handling the situation. He also goes on to praise the airport police and the fire crews.

With that the reporter faces the camera and says, 'Once again, thank you, Mr Kane, for speaking to us. That was Oliver Kane, the new chief executive of Irish Airways.'

Rule Twenty-one: Don't date the boss.

Actually you can forget Rule Twenty-one because when your boss is Oliver Kane, it would be scandalous NOT to date him. We've been blissfully together for four months now and are both looking forward to the wedding this afternoon. I got my dress, a simple Donna Karan number, in a hurry and Oliver already had a black-tie suit.

Edel is coming too and so is Ben, naturally. Thankfully, he hasn't been too traumatised by the incident with the gunman, although he does tend to yell 'bad man' at the telly at any character brandishing a weapon.

Even my parents are coming to the wedding, although my mother has her reservations claiming that everything seems to have happened so fast, and that maybe Robert and Julie are rushing into things.

Oliver collects me at my parents' house. He meets Mum and Dad for the first time and it's clear that they approve, which is enough to make my heart sing. Mum even offers to make him a cup of tea and Dad offers to show him the garden, which is a very big deal in our house.

Oh yes, I forgot to tell you, I'm back living at home for a while because my place in Gardiner Street is up for sale at the moment. I'm hoping to move to Portmarnock sometime soon. I'd love something by the sea, not too far from work. At the moment I have my eye on a few places, and thanks to my considerable raise in salary, I hope to afford a decent new apartment.

I'm no longer working as an air hostess, you understand. Well, as you can imagine, I just couldn't face getting on another plane for a while after the last drama so Oliver arranged for me to get an interview as press officer for the airline. Since I'd already racked up a good deal of experience talking to the press about my hair-raising in-flight experiences, I sailed through the interview surprisingly well and now I have a lovely office not far from Oliver's with commanding views all the way over to Howth. I sometimes meet Oliver for lunch and work but we try not to mix business with pleasure too much in case it would look unprofessional. Oliver, you see, had been meaning to tell me about his new promotion with the airline at the romantic dinner we were supposed to be having. He'd been meaning to tell me, of course, but then I got to hear it on the news instead.

Life is great for me now. I'm at peace with myself and I still talk to Emily every day. I honestly believe she was the one who organised the peaceful ending to Anto's siege from above. And I also believe that she thinks the Anderson family is doing the right thing today by supporting Robert. It's not going to be easy for us of course, but we're going to be brave. It really is the best thing for little Ben. He deserves to have a happy, stable family life. And the Andersons will never be too far away.

And as for Danny? I really don't like to talk about him much, especially after the full extent of his lying and commitment-phobia was revealed, but since you're probably wondering what became of him, I'll fill you in. Poor Danny turned up for an early-morning flight stinking of booze and was immediately breathalysed. It turns out he was two and a half times over the safety limit and was suspended on the spot. I don't know what Sylvie has to say about the matter, but I doubt she'll be going about on her high horse too much any more. I haven't heard from him since the ball and don't expect to hear from him again. Sometimes though, I think being involved with Danny was the best thing that ever happened to me because it really made me appreciate Oliver.

En route to the church we stop to pick up Edel. She's living with her sister as she has split up with Greg and felt she needed a complete break. Now she is dating a completely respectable medical rep who treats her like a princess and never wants to watch videos. 'However,' she says, getting into the car after thanking Oliver profusely for the lift, 'my sister is driving me mad, so I'll have to get a new place soon, something near the airport.'

'And how is the new job going?' Oliver enquires as we head out to the church.

'Oh it's wonderful, Mr Kane. Thank you so much for putting a good word in for me. I'll always be very grateful for your input.'

'No terrorists or anything yet?' he enquires as I give his arm a playful thump.

'No,' says Edel. 'I think we've all had enough drama for

this year, thank you very much, but do you know something?'

'What?'

'Smiling all day and wearing those high heels is an absolute killer. God, I thought the shoe shop was bad enough but my feet are always aching these days.'

'You see?' I wink at her in the rear-view mirror. 'Didn't I always tell you being an air hostess isn't all it's cracked up to be?'

AMANDA TRIMBLE

Singletini

Singletini (*noun*): 1. A glamorous and increasingly common type of girl, typically found in urban settings 2. One possessing an unusual fear of growing up and settling down

For a girl like Victoria Hart, being a singletini means life's a continuous party. The aim is to have fun with no thought for tomorrow. So she's delighted when she finds a job that involves her favourite thing – becoming a wingwoman, helping shy guys navigate the perilous dating scene in Chicago.

But while she's happy with her life the way it is, her friends are moving on in the real world with jobs, houses, relationships. Hadn't they made a pact to be footloose and fancy free with her for ever? Soon Victoria begins to realise that going solo might not always be the best option . . .

A delicious and more-ish cocktail of glamour, fun and true love, this is a sparkling romantic read that's not to be missed.

0 7553 3722 0

little
black
dress

SWAN ADAMSON

My Three Husbands

What's a girl to do when husbands just keep lining up?

Meet Venus Gilroy: twenty-five, carefree, irresistible, and with a nasty habit of getting hitched to the wrong guy.

Husband No 1: would have been a winner, if it hadn't been for the forgery and embezzlement charges.

Husband No 2: sometimes a girl has to realise – meeting a husband in a strip bar will never end well.

Husband No 3: is the real deal. Isn't he? Surely sexy, rugged, *principled* Tremaynne is finally the right one for Venus?

With her insane mother, not to mention her two gay dads, plus porn-video-store-owner boss, all weighing in with advice, it's time for Venus to learn for herself – how you know that Mr Right . . . doesn't turn out to be Mr Wrong.

0 7553 3364 0

little
black
dress

little
black
dress

**brings you
fantastic new books like these
every month - find out more at
www.littleblackdressbooks.com**

**And why not sign up for our
email newsletter to keep
you in the know about
Little Black Dress news!**

You can buy any of these other **Little Black Dress** titles from your bookshop or *direct from the publisher*.

FREE P&P AND UK DELIVERY
(Overseas and Ireland £3.50 per book)

TO ORDER SIMPLY CALL THIS NUMBER

01235 400 414

or visit our website: www.madaboutbooks.com

Prices and availability subject to change without notice.